A year after her sister's death, Katey Philips receives an mysterious message. The message suggests her sister didn't die by accident on the night she hosted a work party. Disguising her identity, Katey moves across the country to work at the public relations firm that employed her sister.

Katey quickly learns she doesn't work at an ordinary PR firm. The company runs a second line of business her sister never spoke of. This secret work is dangerous and shameful, and participating in it is the only way Katey can uncover what happened to her sister. Katey must choose how far she'll go to find the truth, even if it means sharing the same fate as her sister.

At Her Will
Copyright © 2023 Andrea Brellick
ISBN: 978-1-4874-3727-5
Cover art by Angela Waters

Published by eXtasy Books Inc

Look for us online at:
www.eXtasybooks.com

At Her Will

By

Andrea Brellick

CHAPTER ONE

I peeled my thin glove off to call Jackie for the third time since my delayed flight landed in Toronto.

No answer.

She'd insisted I fly for five hours to hear her big news. Now, there I was—no sister and freezing to death outside her condo at midnight.

If only waiting alone in the dark had topped my list of worries. When we'd spoken on the phone, Jackie said she had something to tell me. But then she gave one-word answers. She wanted off the phone. That meant she'd been hiding something. Something she wouldn't tell me unless I arrived at her doorstep and pried it out of her perfect peach-coloured lips.

Stepping back, I looked up toward her unit, which faced the street. No one was out on the balcony at this time of year. I couldn't see anything, let alone the party she was hosting.

I sent another text message—*Where the hell are you? It's freezing out here.*

I wasn't dressed for this. It was my second winter visiting Toronto, but I'd forgotten how frigid it got. My phone said it was -14° C. *Christ.*

Maybe Jackie and her sometimes-sober public relations colleagues moved the party to a bar.

I could have checked a nearby drinking spot, the one we went to on my last visit. But I didn't want to lug around a suitcase in the snow. And if I caught her drinking, I'd lose it. She knew not to drink with a head injury. That girl thought

1

she was invincible.

The wind slapped snow from the street into my face before I could turn my back. I couldn't stay outside much longer.

As I pulled my suitcase away from the building, a guy with a hockey bag held the door open for me. I rushed toward the elevators.

Once on the twelfth floor, I knocked on Jackie's door.

It was unnaturally quiet in the hallway. No elevator dings, no footsteps. I couldn't hear the sounds of a party inside. The only noise came from my knuckles rapping on her door.

No answer.

I tried again, this time with more force.

Nothing.

I pressed my ear against the door. Something? A chair being dragged, maybe? Was the sound coming from Jackie's condo or a neighbouring unit?

I twisted the handle, and the door opened. *Why isn't it locked?*

"Jackie, you here?" I took a few steps inside, then paused, waiting for the sound of her voice.

It was a spacious one-bedroom condo, but there were a few places to be unseen.

I looked down. No extra shoes were scattered by the door. I guessed they'd decided to go out after all.

The only light came from two white candles. One was burning in the kitchen, the other in the living room.

Empty wine bottles and red-stained glasses were scattered across the counters and coffee table. Definite proof of a party.

I circled the kitchen island, treading on the remnants of cheese and baguette on the hardwood floor. Taking the cheese platter from the counter, I held it up to my face and examined the surface. Blue cheese—her favourite. And mine.

Peering out the floor-to-ceiling window in the living room, I studied the balcony. A small table and two chairs were covered in snow.

As I placed the platter on the counter, the same noise re-played. I jerked my head up. It was coming from her bed-room. "H-hello?"

I made my way there, hesitating in the doorway.

Stop being such a baby. Go.

My feet remained planted on the floor. *What's inside? I don't want to know.*

With the curtains drawn, the bedroom was pitch-black. I fumbled my sweaty palm along the wall, searching for the light switch. *Flick.* Nothing. I'd forgotten. Jackie only used her bedside lamp.

I activated the flashlight app on my phone and shone the bright light into every corner of the room, including the crack between the door and wall, separated by the door's hinges.

The bed was perfectly made and undisturbed. I shoved my phone against my thigh, hiding the light. There was only one other place to hide in this room — the closet. It was closed by double-doors that opened from two center knobs.

The closet doors were solid. If someone was in there, they couldn't see me coming. If I approached carefully enough, they wouldn't be able to hear me, either.

Stop it, doesn't matter. No one is in there.

I inched forward.

That noise again.

It sounded like something light, maybe a shoe dropped on the closet floor. I spun around and sprinted to the kitchen. There was a block of knives on the counter. I pulled one out, my heart pounding.

I should call the police. And say what? The couch squeaked?

This is ridiculous.

I stalked back into my sister's bedroom, holding the blade at eye level. Tossing my phone on the bed, I yanked the cur-tains open, flooding the room with streetlights. Taking my courage into my free hand, I wrenched the closet doors open.

Dresses, skirts, and blouses hung from a rod — exactly what

should be in a closet.

With a sigh of relief, I dropped the knife on the bed and took off my coat and scarf. Nothing out of the ordinary was there.

Stupid girl. I took a selfie showing mousy hair stuck to my forehead and a butcher's knife across my lap. I sent it to Jackie. *This is what happens when you don't pick up your phone.*

Still no new messages. I'd watch something on Netflix while waiting for her to come home.

I returned the knife to the kitchen and flopped on the L-shaped gray couch. And looked up. A light from the bathroom on the other side of the living room caught my eye.

How did I not see it earlier?

A dim light shone through the crack beneath the door. I tapped lightly. "Anyone in there?" I whispered.

No answer.

I took another moment to listen.

No sound.

This time, it felt different. I wasn't waiting for a man wearing a ski mask to jump out of nowhere.

I repeatedly swallowed, even though there was nothing to push down.

I moved closer. Held my breath and listened. More silence.

I couldn't take it. I slowly pushed the door wide open. My heart skipped a beat before I rushed to the side of the bathtub. Knocking over a glass of red wine on the floor, I plunged my arms into the water. I grabbed the back of her arms and shoulders and pulled her from underneath the water. "Oh, God, no. Jackie"

I was on my knees, holding her, willing her to open her eyes. I moved her dark hair away from her face, frantically listening and feeling for her breath.

Oh, God. I don't think she's breathing.

The water was warm. Her body was warm.

CHAPTER TWO: ONE YEAR LATER

Ben squeezed my left shoulder gently. "Katey, what would you like?"

"Sorry, what?"

"Like to drink?" He turned toward the waiter but kept his worried eyes on me.

"Oh, ginger ale, please." Sitting up straight, I forced a smile.

Ben leaned toward me, tipping his giant frame to my level, his sandy hair almost blending with mine. "I appreciate you coming out for my birthday. Stay as long as you're comfortable."

I leaned away from a bottle of wine being uncorked by a waiter. I'd be better if we weren't at a bar. The scent of red wine was my last memory of Jackie.

I nodded.

Happy hour at a *I-want-to-be-seen* bar was the least I could do to thank him for his support since Jackie's passing. Or, as my parents said, "The accident."

I supposed that was correct. The coroner's report ruled it was an accidental death—she slipped in the bathtub, hit her head, was knocked unconscious, and drowned. At the time, she was recovering from a cycling crash that had left her with a concussion and a fractured ankle. The biking injuries could have affected her balance and contributed to the fall.

Just like that—one, two, dead. It wasn't that simple. There was more to it than that. I'd never been wrong when it came to Jackie.

5

I called the police officer who took my statement the night she died. There was something off before I found her. It was right there in front of me, but I couldn't recognize it. Then I realized—the bathroom door was closed. Jackie never closed it, ever. Not when she took a shower or went to the bathroom. Why would she? She lived alone.

The policeman said there were no signs of foul play and swore by the coroner's report. The coroner, who spent a few hours with Jackie's cold dead body, knew everything, the officer assured me. Then he advised me to get some rest.

Mom and David shook their heads when I tried to tell them what I told the police.

Ben listened, then suggested I see a therapist. So every week, I met with Evelyn. Ben thought the sessions helped because I no longer locked my office door and emerged when everyone else had left for the day. Progress, I supposed. Evelyn met my needs for the bare-minimum human contact. I didn't need obligated company—family, work colleagues, or *friends* who came out of the woodwork. A therapist wouldn't spend time with their clients out of pity.

I'd made some progress, but I was still having *the dream*. Evelyn wanted me to talk about it—not a chance in hell.

The dream was always the same. I walked into my sister's bathroom. The bathroom fixtures were missing—no toilet, sink, towels, shower, or mirror. Only the bathtub, filled to the brim. The lights were bright. The water in the tub had a blue tinge. Jackie lay flat beneath the surface as if she was in a casket. Her eyes were closed, black hair arranged in a perfectly straight line that disappeared behind her shoulders. When I tried to reach out to her, I couldn't move. When I tried to scream, no sound came out. I kept trying until I woke up, gasping, with a sharp pain in my gut.

The dream had coloured my memory of that night. Things that happened were a blur, and that was how I wanted them to stay. From the little I'd told her, Evelyn said it was a typical symptom of shock, a defence mechanism that prevented me from revisiting the events.

"Thank you," I told the waiter as he placed a tall glass in front of me, nearly spilling the clear soda. He hovered with a glass of red wine inches from my chin before putting it down. Acid crept up the back of my throat, and the insides of my knees bounced off each other.

Ben was staring at my drink and caught my eye.

"Sorry, I'll celebrate next year," I said. Maybe by then, alcohol wouldn't smell like cat piss.

"Don't apologize."

Ben nudged the food platter toward me. I wasn't hungry, but I dipped a piece of fried squid into the mayonnaise and chewed the rubbery texture.

He'd done so much. He'd given me whatever time off from work I needed and didn't flinch on days when I left abruptly. And he allowed me to keep my senior consultant title and pay grade. If there was a time to ask for more help so I could maybe be more normal by next year, it was now.

"If it's okay with you, I want to see Evelyn more frequently. I'll take a pay cut."

"Take whatever time you need."

I clamped my straw between my teeth, still holding a smile.

He leaned in once more as the tables flanking us filled. "You've come a long way."

"Yeah, I can hear her name, and my eyes stay dry."

His eyebrows sank and moved closer together. *Shoot, that was meant to be a joke.*

"And I went out for lunch with the team and the video game guys from down the hall."

"Ha." His broad smile returned. "You went out with strangers?"

"We ended up at the same place. But I stayed the whole time."

He laughed. "I was going to say . . ."

"Sorry, what?" I couldn't hear him. I twisted around. A rowdy group wearing yellow t-shirts was swarming us.

"If your therapist can get you to mingle with strangers, I need someone with that kind of magic in my life."

A stocky, middle-aged man from the loud t-shirt crowd squeezed up against our table.

"Heard you're talking about therapy. It's your lucky day. I'm with the Nikall workshop. Do you know who Oscar Nikall is?"

Ben and I stared at him in silence.

"He's a famous hypnotist," the intruder persisted with spread arms. "We just graduated from his seminar." He pointed to the group wearing the t-shirts. "Would you like to meet Oscar? He's over here."

"No," we replied.

"That's okay. Right here is perfect."

"For what?" Ben asked, not glancing his way.

"Hypnosis. It's therapy. It gets rid of your worries and problems."

The man looked downward, shifted his weight, ground his toe into the floor, and then addressed me alone. "Do you want to try it? It'll only take a few minutes."

"I don't think so."

"C'mon."

People sitting nearby were watching. Some banged on their tables. "Show off your witchcraft," someone hollered.

"Piss off, asshole," another voice called.

Captain t-shirt lowered his voice, pleading a little. "I want to impress this girl in the seminar."

Ben motioned to the t-shirt crowd. "Use your voodoo to solve her problem of not wanting you."

If I can do this with a stranger in front of a drunk crowd, it'll show Ben how far I've come and that his kindness has paid off. It'll be over soon, anyway.

Ben took a long gulp of beer and placed the empty glass beside the uninvited company with a thud.

Better get going. I stood. "Proceed."

Patches of bald skin appeared in his short beard as his grin spread. "It'll only take ten minutes. Maybe we can go to the corner."

"You've got five, buddy," Ben said. "And you're staying right here."

It would be nice to get away from leering eyes, but Ben's right. Best not be alone with this character.

The captain closed the space between us, his eyes level with mine. "Close your eyes and think of a minor problem."

I leaned back, closing my eyes. *Minor problem. That's rich.* A year ago, my problems ranged from unripe avocados to being late for yoga. There was only one problem now. Everything else was just noise.

"Now, squeeze my two fingers." He offered the chubby index and middle fingers of his right hand, parallel to his chest.

I grabbed them and squeezed.

"Relax. Squeeze harder."

My grip tightened as his hot breath hit my face.

"Relax." He used his free hand to push down on my shoulders. "Squeeze harder."

I did.

"Now, pose your problem as a question, but don't say it out loud."

I knew the response, but I asked myself anyways — *why did my sister leave me?*

"Listen carefully. Let go of my fingers, but keep squeezing."

My grip loosened, and his fingers wiggled free.

"Open your eyes. Good. Now follow my hand with your eyes." His hand started at the top of my head, barely in my peripheral vision, and slowly moved from left to right.

"No, no." His fingers snapped twice at my forehead.

"Concentrate. Don't move your head."

Laughter and howls from the audience grew.

Everyone was looking at me. *God, is this over yet?* "Maybe I can't be hypnotized."

"Everyone can be," the captain shot back. "We're trying again."

I formed a stop sign with my hand and held it toward Ben before he got any ideas.

The captain waited for the laughter to subside. "Close your eyes. Focus on your question. Squeeze my fingers hard."

I obeyed.

"Maintain the tension. Keep squeezing. Let go of my fingers."

I released his hand.

"Good. Now open your eyes. Follow my hand."

His hand drew a straight line, crisscrossed, and formed a block. It slowed, and I started to feel light. I could still see, but everything was moving in slow motion. The smell of fish and grease disappeared. The sound of crashing dishes was gone.

I drifted, feeling aware but also in a deep slumber. And slipped further into another space. And stayed there.

"Katey, open your eyes."

I did, slowly.

Ben stood over me, and I read his lips to make out his words. "Are you okay?"

I rubbed my eyes. "Yeah. Why wouldn't I be?"

"Beat it," Ben told the captain.

The captain puffed his chest and rejoined the t-shirts.

Ben waited for me to sit down before taking his seat across from me.

"You were muttering something. A door? Something about a number. Are you sure you're all right?"

I scanned the room—the identical dark-wood adjacent tables, the waiter wearing all black, and the standing crowd dressed the same. I felt like I'd just awakened in the morning but in an unfamiliar place. "I'm absolutely fine."

Ben signalled for the check. "I'll see you home."

Thirty-one years old, and I still faced twenty questions every time I came home. I loved my parents. I just didn't want to see them.

The last time I did anything social, outside of lunch with colleagues, was months ago. Jackie's old friends from high school invited me to a movie. They're the ones who held a community vigil for Jackie and invited me last-minute. Haven't heard from them since. I went out with them for the same reason I moved back home to sleep in my single bed — to console my mom's maternal void. A space that I couldn't fill, but I would be there until she was ready to accept that.

I reached the second-floor landing. Miko was there, nudging her ball toward me, yelping with joy. "Shh, not now."

Her begging hound eyes got me every time, even when she ratted out my presence to the household. I threw the ball against the wall, and she caught it off the first bounce.

At least one of us should have some fun. I rubbed behind her ears before tossing the ball down the stairs and escaping to my room.

Within minutes, there was a knock on the door. It was my stepdad.

"Hi, honey."

"Hi, David."

"We weren't sure if you had dinner. Brought you a snack," he said from the other side of the door.

"Thanks." I opened the door, took the pizza, and gave him a kiss. I ate dinner alone in my room. We didn't argue about it anymore.

It was times like that when I regretted keeping my biological father's surname — the man who dropped me off at school and promised to pick me up later that day to take me to T-ball. He hugged me goodbye with one arm.

When David and Mom married, they asked me if I wanted to change my name. I thought about it, then looked in the mirror. Nakajima seemed weird on a green-eyed blonde. So I stayed Katey Philips.

Jackie was my half-sister. When people learned about our relationship, their condolences changed to a tilt of the head and a sigh of relief. As if a half-sister wasn't a real sister.

I tried to make a life of my own in Vancouver. When I finished my MBA, Ben hired me and promoted me every year. Senior Project Management Environmental Consulting kept me busy. My assessments supported court-ordered fines and even jail time for the white-collared environmental criminals that David advocated were just trying to cut red tape. But then Mom and David would change the subject and ask where Jackie was travelling for work that week.

Now that Jackie was gone, my parents cared about the maintenance of my car and my vitamin D intake. But I didn't want that or their concern in the form of late-night snacks. I just needed my sister.

I waited for my parents to go to bed, climbed out my bedroom window onto the roof, and lit my pipe. When we were teenagers, Jackie and I used to meet late there at night to smoke joints.

The last time we were on the roof, we stayed out for a long time. It was cold, but we didn't care.

"I'm getting you outta here." Jackie shivered and topped off my glass of red wine. "You're gonna move to Toronto."

"And do what? Surf on your couch?" She was living life in a city built for her. She didn't need me dragging her down.

"I have a plan."

"What kind of plan?"

"Can't tell you yet, but I'm almost ready. It's going to be perfect."

"I won't fit in with your friends." I'd told her that so many times before, and she'd always brushed it off.

She drew close, giving me her lopsided smile, always a little wicked. "They aren't my friends, Kitty Kat." She took a long swig from the bottle. "I'm getting away from them, from all that. And soon." Before I could ask anything else, she switched the subject and flung her arm around my shoulder.

"I'm gonna set you up with some good guys."

"Because that worked so well last time."

"He was a loser. I should've known better."

"He shouldn't have called me your name all night."

My date made it clear that he wanted a trade. But I was used to that. After all, the old me — overweight thigh-chafing sister — disappeared next to her model-scouted sister.

She linked her arm through mine. "You're leaving all of that here."

I turned my face to hers. She was gone. It was cold and dark, and I was alone.

That night, the dream was different. I walked into the blindingly bright bare room. Jackie's pale, motionless body was submerged in the clear water filling the bathtub, but this time she was turned to one side, her ribs exposed. Jet-black hair was floating in hundreds of tendrils around her head. The light became brighter. I moved toward her and saw something dark on her body. A mark running from the top of her rib cage to her waist. A tattoo? But it wasn't a symbol or letters. *What is it? Focus.* I leaned forward. It became clear.

I woke up and turned on the bedside light, almost knocking it over. Grabbing a pen and an envelope from my desk, I wrote down what I saw before the image had a chance to fade.

CHAPTER THREE

804260636. I'd seen this before. I knew I did. But where? Or when?

Was it a phone number? Not enough digits. A date? Nope. Her SIN number? Hers started with five, same as mine. Pacing, I looked for something to jog my memory.

It wasn't like me to be forgetful. That was Jackie's thing—Jackie was always misplacing everything—her keys, wallet, phone, anything she would need to get through the day. Every time, I told her, "*Look under your bed.*" And she usually found whatever it was down there.

Right, her bed. I needed to get under that bed. One problem, though. If I went into her room, my parents would kill me.

When Jackie died, the only thing David asked for was Mom's blessing and mine to bolt her bedroom door and keep it shut until two birthdays passed. A family tradition, he said. If the door was opened prematurely, it would bring further suffering to the family. I figured it was some bizarre Japanese superstition, and I didn't care what he wanted at the time because nothing could have made things worse. So it had stayed locked ever since.

If I unlocked it, David would be crushed. If I did it and David told his family—which he would—they'd label me insolent and disrespectful to the man who raised me. And, once again, I would have embarrassed Mom. That's the story they would tell. Not the real one—that David wouldn't read to me at night until my biological father was gone.

I needed to get into her room. But my promise . . .

What would Jackie do? She wouldn't ask. And she'd be right. David installed a slide bolt on her bedroom door but no padlock. I just couldn't get caught. But if I did, I'd be in the shit. *Big shit.*

The sun would rise in half an hour, then David–superboomer–got up for his morning run. Had to be quick. Ninjaquick.

I scurried down the hall to Jackie's room, slid the bolt, swung the door open, and stepped onto her white shag rug.

I breathed deeply. Jackie's scent still lingered.

My eyes adjusted to the dark. Her room was exactly as she'd left it. Overpriced constricting exercise clothes were scattered on the chair, and a bath towel hung on the back of the door. The heeled slippers she wore when she blow-dried her hair lay beneath her desk.

I opened her closet and took out the summer dress that she'd bought for me before she moved to Toronto. It was too tight, so I gave it back. And that was the truth. I didn't give it back because of the you-are-too-big-to-wear-anything-revealing glares. Jackie had always made me feel beautiful. More than beautiful — like I was her world. It was her voice — one word from her, and what everyone else thought of me faded to nothing. I placed the floral print back next to her *James Bond-girl*-themed prom dress.

Get to work.

I rushed to her bed, got down on my knees and stomach. Reaching under the bed, I felt only dust and carpet. I grabbed a mini flashlight from the top drawer of her bedside table and shone the light beneath the bed and around the bed frame. Nothing.

I checked her computer. *Yes,* the security password was the same — *chunkeymonkey.* Searching her files, it didn't feel like any time had passed. I could have navigated this system with my eyes closed. Picking up the pace, I scanned through photos—images of her first high school trip to Vegas and baseball stadiums in the states. Nothing came up resembling the numbers in my dream. Her browser history was gone.

Next to the mouse, the light from the monitor caught a thick gold bracelet wrapped around a bouquet of pens. I hadn't seen this before. She must have left it the last time she was here. I picked it up. It was clunky and had no give. Not really her style. But the snug metal band felt warm around my wrist, so I took it.

I looked out the window and saw pink shades of light on the horizon. David would be up any minute now. *Move it.*

My eyes were darting around the room. The bookshelf. I was there in a flash, shaking her favourite books upside down—the *Fifty Shades of Grey* series, which we used to read out loud and laugh over like assholes. Nothing was there, either.

Her old university textbooks caught my eye next. Ha, no, she'd never leave a clue in something related to school. The thought almost made me laugh out loud. I used her textbooks more than she did, and I didn't take her courses.

I used my sleeve to remove dust from her snowboard trophies resting on top of the dresser. And that would happen to her memory if I couldn't figure this out.

Through the wall separating Jackie's bedroom and my parents, I heard the sound of water from the shower in their bathroom. I had five minutes.

What the hell am I looking for? And where the hell is it?

I tore through her dresser drawers, still full of clothes, but I turned around every few seconds to check the time on the computer clock. My shaky fingers ran along the drawer cracks where we hid joints. Empty.

Three minutes.

I lifted the corner of the mattress. Nothing. And the bed skirt. Bare.

Two minutes.

Beside her dresser, I pulled the cover off the air vent where Jackie hid pot. Zip.

Shut off the computer. The e-mail icon stood out on the screen. I'd already deactivated her account, but mine still had all our messages.

The sound of running water stopped. *Time's up. Get out.*

Couldn't use the hall. He would see me. I glanced over at the window. The roof.

I pulled the sliding window panel upwards to open it. Wouldn't budge. Again, I used my legs for leverage and pulled. *Ow.* I took my hands off the frame and gave them a shake. I pulled as hard as I could, *c'mon* — it slid open with a jolt and crack. Piercing cold air flooded the room. Gripping the icy shingles, I hoisted myself onto the roof and crawled towards my room window. Sharp square corners jabbed my hands and knees, but I didn't care.

Crunch, crunch, crunch. I was close to my room now. *Crunch, crunch, click.* That wasn't me. I froze. That was the front door. Miko's nails were clicking on the driveway.

Stay still. My hands on the frozen shingles were trembling. I pressed them down harder until it felt like a hundred hornets were stinging my palms. *Don't move.* The sound of a pin dropping could be heard that early on a Saturday morning. Not that it would matter if Miko smelled me — she'd bark loud enough to wake up the entire street.

David passed the house next door, then the one after that. At the third house, Miko was barking, using that high-pitched tone she had when someone came home.

He stopped running.

Oh crap.

I lowered my head and pinched my eyes shut and wished I'd turn to stone.

Not a sound. He saw me. As I raised my head to acknowledge David, some guy approached him on the sidewalk. It was a neighbour and one of his developer friends. Thank God. They chatted, but Miko was still looking my way and whining.

Shush, Miko.

Get the hell out of here before they see you.

David tugged the leash, Miko followed, and they continued jogging up the road. They were gone.

My heart slowed down, and I peeled my hands from the frozen roof, wincing out loud. I climbed back into my room, into the hall, and replaced the bolt on Jackie's door. Ignoring the numbing pain in my fingers, I grabbed my phone and continued my search with my phone from my bed.

Hours and hundreds of e-mails later, I'd produced nothing but a sore jaw from grinding my teeth.

By evening, I was still lying in bed and was rotating between staring at the ceiling and smothering my face with a pillow. Nothing remotely related to that number had turned up.

I revisited our e-mails leading up to my final visit to see Jackie. This was how we said goodbye to each other.

She never received the gift I carefully packed in that suitcase. It was still there one year later. It had stayed in the basement, undisturbed. My version of Jackie's locked room, I supposed.

It was perfect—a custom-made dress for her. Exactly the type of floor-length dress she wore to her fancy work events. A gifted tailor turned my design into a runway-ready look— a full-length black lace, high neck, mesh back that formed an arrow to the center of the lower back, and a slit that ran high up the left leg.

. It could stay there.

My e-mail flashed an inbox capacity warning, so I began deleting old messages, starting with spam. In the *Trash* folder, there was an e-mail from Jackie sent right before my final visit. I remembered the message, but had no idea how it landed in the *Trash* folder.

The message was her to-do list for the party she threw the night she died.

1 – Wine, martini stuff

2 – Cheese, baguette, olives, shrimp, butter

3 – Clean bathroom

4 – Remind co-workers

5 – Play list

6 – Refill soda water canister

7 – 804260636

The phone slid from my sweaty palm to the floor. I remained as still as a statue until I couldn't and let the corners of my mouth take over my cheeks.

I listened to the strong, steady beat of my chest. I knew I was right.

Nothing about this had ever felt right. She had news to tell me that night, but she said she couldn't talk about it until she saw me. She didn't trust her job—her colleagues were at the party the night she died. My mind flashed once more back to the night—the night the dim light shone through the crack of the bathroom door. She never closed the bathroom door. And now this number from that night appeared. It wasn't a coincidence.

The police, Mom, David, and everyone else quoted me statistics on how many people died from slipping and falling in bathtubs each year. She was never another number. And I could prove it. But not by staying there.

CHAPTER FOUR: THREE MONTHS LATER

The car hit a pothole, and my lip liner streaked in a straight line across my cheek. *Sigh. Wipe. Try again.*

Applying makeup in a moving car, especially an Uber ride, was never a good idea. But when I checked my reflection in the rear-view mirror—pre-makeup application—I could almost hear Jackie scream at me—*where's the rest of your face?* And she was right. For a job interview at DMI, the public relations firm Jackie worked for, I had to take it up a notch. Or ten.

I barely recognized myself in my compact mirror—white-blonde hair, bronzed skin, rosy cheeks, and glossy lips. It wasn't me, but it was DMI.

My makeover began long before I saw the job advertisement for an event planner at the company. I looked down at my waist, hips, and thighs—parts that would have jiggled and blobbed during a car ride a year ago. The people who knew the former larger me saw me now and cheered. When they asked how I lost the weight, I told them it was simple— become so depressed you couldn't get out of bed to go to the kitchen. Then I'd ask them if that sounded like something they would want to try.

I ran a wood comb through my brittle hair one final time. *That should do it.* I looked like one of them, and more importantly, not like I used to. There was a chance Jackie's colleagues may have seen me on her social media posts. I disabled her accounts, as well as mine, shortly after she died, but there were photos of me the day they were shut down.

My gloves were moist. I flipped my palms toward the sky. My body would need to cooperate if I was going to pull this off. I didn't have any event planning experience, but neither did Jackie when DMI hired her. She was confident, though, and could pull the best answers out of her ass any day. The only thing I had going for me was my memory. I paid attention when she talked about her work and kind of know a few industry tricks.

They might see through it, though, and cut the interview short. And there goes my plan. Focus on what you know, what's real, and build from there. I closed my eyes. *You've drawn up million-dollar contracts. You're a senior event planner. You've planned weddings, massive conferences, and art shows. Like Jackie used to say, fake it until you make it.*

Glancing up, I noticed cars idled bumper-to-bumper and were filling the road ahead. "Can you take another route?" I asked the driver.

The company's general manager, Claudia Lanley, agreed to interview me while she was in Vancouver on business. I couldn't blow this by arriving late.

A hotel room door swung open. A woman with thick square glasses and prominent hip bones answered. "What do you want?" she said.

I looked up. "Claudia? I'm Katey Philips."

"Who?"

Maybe I had the wrong room. "I'm here for the interview."

Her claw-like, manicured dark purple nails drummed on the door. "Oh right, you. Go by the window."

Claudia runway-strutted into another room. I followed, tracking the slick tight bun at the top of her head. Not one loose strand of hair strayed from the arrangement.

She must not have been there for very long. In fact, it was as if no one was staying there at all. There was no suitcase in sight. And nothing rested on top of the dresser or the small bedside table—not even the complimentary hotel pen. Not a ripple on the king-sized bed duvet.

I waited for her to sit at the small round table by the window. She remained standing, hands on her hips. "Where did you get that outfit? It's adorable."

My head dropped to examine my black pencil skirt and matching blazer covering a cream-coloured blouse. *What does she mean by adorable? Girl Guide outfit adorable? Wouldn't-be-caught-dead-in-that adorable?*

"It's Tahari, inherited from my sister."

Shit. I did not just say that.

My face was hot. I practiced that and reminded myself over and over not to make any reference to my sister.

I tried to clarify. "It was a present that I helped myself to. Same thing, right?"

Get it together, you idiot.

"Spin around," she instructed, pointing toward the ground and circling with her index finger.

Spin? This is freaking weird.

Trying to rotate naturally, my knees locked, and I was moving like a penguin.

Claudia rolled her eyes to the ceiling. Maybe she was working through my Jackie blunder.

Don't let her go down that path. Forget the slip-up. She was more interested in my wardrobe than anything I had to say. Maybe I could offer her my outfit in exchange for the job.

A laugh-snort almost surfaced at the thought of walking out of here in only a peacoat. Wrapping my hands around my waist and shoulders pushed back, I twirled like I was wearing a poodle skirt. "Thank you, my mom's friends love this outfit."

"Sit," she barked.

We sat opposite each other. She didn't look at me as she was scribbling in a small, black leather-lined notebook.

"If you had to choose between giving birth or a shattered

22

femur, which would it be?"

What kind of interview question is this? Is it a trick question?

Okay, think like her. No, wait. Think like Jackie. Remember what she told you about Claudia. Claudia was single, late thirties, no friends, the boss's pet, sucked at her job and delegated her responsibilities to junior staff. But when she was working, she always looked good doing it.

"Shattered femur."

"Why is that?" she asked, not looking up.

Jackie never mentioned colleagues who had kids. Not a problem. A family wasn't in the cards for me. "Both are horribly painful and cause damage that can never be undone. However, the burden of a child will sting far longer than the time it takes a broken bone to heal."

Claudia made a tick on the page. *I think she bought it.*

"Who would you rather go on a date with. Harvey Weinstein or Hannibal Lecter?"

I paused, taking time to craft my response. *Image, think image.*

Claudia was using her pen to let me know she was waiting. *Tap-tap-tap-tap-tap-tap.*

"Hannibal Lecter."

She tipped her head upward.

"Hannibal Lecter would treat me to the best restaurants with the finest wine. I could order whatever I wanted. With Weinstein, we couldn't go out in public. I'd have to settle for a Subway sandwich. I'll take my chances with the host who might see me as an ingredient of fine dining."

Claudia finally looked me in the eye. I looked right back.

She gripped the pen tightly and made a few short notes. *Bring it.*

"Correct this sentence . . . the conclusion of *Sex and the City* has polarized Carrie Bradshaw fans."

Anyone can spot that error. "The conclusion of *Sex and the City* has polarized fans of the show."

Claudia scribbled furiously.

"Do you believe in bears?"

Sweet Mother of God. What's she testing now?

"Yes, being from British Columbia, I've seen many bears —
"

"I've never seen a bear, so they don't exist."

Point taken. I can lie, too. "Then let me tell you about these four-legged furry creatures. They communicate with trees, the bears eat the insects that destroy the leaves, and in return, the treeline moves, expanding the bears' territory. Every year, the trees encroach, closing in on remote homes in the forest. If trees are chopped down, they migrate closer until the branches break through windows and roofs. People can try to leave, but bears run faster."

Claudia stared at me and parted her lips. *I'll leave it there.*

"Those who are fortunate to work at DMI live a blessed life," she said. "They travel the world, attend the most desired events, even bypassing celebrities." She paused, glared out the window, and hummed a longing tone.

I interrupted. "I would do whatever you ask to show my gratitude for the opportunity."

She took a moment to look at me before starting again. When she did, she talked about the firm, occasionally distracted by the mirror behind me. I didn't learn anything new from her spiel. I knew who the owners were when the company was established and its services — crisis management, social media campaigns, branding, events and media training.

When she finished, our session finally began to feel like an interview. "Tell me about an event you managed," she said.

As I delivered my rehearsed response, tweaking Jackie's experience organizing a high-profile art show, Claudia answered her phone and was talking over me.

I stopped.

"Keep going," she said to me and continued her phone

conversation.

This might have been a test to determine how easily I was thrown off, so I talked on. And so did she. This was so strange. There was no way she could follow her conversation and my solo discussion at the same time. I wondered what would happen if I started talking about my favourite kidney?

"We're done," Claudia said, rising to her feet while still holding her phone to her ear.

Clutching the envelope with my references, I hesitated to release its fabricated contents to the woman who saw my sister more than I did in her last years.

She pointed to the door.

"Have a great afternoon." I smiled, placed it in her hand, and turned away.

Back at home, I was pacing back and forth in my room. I replayed the interview in my mind over and over, followed by a smack of my palm to my forehead.

My clothes? All I had to say was I didn't remember where I got them. Maybe mentioning my sister didn't click with her at the time, but that didn't mean it would later.

Lecter or Weinstein? I should have chosen Weinstein. DMI probably had clients like him.

And because I didn't have enough to worry about, I submitted fake references to Claudia. I had no choice. I had no event planning experience, and I didn't want to ask Ben to lie for me, even though he would have. Maybe. So I did a Google search and found a service that would falsely attest to my event experience. I met a guy wearing aviator sunglasses, a toque, and a hoody in an alley behind a shady nightclub. I paid him twenty-five hundred cash to create a few websites for non-existent companies that I'd claim I worked at. He also agreed to pretend to be my references when contacted. When I asked how he would pull this off with one voice, he left with my money.

My cell phone vibrated on the wooden desk. It was DMI. "Hello?"

"You can start on Monday."

It was Claudia's voice. My heart pounded. The DMI job was meant to be. I'd be with the company that I *knew* somehow had something to do with Jackie's death.

"Thank you so much, Claudia. I—"

"I'll e-mail you more details."

"Wait, you mean start this coming Monday, three days from now?"

"Do you want the job or not?"

"I'll be there."

"Eight AM sharp."

Click.

CHAPTER FIVE

"Ben, sorry to call you at this hour."
"It's okay. I'm watching TV. What's up?"
"Remember our conversation at the bar? How I'm doing better?"
Ben paused. "Yeah. Saw you went out for lunch with the team again. Did a double take."
"That was before pedicures."
He chuckled. He was in a good mood.
"To get more better, I think I'm going to need more time. A long time away from work."
He was quiet.
"Of course, the offer still stands."
Ben, you are the best.
"I'm going to Toronto."
"I knew you would." He paused. "For how long?"
"I don't know."
"Come back when you're ready."
"Thank you for everything, Ben. I wouldn't be where I am without you."
I meant every word. He was my boss who was better than any friend. There was a time I thought we might be more. But after Jackie died, I couldn't, I don't know.
"Call me for anything, understand?"
"Of course."
"When are you going?"
"I'm leaving this weekend."
"Be well, Katey. Stay safe."

CHAPTER SIX: JACKIE

June 2016

"This one, the whole family is together."

The roar of the powerboat was our cue. We sprang out of our Muskoka chairs and got in position at the edge of the dock bordering the narrow lake channel.

"Raise your beer higher. Wave."

"Drive closer, Daddy. He sees us. Now make his day."

In unison, we turned around, pulled our bathing suit bottoms to our ankles and stuck out our bare bums, and bounced them in the air like balls.

"Did you see their faces?" Katey shrieked.

"No, but I can ask my asshole."

"Pull your bottoms up before you blind someone with those pasty cheeks," she told me.

I grabbed her oversized brimmed sun hat. "I'll put it on when you take the seniors' garden tour outfit off."

I yelped as she pushed me off the dock.

Splash. I could see the lake's stony bottom and would have stayed underwater longer, but when I flipped over, Katey was standing on the balls of her feet on the edge of the dock.

I broke the water's surface.

"Your beer is ruined," she said.

"Then I'll have another." Treading water, I poured the contaminated can contents into my mouth.

"I'll get you another one."

"Why don't you get one for Mom-shorts?" I flicked my ponytail at the refrigerator-shaped neighbour wearing knee-length fire-truck red shorts, stomping on her golf-green lawn.

All week, I had to hear, "*Don't wear your wet bathing suit in the house, no swimming until two hours after eating, no pushing off the dock.*"

"She needs to get laid. Pretty sure that was the last time for her." I drew an arrow in the water toward the pre-teen boys making their way to their dock.

"Shh." Katey brought her index finger to her lips. "I wanna come back here next summer. They won't rent to you if the neighbours complain."

"Then I'll have to buy it."

"Do you know what this place would go for? Be extra nice to Dad."

"No need. I've got this."

Katey swatted the air. "Can we wait until the end of the week to make an enemy?"

We wouldn't be there for a week. DMI cut my vacation short. And I had let them. I couldn't afford a lakefront cottage, or anything I wanted, without DMI. I hadn't told Katey that we were leaving early yet and she couldn't come back to Toronto with me. She wasn't the type who would help us bypass the line at the bars. My work knew this. They didn't want her around. And neither did I, not there.

I turned away from my sister, dropped my head to the lake, and bit my lip.

"Wench reminds me of that French teacher."

Katey giggled and lowered her voice. "Except *she* was getting something at those Dungeons and Dragons conventions."

A picture of our high school teacher wearing a too-sexy medieval-warrior outfit with an empty scabbard made its way to social media. "She just wanted a proper sword fitting."

"Eww." She kicked water into my face. It felt good.

"You'd feel differently if Ben offered his sword."

I left my eyes open as more water from Katey's kicks flew

into my face.

"Oh, my God. Ben is my boss, " she squealed.

"Nothing wrong with going out to dinner, followed by a sleepover with your boss to unwind after a long, busy week."

"Oh, my God. I'm getting more beer." She got up, wrapped a beach towel around her waist, and headed up the stone path winding through the grass to the cottage.

"Do we have any left?" I called.

"We'll need to go into town for more soon. I want to confirm the township's organics disposal policies anyways."

I whipped around and pushed my beer can underwater. *Tell her.*

Mom-shorts was stomping over to our dock. I would have gone back underwater if Katey wasn't trapped on land with her.

"Excuse me, girls," the neighbour called in a high-pitched nasal voice.

I climbed the dock ladder out of the water. I bunched my wet hair over my shoulder and twisted it into a knot. Water dripped over me and landed on the dock. "Can we help you, madam?"

She pointed to her house, "I'm the owner of the cottage next door." She kept her arm pointed straight. "My family and the other families have been on this lake for generations." She swept her arm from the ground to the sky, and her triceps fat flapped like a flag.

Katey and I looked at each other.

"New people have started to use this cottage," she said, pointing to where we were staying.

"We're up for the week," Katey said, adjusting the knot holding up her beach towel. "Is there something we can help you with?"

"You're visiting. I understand you don't know any better."

"Won't you help our fresh blood understand?" I asked.

The woman crossed her arms, separating her unsupported boobs and solid gut. "As I mentioned, this is a *family* lake. Many of us have young children." Her eyes skipped over my frame for a moment. "Modest swimwear is more appropriate for this lake." She turned to Katey. "Like this young lady's maternity suit."

Katey lifted her towel to her armpits after struggling to grip it.

"Oh, is my bikini showing too much?" I tugged the strings holding together the bottom by the sides.

Mom-shorts glued her eyes above my chest. "Yes."

I nodded. "I will rectify the situation immediately."

The woman dusted off her pudgy hands and raised her chin.

Smiling at my sister, I reached my hand behind my back and pulled. My bikini top landed on the grass.

I paraded to the end of the dock. When I reached the edge, I spread my arms apart wide, dropped my head backward, and let my hands fall to the sides. With one more pull, my bikini bottom landed at my ankles, and I kicked it into the lake.

Later that day, Katey asked me to repeat my dock display every time the neighbour came outside. Her eyes were wide, hands clasped under her nose. I promised her I would do so.

I decided that I would tell her about my early departure the next day. I wanted the day to be ours. And it almost was. That evening, we sat on the dock to watch the sunset. I faced our neighbour's cottage. I gritted my teeth and fastened my eyes on the blue bathing suit trunks hanging on a clothesline. Choose another swimsuit, she said. I hadn't chosen my clothes in years.

CHAPTER SEVEN

"Mom, I'm getting on the elevator. Love you, too. Bye."
The trade-off for moving across the country was frequently calling my parents. I told them my firm had temporarily reassigned me to Toronto. They told me to quit. Then I told them that when I was home, all I saw was Jackie. My room overlooked the backyard pool where we learned to swim, the tree house we told ghost stories in, and the tomatoes in the garden we grew, picked, and sold at the side of the road. And then I added my trump card—that my therapist suggested trying some distance. That was the most useful thing about therapy—no one could verify what happened in those sessions.

And the move *was* temporary. I was in Toronto for one reason, and when I was done, I was outta there. And when I found out that *natural causes* didn't end my sister's life, I would ensure those who were responsible met the maximum punishment of the law. I didn't know much about uncovering these types of crimes, but I was experienced with environmental offences, and I was confident the same cycle held—polluters could dump their waste, and it may have appeared like the earth just absorbed it. But nature always resurfaces our sins.

I was looking up at my destination—a window-covered Jenga tower, and I squeezed my knees together. I brought a three-tier pyramid to the skyline of rectangular skyscrapers—a number from a party on top of a witch at a bar and a bottom layer of suspicion and unresolved guilt. The three layers didn't form the strongest structure, but they had given me purpose, and really the only feeling I'd had in over a year. And I would rather feel blind, stupid hope than numbness that hardened like a candy apple that was missing its core.

I stepped off the 22nd floor and smoothed out my black tweed skirt suit. Double-frosted glass doors opened to a reception area straddled by curved hallways. I walked to the right side of the unoccupied reception desk and peeked down the hall. Cubicles lined the wall of windows that flooded the space with rare March sunlight.

This was where Jackie started on her first day. She would have marched right into the office and had everyone on their feet, gawking. I needed the opposite. No attention, no stares, no curiosity. I needed to find someone who would talk. Someone who was at Jackie's party the night she died. Someone knew something.

"Good morning, Kaitlin."

I jumped and spun around.

"Good morning, Claudia." She was way too close to me. *No, be like them. Stay put. Smile.*

"How was your flight?"

"Flight was good. And it's Katey."

"All settled in?"

"I'm staying at a hotel up the street, but I'm looking for an apart—"

"I'll show you around."

I followed Claudia's topknot bun as her snakeskin stilettos clicked on the stone floor. "Take it." She handed me a folded piece of paper. "Your e-mail isn't set up yet."

I unfolded it. *Code of conduct, blah, blah, blah.* But at the bottom, in bold, it said I had to recruit three new clients by the month of May. *What?*

"What is this?"

"The terms of your probation."

"I have to bring on three new clients in three months?"

"You can read."

God, that seems like a lot. Once, at my consulting job, I brought in two clients in a similar timeframe, but that was a fluke. This must have been new. Jackie didn't mention a client quota.

"So I'll be working on the sales end?"

"A mix of sales and execution."

"This is only a target, right? Based on previous years' sales?"

"It's your required sales. We need to know if you're going to fit in here."

How am I going to meet this? Shit, I might only have three months to figure everything out.

I edged beside her. "Most DMI staff meet their targets, right?"

She grinned. "The ones here met their targets."

Claudia halted at the space lining the windows where the desks were set up in quads.

"The intern," she said.

A girl with artificially swollen lips pouted at a round compact mirror surrounded by make-up on her desk. She hoisted a lipstick in one hand, "Should I wear Sex-in-a-Vegas-Pool or"—and lifted the other hand with another lipstick—"Flirt for Freedom?"

Our future was in good hands. "They're both nice. I'm Katey. Sorry, didn't catch your name."

She removed the cap off a lipstick. "I need more lip liner."

"This place is a disaster." Claudia picked up the loose paper with her index and thumbnail, knocking over a paper coffee cup. "Were you raised in a pig stye? Clean this up now. And then—" Claudia reached into her Birkin purse and took out a twenty-dollar bill and something else. "I'll take a soy triple-shot latte, no foam, and an omelet–egg whites only. Quebec dairy only. And here's my ticket for my dry cleaning."

Claudia dropped the bill and ticket on her desk.

The girl snapped her mirror shut.

She's the intern — probably wasn't here at the same time as Jackie.

"Joan, our accountant." As Claudia tapped the cubicle wall with her fig-coloured fingernails, a woman with short gray hair turned her head, squinted at me, then returned to watching multiple computer screens.

Probably not the partying type.

"This is Larissa, Trish, and Ravi, our account managers," Claudia continued.

They were young, maybe 28 — the age Jackie would have turned this year. They might have been at Jackie's party. My stomach tightened.

The guy got up as the others who *appeared* to be on calls stayed put in their chairs. He reached for my clammy hand.

Make eye contact. Don't squeeze their hands too hard. Remember to blink.

I studied their faces with no idea what I was looking for.

Ravi took a bite from a chicken drumstick, skin hanging from the side of his mouth as he chewed. "Keto."

"You can eat your lunch at lunchtime," Claudia said.

Ravi hid the drumstick behind his back and turned to me. "Have we met? You look familiar."

My cheeks grew hot. "Nope, just moved here."

He tilted his head to the side, and dark greasy bangs covered one bushy eyebrow.

He'd probably seen a picture of me before but couldn't place it. *Suggest something before he figures out who you are.*

"I've gone ice fishing north of here," I said. "Near Barrie. Have you been?"

Ravi moved his lips to one side.

Oh God, he might recognize me.

"Risky behaviour is not permitted," Claudia said. "It's in your contract."

What contract? Lady, all you've given me is a sweaty ball of paper.

"Of course. No more ice fishing."

"Nah," Ravi wagged the drumstick at me, chicken veins dangling. "Pretty sure I've seen you at my show. I'm DJ Bro-Spin."

Ah ha. Someone who will talk to me . . . about himself, but a start nevertheless. "Haven't been to your show, but I would love to."

"Moving on," Claudia instructed.

As we continued down the hall, two girls in short dresses and a guy in tight pants huddled around a cell phone. Once they saw Claudia, they dispersed.

"Hillary and Christine." Claudia flicked her wrist at the girls with identical waist-length balayage hair. "They do social media." She addressed them. "It's nice to see you in the *morning*."

"That's Hillary, with two *L*'s," the darker one said, showing off her tongue piercing.

"Got it. Nice to meet you, Hillary, and . . ."

"I'm Christine, with a *Ceee*."

"Fabulous to meet you," they said in tandem.

They squealed, giggled, and flipped their hair. "We finish each other's sentences."

"If only you finished each other's work," Claudia said.

The long-haired girls looked at me. "She would look gorge in the navy Dior."

"OMG, yes! Would really . . . mmm . . . yeah, give her a waist."

Claudia turned back. "That's an old dress. We get rid of worn, tired things, don't we, girls."

"It's from this year's spring collection," Hillary jabbed. Her twin folded her arms in solidarity.

Claudia whipped half a turn the other way. "Jacob, our web developer and graphic designer." She gestured to the guy with acne scars on his face, standing by the window.

His muffin top spilled over the side of his pants so tight

you could see the date of a nickel coin. He squared his hips, pointed his finger at me, and winked. "S'up."

I waved.

Claudia stopped where the cubicles ended and tipped her chin. "And these are the executive offices for myself, the DMI's CEO, Sandra Maile, and the owner, Daniel Maile."

She waited. "This is my office. Enter."

She remained at the door. I walked over to the window. Tall grey buildings, grey streets crawling with grey cars under a grey sky. *Hideous.* "Gorgeous view," I said.

I followed Claudia toward the other offices. "Sandra and Daniel are probably too busy right now."

Through clear glass walls at the end of the hall, I saw Sandra standing behind a desk, fingertips splayed and firmly pressed on its surface. She leaned toward Daniel like a boss did when their employees were about to get it.

Jackie told me about them. Daniel Maile owned the company because he put up the financing and used his family connections to bring in clients. Sandra was the president, the heavy-lifter, and the mastermind behind its success.

Jackie said as a teenager, Sandra moved to Canada with her mother from somewhere in Eastern Europe. They both cleaned houses. Daniel noticed the redhead who filled her uniform beautifully and folded his underwear. Daniel fell for the girl who he would never have to answer to.

In DMI's early days, Sandra worked her ass off to build the business while Daniel took on late-night partying and flew clients to boxing matches. Although still considered *boutique*, DMI was now an up-and-coming PR firm.

Now in her mid-forties, Sandra easily put her younger female staff to shame. Her soft auburn waves fell midway down her back, complementing the crocodile-textured blush blouse and leather burgundy pencil skirt, pinching in the right places. She was at least a foot shorter than Daniel, but her high leather boots levelled their conviction.

Sandra turned her head and noticed me. We locked eyes. She stopped speaking.

Claudia waved me in the opposite direction. "I'll introduce you later."

I tore myself away and went with her.

Back near the entrance again, I noticed two small cubicles I hadn't seen before—one overlooking the hallway, the other facing the window.

"This is your workstation." Claudia pointed to the window desk. "Next to Isabella."

I took a step back to view my neighbour typing feverishly—a curly-haired faux blonde with dark roots, wearing a low-cut mesh shirt.

She swivelled her chair around and extended a French-manicured hand, silver bracelets jingling. "Hi, honey. Welcome." She flashed bright, perfectly straight whitened teeth. Her smile was warm, and I leaned in.

"The Crompton VIP event is tonight, right?" Claudia asked Isabella.

"Yes, I'm stoked."

Claudia waved the back of her hand at me. "Here's your help."

"I would love another pair of hands. Sophie will be late," Isabella said. Then she turned her attention to me. "You'll be outside tonight." She brushed her fingertips on my nylons. "Not warm enough."

Well, well. That was the most helpful, and personal, thing anyone had said to me today. Still feeling her touch on my leg, maybe I'd get somewhere with her.

"Do you have something to wear? If not, I'll hook you up." Isabella asked.

"Nothing casual," Claudia interjected. "High leather boots, black tights, and a black dress or skirt just above the knees.

Don't wear anything stuffed with feathers or fluff, either. A full leather overcoat is appropriate."

I blinked and tried to remember one of those things. "I'll be ready."

Claudia swivelled her ostrich neck in the other direction. "Ravi. Come here."

He made his way over, stuffing his face with a Danish.

"Katey will help with the AleAngels proposal," Claudia said. "Can you get her up to speed?"

She kind of paused.

"Wonderful. My next appointment is starting." She walked away.

Isabella peered down the hall towards the fading sound of Claudia's heels against the floor. "Don't mix leather with leather," she told me.

"What?"

She wagged her index finger from side to side. "Leather boots and a leather coat. Nuh-uh."

I licked my lips. *How else can this nice girl help*?

She continued, "How you look tonight equally reflects on how DMI is perceived at that moment and the impression carried with them." With her fingertips, she hooked the front hem of my dress. "Let me help you."

CHAPTER EIGHT

I was rummaging through my suitcase, looking for a hat and scarf that would match the back U-shaped neckline dress Isabella insisted I wear. So weird, I didn't think the dress was Isabella's—it looked too big to fit her.

I pulled out ski mittens—pretty sure Isabella and Claudia would throw me in the pig stye if I showed up at a corporate event in these. I dug deeper and found a pair of dark purple leather driving gloves that Jackie gave me for Christmas one year. I told her I didn't want new clothes, given the environmental impact of the fashion industry. She wouldn't take them back and told me they might come in handy for committing a crime. She was right, always was.

One final check in front of the mirror. I saw the image I needed to be—knee-high, faux suede boots, long-sleeved black dress under a black lambswool coat, cashmere scarf, and shoulders covered by hair so bright I could have been a human flashlight.

I slowly pulled on the gloves. They really were beautiful.

I arrived at the hotel to find Isabella pulling a dining table across the floor.

"What's going on?" I asked. Rectangle, square, and noodle-shaped tables were artfully arranged on the dining floor. They were topped with bright green, blue, and red gemstone centrepieces attached to cement bases. They looked like sparkly snow cones. Isabella was sandwiched between a handful of tables with off-white lopsided tablecloths and more decorative rocks on the floor on the other side.

"The hotel screwed up," Isabella wiped her forehead with the back of her hand. "Sandra will blow her anal glands if she sees this. We have to fix it."

"Let me know what goes where."

"You're a doll. And you look very nice. Well done." Isabella passed me her phone with a blueprint of the room. "Copy this scheme." She sat down. "I need a breather. I can't look like I came from the gym."

I studied the schematic. Ah, some rocks needed to be moved this way and a few tables that way. No big deal. I got to it.

After hauling around a dozen or so tables, I felt sweat trickle down my back and soak my tights. Fantastic.

"I'm boiling. Need to take off my tights."

"I'll help you." She advanced.

Do I look that helpless? "I got it," I told her.

"Go behind this table in case the AV crew walks in. And keep your boots on. Do you know what happens when a twenty-pound rock lands on your foot?"

"I upgrade to steel-toe Pradas?"

She laughed through her nose. "I'm going to chat with the kitchen. Keep going, be right back."

Whatever. Do everything she says, and she'll feed me information on Jackie in no time. Piece of cake. I just need to survive my probation to receive the intel.

With fewer clothes on, I got back to work. One by one, I picked up the rocks and steadied them by hugging them close.

Isabella returned. Her jaw dropped.

"What's wrong?"

"Look down."

Damn. Those stupid rocks left a white film all over my black dress. I looked like that famous intern, fresh from under the desk.

"We'll keep you outside for the night," Isabella said.

Next to her, it was addict Barbie meets glam Barbie.

Hmm. I ran my tongue over my teeth and took a step toward her.

"Got my target today. Maybe I'm paranoid, but signing three clients seems like a lot in a few months."

She twisted a red rock on the table.

"Is this a firm target? There's wiggle room, right?"

Addressing the rock, she said, "It's for the best. You want to know sooner rather than later if you like the way we do things."

"Could you give me some tips?"

"Sure."

More silence. She brushed the tablecloth and checked her fingertips. *Am I talking to myself here?*

"So we'll talk later?"

"I meant to tell you. Dinner looks good. I checked that the dietary requests were marked with photographs. The kitchen and wait staff hates it, but someone screaming bloody murder over gluten can throw a wrench into the night."

I should have known better than to fall for the pretty nice girl.

"Let's get ready. I'll need more time than you. Go to the main bathroom, and I'll meet you outside. Sophie will arrive soon."

Dare I ask where she was going to get ready and why I couldn't join her? There probably wasn't room for me because she invited the tablecloth.

"One more thing." Isabella pulled a tablet from her bag and passed it to me. "The password for InvitePro is DMIone-two-zero-one-eight."

I didn't know what that was. And I needed to last beyond my first day. She'd probably tell me to figure out how to work the software by myself, but I had to try.

"At my old firm, we used different software. Could you give me a quick one-oh-one on InvitePro?"

"Oh, sure. Did you use EventWiz before?"

"Yes," I responded and held my breath.

"It's similar. You'll be fine."

I bit my lip and scanned the room, orbiting my head.

Isabella took the tablet from me. "Enter the guest's name or organization. You won't know the names, though. Don't ask. We're expected to know everyone who's been invited. You can take a picture of the guest, but be careful. They can't know."

Isabella took a photo of herself. "You can see my name, title, picture, and company pop up. I've already checked in, so click here to confirm that I showed up."

She lowered the tablet. "Hmm, it *is* cold tonight, even with the heat lamps. Forget the outdoor check-ins. Those will be done at the second point, inside the hotel."

"What will I do outside?"

She clicked another icon. "Greet."

"Just say hi?"

"Silly. Enter details on what guests are wearing, the type of car they arrive in." She winked. "You know, the stuff that matters. The stuff that drives our revenue."

A welcome in the PR world was synonymous for determining someone's net worth. Got it.

"Two of us will be inside, two outside," she said.

Isabella looked both ways over her shoulders—hair curls bouncing into my face—then turned back to me. "The fun stuff is in these tabs." Returning to the guest list, she clicked on the name Burke. When his picture popped up, she clicked on his profile tab. A password request was prompted. Isabella pulled the tablet toward her chest, sheltering the entry, before positioning the tablet back in my view.

The screen displayed a headshot of a bald double-chinned middle-aged man. "You can see the company's financials, business history with DMI, and our competitors. Blah, blah—the good shit is recorded here." She tapped another tab. "See this guy. Only the smell of newspaper gets him off."

What? I searched her face for a sign of embarrassment or an accidental slip. She was typing away as if we were talking about the weather.

Why does a PR company want that type of information?

She was happy to share some guy's fantasy, but not a word of advice on making it through my probation?

"When Burke arrives, I'll offer him the personal section of the newspaper," I said.

Isabella touched my forearm with her fingertips, and her nails grazed my clammy skin. "Bad girl. You go and clean up. See you outside, better than new."

She left. I pulled on my gloves, high up my arm, and made my way outside.

Sophie was stationed at the greeting spot. I took the position across from her.

"I'm *so* happy someone else is working events," she said, teetering toward me in five-inch-heel, mid-thigh boots. "Did Isabella tell you what to do out here?"

"Yep." I brought the tablet closer, picked a guest at random, selected the password-protected tab, and entered the number from my dream — 804260636.

Access Denied flashed in response. That was fine. I'd try it on each guest.

I looked up. I had time to go through each guest. Sophie was taking selfies of her enlarged cherry-coloured lips with the hotel in the background.

"How long have you worked at DMI?" I asked.

"A few months."

Darn. She wouldn't have overlapped with Jackie. Still, she might know something helpful. "Sounds like you've been to some cool events, parties?"

"Girls. Where is Isabella?" Claudia, once again, appeared out of nowhere and posed in the center of the red carpet — one hand on her hip, feet facing twelve and two.

Isabella was probably planting cameras in the bathroom.

"She's getting ready."

Claudia riffled through a shopping bag. "We will be the first faces, the first impression of DMI." She pulled out and distributed matching emerald-green scarves, earmuffs, and gloves thinner than mine.

Claudia held a compact mirror up to my face. "Your eyes are leaking."

Oh no. I thought I had cleaned up all the makeup sweat.

She reached into her purse, took out a tissue, and wiped hard underneath my eyes. The cold air was stinging my eyeball. She stopped, licked her thumb, and continued scrubbing with surprisingly rough skin.

"Next time, you'll need approval before you present yourself," she told me.

Claudia turned towards Sophie, removed her neck warmer, then turned back to me. "Change those heinous gloves."

Sophie prodded at the gifts from Claudia. "These aren't warm enough. We're gonna freeze."

"One lucky person will be inside with me," Claudia said, looking over at the hotel entrance.

Sophie couldn't stay out here. Whatever was in her lips would probably freeze and break off.

Yanking me forward, Claudia unravelled my cashmere scarf. She wrapped the new green fabric around my neck and hooked the earmuffs on my head.

I slid off my gloves and placed them into my coat pockets.

"What are you doing?" Claudia squawked. "You look like you have two hip tumors." She pulled them out.

"But—"

Isabella joined us.

"There you are." Claudia handed her the green combination. "Wear these."

Give those back. My open hands reached for Claudia. "You don't have to hold my things."

"I won't. The trash can will."

She retreated into the hotel. I watched her all the way.

"Go," Isabella shooed Sophie toward the hotel. "Me and Katey will stay."

Sophie held up the green ensemble on her way to the hotel. "These don't match. They're different shades of green."

Attendees kept coming. Isabella's energy somehow escalated with each arrival. And somehow, she delivered a unique compliment for each person.

I continued entering the nine-digit number into the tablet, trying to hack the protected profiles. It wasn't working.

It was freezing outside. The heat lamps may as well have been streetlamps. I removed the paper-thin gloves. I'd rather let the cold burn my skin than wear them. Isabella demanded I put them back on or go inside when my fingers turned blue. I told her the blue went well with the green, and she shook her head.

People arrived in droves. When they entered the hotel, Isabella ran over to my side and showed me the details she was recording. Everything was there—cosmetic surgery, diamond carat count, designer clothing brands. I showed her my one entry—*skinny* and *blonde*. Isabella's breath coated the tablet screen.

A black *Mercedes* stopped in front of the hotel. I took down the plate number. A tall, well-built guy in a tuxedo that fit like a glove got out, tossed his keys to the valet, and glided our way.

Retaking my position, I practiced my greeting. Smiled, waited for Isabella to announce the title and name of the attendee, said nothing, and smiled again.

A tall, rail-thin woman with pin-straight ash-blonde hair exited the same car and followed quite a ways behind the guy in the tux. She hurried when gusts of snow hit the entrance path and slowed as he got closer to the hotel.

Pretty girl and prettier guy pretended to arrive separately. I typed into the tablet and showed Isabella.

Ignoring me, Isabella stood taller and smiled generously as they approached. "Good evening, Daniel."

"Nothing dampens your spirits, Isabella, not even the frigid weather." He squared his shoulders towards me and approached. Then he took another step closer. "I'm lucky another trooper joined my team."

Shit. That was Daniel, my new boss, Daniel. Or boss' husband. "V-very nice to meet you." Dimples formed below the corners of his smile. I brushed my hair behind my ears.

He continued to address me. His voice was slick. "Take tomorrow off for doing the graveyard shift, ladies."

His attention remained in my direction as he made his way toward the hotel.

Isabella looked around once he was gone. "Don't record that one."

"I'm so sorry, so sorry." I'd never seen him up close before. *Stupid, stupid, stupid.*

Isabella laughed. "Don't worry about it." Her voice turned to a whisper. "They are kind of apart, but still together for DMI." Her tone shortened. "Stay away from him."

Geez, all I did was say hi. Whatever, I was the last person she needed to worry about in that department. I wasn't in pursuit of a husband.

"Can I ask a huge favour?" I asked her.

She squeezed my cold, stiff hand. "I'm not going to say anything."

I didn't trust her, but for the sake of my survival at the firm, I squeezed her hand back.

"Just don't say anything about what you saw," she said. "And don't take tomorrow off."

I nodded. "I'll have this down for the next event."

"Don't forget what you learned. There are no events in the pipeline."

Isabella glanced at the incoming traffic, rushed over to me, undid the top and bottom buttons of my coat, and spread each side, revealing my black dress. "You can do it back up in a moment." She rushed back to her position.

"Welcome to the team," a full, rich voice interrupted.

It was Sandra, wearing a faux fur-trimmed white cape that sank into a *V* to highlight her flawless cleavage.

I couldn't help but stare at her. She was a tractor beam. I wanted her to invite me into her sleigh and offer me Turkish delight. I would have folded her underwear.

"A pleasure to meet you," she said, then turned to Isabella. "Is everything going well?"

"So far, so good," Isabella said, her tone less bouncy, more composed, like Sandra's.

"Excellent," Sandra replied as if Isabella communicated something more. "Can I get you anything?" Sandra asked me.

"We have everything," Isabella said before I could answer.

Out of all the arrivals, Sandra must have been wearing the least amount of clothes and had spent the most time outdoors. She didn't produce a goosebump or a shiver. The wind was gone — even it knew who the boss around there was.

"François," Sandra said and kissed a tall, bald man on both cheeks. She linked her arm, covered in a long white glove, with his before they disappeared into the hotel.

I realized I was sucking in. I felt like I'd had a brush with royalty.

I didn't notice Isabella had left until I heard running footsteps back from the hotel.

"Here you go, honey," she said, handing me two scrunched purple leather gloves.

By the time I got back to my hotel room, it was past midnight.

I watched a tea bag floating in water until it went cold.

Isabella made me look and smell stupid on my first day. She wasn't willing to help me recruit clients, but she got me my gloves. And she taught me how to use the creepy stalker software. But the back and forth between quasi-catty behaviour and overly friendly hands wasn't keeping me up. There were no upcoming events. Isabella said so. Why did they rush to hire an event planner to work on events that didn't exist?

I parked the thought—maybe Isabella forgot or Claudia didn't tell her of some upcoming event. I rested my laptop on the hotel armchair and began researching the AleAngels' bid.

I rubbed my shoulders and looked outside. The windows in my hotel met energy efficiency manufacturing requirements from fifty years ago.

I put on a raggedy old sweater that Jackie used to call a *rat's nest*. It was her sweater at one point. After she graduated, she took a year to teach English in China. When I flew to Beijing, we visited the Great Wall. It was so cold that day my bones felt damp. I found a corner sheltered from the wind and curled into a ball. I told her through chattered teeth to keep going. Jackie took off her ski jacket, and her long hair thrashed her face. She wouldn't move until I put on her jacket. We continued, me in two winter coats and her in the long wool sweater that tied at the waist.

I curled up on the bed and fingered the piece of faded, balled-up fabric tied around my waist. I brought it up to my face. It still smelled like Jackie—baby lotion.

I was settled in bed when my eyes peeled back open to a sound coming from my laptop. It was an e-mail notification. *At this hour?* I climbed out of bed and checked my inbox. It was from Daniel. I opened the e-mail. It was for a reservation for brunch tomorrow for me and Isabella. *Totally unnecessary.* I hit *Reply All* to thank him, but only Daniel's e-mail appeared in the *To* line. Daniel only sent the e-mail to me.

CHAPTER NINE

A windowless meeting room lit by stadium-intensity lights had become my new home. For two weeks, Ravi, Jacob, and I had been working in a locker-sized space to complete the AleAngels product launch bid.

I wasn't sure why we were putting that much effort into the bid. It was way out of our league. The big firms would beat us out. If we had a chance, it was because Daniel went hunting with the CEO in the Yukon.

And surely spending that much time with my colleagues would make way for hours of gossip. More like hours of learning how to bleach my asshole. Not a word on Jackie. When I asked about projects she worked on, they left her out of the story. I got it, it's weird, and most people don't know how to deal with dead people. But that purposeful omission was not normal. *Something wasn't right around here.*

And, of course, no help from my new cellmates on meeting my client recruitment target. It turned out that neither Ravi nor Jacob had one.

When I asked who could help, Ravi told me to see Isabella. The *office Mamma* he called her. More like the office stepmom.

Claudia marched into the meeting room and planted her hands around her waist. Her fingers almost touched. "The bid done yet?"

"Almost," Ravi said. "It's with Jacob for final touches."

"Be ready to brief me first thing tomorrow. And turn that off." She pointed to his phone, which was playing music that sounded like a cat in heat.

"You said we're meeting tomorrow afternoon to discuss the bid," Ravi said, shutting off the noise.

"Daniel wants to see it tomorrow. I need to be briefed first thing."

"I have tomorrow morning off. My set is tonight." He held his phone closer to Claudia. "See."

Claudia stayed where she was. "Katey can brief me." She ran her eyes over me. "In feminine attire, of course."

I glanced down. I was wearing one of my nicer pantsuits.

"It looks like you're at a standstill until Jacob finishes. Katey, go help Isabella with the website refresh."

We'd had five minutes of downtime. "On my way." I used the table to get to my feet.

"And clean this room before Sandra sees." Claudia pointed to empty chip bags and soda cans and looked at me. "This crap will make you age twice as fast."

"We don't have time to eat healthily. Or get a good night's rest," Ravi muttered.

Not true. His mom packs his lunch every day.

"I understand. You're working long hours. Must be exhausting." Claudia smirked. "Don't worry, I'll sleep for you."

We cleared the table once she left.

"It's not like she's going to add value to the bid," Ravi said.

"I'll try to talk to her. Move the briefing."

"Don't bother." He crumpled a soda can. "We're not gonna win the contract."

"Let me know if you need me," I said. "I'll come right back."

"Kay."

Isabella was listening to music on her earbuds.

"Hey, Claudia said you need help with the website."

"You're an angel." She waved me over and slid her chair, giving me a clear view of her computer screen, and opened the shared drive, revealing about ten folders. "Can you move each photo from the folder labelled *Website Refresh* into the folder called *Twenty-eighteen Refresh Meeting*. Create a slideshow, sort by date, and start with the most recent."

"No problem."

"Bring the laptop to the boardroom, and we'll review on screen. We were supposed to finalize earlier this week, but the meeting kept getting cancelled. They'd better like what I've come up with or be ready to buy us espressos tonight."

"Got it."

"I'll send you the link to the folder on the shared drive." She slapped my hip to send me off. "Thanks so much, sweetie pie." She returned the earbuds to her ears.

I opened the folder path Isabella e-mailed me. No wonder she sent me the link—there were twelve, thirteen, or more subfolders in the path.

Some folders were organized by date, others by client events. There were a couple of events already in 2018. I clicked the folder. The DMI girls in the photos had their hair up and wore wide, strained smiles under bright lights.

Don't care.

I clicked back until the 2016 events folder appeared and entered it. That one, I knew. Jackie worked on it. My heart fluttered, just like it did when we were reunited after being apart for months.

The folder called Jackson opened. Jackie said something about drunk lacrosse players hitting on anyone with a pulse at that party. There were plenty, or too many, images of Sandra and people with smooth faces and droopy necks. But no photos of Jackie.

I searched the other folders. More photos with Sandra—her hair always down in perfect loose waves, piled over her shoulders. Daniel was there, and a few photos showed Claudia, Isabella, and some other DMI girls whose names I couldn't remember. That was odd. Surely Jackie would have been there.

I should organize the photos for the meeting.

DMI 2016 Christmas Party.

What is this folder? According to the date—Dec. 16, 2016— it would have been a few weeks after Jackie died. There were pictures of them drinking at a restaurant. *They were out partying?* I eyed the black stapler on my desk and then the monitor, and breathed in and out through my nose. *Stop it. Jackie would have wanted her co-workers to enjoy themselves and drink in her honour.*

I clicked backward and kept clicking and clicking.

Scrolling and clicking loudly.

I paused at a folder called Archive 2016. It opened to thumbnail images.

I scrolled down, stopped, and went back up.

My heart swelled. She was there—standing in front of a backdrop at a red-carpet event, she was wearing a low-cut, metallic floor-length dress. She looked stunning, in a different league than the guy, a larger guy, but in a well-fitted suit standing next to her. My face crowded the monitor for a closer look. He was really close to her. His arm was wrapped around her waist but rested much lower than the friend zone.

The photo was dated July 6, 2016. She didn't have a boyfriend that summer.

"Katey, we're meeting now," Isabella called from down the hall.

"Be right there," I hollered back.

As I jogged into the boardroom, Claudia glared at her watch, then at the wall clock, then at her watch again.

"Sorry," I said and sat beside her. Isabella was on her other side. I connected the laptop to display the images on the TV screen.

"Create three folders," Claudia commanded. "One for the photos going on the website, another for the rejects, and a maybe pile. I'll brief Sandra when we're done."

The slideshow started. *Be patient, steady hands.*

The first photo was from a Toronto International Film Festival press conference. Sandra and five other women, their legs crossed in the same direction and holding microphones, were sitting on a raised platform.

"The one in the middle, the director. She looks like she wants to shove the entire microphone in her mouth," Isabella said, swivelling side to side in her chair.

"This one goes in the *Yes* pile," Claudia instructed. "Next one."

I flipped to a photo of two women on a celebrity cooking show. If you didn't know the show, like me, you wouldn't be able to pick out the chef. Both were wearing feather-dangling earrings, hair extensions, and aprons that cut higher than their shirts.

"Hmm. This is a good one. Julia is planning her divorce," Claudia mused.

"Oh?" Isabella probed.

"Early stages. They still have the same security team. Plenty of time before our next refresh." She addressed Isabella. "She'll be out on Saturday. Put it in the *maybe* pile." Claudia rose to her feet. "Next."

With a slight tremble, I switched the screen to the photo of Jackie and the guy latched to her side. This time, my eyes were fixed on my colleagues.

"I had no idea how that one got in there," Isabella blurted out.

Neither of them looked my way.

"Who are they?" I asked before Claudia could order us to continue.

Silence.

Isabella piped up, "She was—"

"He's a writer. And Daniel's friend," Claudia interrupted, as if reading from a script.

I tried to keep my voice level. "Is she his wife?"

"No," Claudia said. "That's not his wife." She leaned over me and smacked the keyboard. The screen displayed the next photo.

My cheeks burned as if I'd been slapped. No recognition for my sister, who worked there for years. No, she was referred to as a *that*.

But an image of my sister offends you. Or maybe it scares you, reminds you of something you'd rather forget.

My hands mechanically maintained the photo review rhythm while my mind conjured other images—Claudia's broken eyeglasses and the pieces carving a half-circle shape right above her high cheekbones.

I used this strategy when I'd been blindsided by fury. If I kept my mind occupied, I wouldn't say or do something I would later regret. It was a trick Jackie taught me after hearing my teeth grind. Usually prompted by David, waiting until he was at the door to leave for work, again in the evening, before he asked me how school was.

"I'll brief Sandra and tell you what to do in twenty minutes," Claudia said, her back to us as she headed out the door.

Isabella waited for her to leave. "We might see her in an hour."

I checked my watch. "Any reason why this needs to happen today?"

"Sandra wants the new site live first thing tomorrow. This is apparently the only time she can review. Everything posted on the company site is cleared by Sandra."

Then I won't waste any time, either. "I'm going to get coffee. Do you want anything? Latte, extra foam, two-percent milk, one shot of espresso?"

"My favourite. You don't have to stay., doll face." She stretched her arms above her head and yawned. "I can finish up."

"I have to stick around in case Ravi needs me to finalize a

proposal."

"Thought I saw him take off."

He did. I shrugged and said nothing.

"I won't turn down coffee. Hold on, I'll give you money."

"Don't be silly. You got the last one. I'll get one for Claudia, too. She seemed like she needed a something nice."

"Claudia always has a stick up her ass. Don't worry." She flicked her wrist. "I screwed up, not you."

"What was the big deal?"

"It wasn't a big deal. But if Sandra saw the slideshow, she'd be . . . well, let's just say, she doesn't like portraying anything less than a perfect image. That guy in the photo Claudia freaked over is getting married to one of our clients. Not to the girl in the photo."

"I see."

"Honey, I know you mean well, but don't interrupt Claudia when she's with Sandra. Even if you're delivering a treat."

"Point taken. Thanks."

"Honey, take my umbrella. Your face looks inviting today. Never know who you might run into."

She handed me an umbrella with a clear plastic dome.

An hour later, Claudia dropped a contact sheet with thumbnail photos on Isabella's desk. "Move these into the Twenty-eighteen Web Refresh folder. Tell Jacob. He'll update the site and notify our distribution list first thing in the morning."

"No problem," Isabella replied.

"Good night."

We replied together, "Night."

Isabella turned to me. "I can do this by myself. It's late. You should go."

"Soon." My head swerved to my screen. "Looks like Ravi wants a few changes."

"Don't let him boss you around while he sits at home swiping left on Tinder."

I smiled as she sipped the drink I'd brought her.

"At least I'll have the pleasure of your company a bit longer."

Thirty minutes later, my coffee run took effect. Isabella shook her empty coffee cup. "I'm heading out after I go to the bathroom. Can I keep you company on your walk home?"

"I'd love to. Can you show me where the museum is? The one with the sustainable fishing practices exhibition?"

She snorted. "I have no idea what that is. Let's go on that adventure another night. The temperature is dropping fast."

Once Isabella was out of sight, I slid into her chair. As if my hand had a will of its own, I opened the *Archives 2016 folder* and dragged the photo of Jackie and the mysterious man into the *2018 Web Refresh* folder.

CHAPTER TEN

Although it snowed last night, Sandra arrived at the office shortly after the website notification e-mail went out at 7 a.m. Claudia, Isabella, and Daniel stormed in a half hour later, went straight to the glass offices, and hadn't come out.

I hid in the boardroom when I heard the elevator from my desk. The snow left from boots on the office stone floors still had not evaporated.

This could backfire. I had no idea if there were office cameras or if there was a way to link me to the photo. The software pointed to Isabella as the last user, but if they didn't buy that and suspected me, Claudia wouldn't waste any time showing me the door.

When Hillary and Christine arrived, I followed them.

I volunteered to be the morning social media conduit, snapping photos of their extra-large caffeinated beverages and unpeeled avocados to post on their accounts, hashtag *PRbreakfast*.

"You're in early," I probed after I'd taken a few dozen pictures. And then another handful.

"No one sleeps when there's a fuck-up," Hillary said.

"Royal fuck-up," Christine said.

"Right before the guy's wedding." Hillary flashed the picture I posted with Jackie and that guy on her phone at Christine.

"We reminded him he's had better." Hillary and Christine cackled and swooshed their Ariana Grande-style ponytails.

So Jackie was dating this guy I never knew about, but these clones

58

did. Doesn't make a lick of sense.

They turned back to their phones. "His fiancée," Christine said. "A turtle neck in the summer—"

"Turtlenecks should never be worn unless it's for a laxative commercial."

They laughed like hyaenas and sifted their fingers through their manes.

"She's gonna get a nice present from Sandra after this shitshow."

"I bet Sandra throws in a trip to Paris."

"My money's on Swarovski crystals glued to her vag in Sandra's initials."

They flipped their hair towards each other.

"Fuck!" they said in unison and looked at each other for too long.

"Isabella can bloody pay for it. She screwed up," Hillary said loudly. "I'm not working and missing the director's party."

"We'll all pay," Christine said, her mocking tone gone.

Why would Isabella pay for a wedding gift from Sandra? These two might still be drunk. This isn't helpful.

Jacob arrived at his desk across from the kitchen. His pants sat lower today, tighter around the ankles.

"Good morning," I chirped.

"Morning." He removed a faded leather messenger bag from his shoulder.

"I made coffee. Can I get you some?"

"No thanks." He glanced down the hall. "Don't go that way." He pointed toward the offices.

"What's wrong?"

He waved me to come closer. "The website refresh didn't go *as planned*. A photo of a client and his former lady friend was posted. You haven't heard the story?"

Lady friend? Your old co-worker, asshole. "Just bits and pieces. I don't want to upset anyone."

"The girl in the photo used to work here."

I studied his chubby scared face. "What's wrong with that? Ugly break-up?"

Dark thick eyebrows sank away from curly hair and moved closer together. "The girl passed away, and the dude's now-fiancée works for a big client. And, yep, she's on our distribution list. She woke up to an image of her husband-to-be grinding another girl."

"I see."

"The poor girl is probably in tears. Spending her last single days in humiliation."

I should slap you for days for empathizing with some who-the-hell-cares bride-to-be instead of your co-worker. "Thanks for the heads-up."

I glanced at Sandra's office. Isabella sat in an armless chair, her hands covering her face. Sandra and Daniel were standing over her, like police interrogating a suspect.

"Do not talk about this around the offices. This wedding is big. Like talk of the city elite big."

"So I helped Isabella with the refresh."

"Then definitely don't talk or go near Sandra."

"I should catch up with Isabella. Make sure I didn't cause this."

He looked down the hall at the offices, then back at me. "If they thought you did this, you would be in there. But that doesn't mean you or any of us are off the hook."

He whispered, "Claudia called me this morning, flipping out while I was still asleep. I had to get out of bed and confirm I only uploaded what I'd been told to. And then listen to her freak out for another fifteen minutes."

"Hope you didn't lose too much sleep."

He smirked. "I went to the bathroom while we were on the phone."

I turned my attention back to the office. I hoped Isabella was only getting an earful.

60

Isabella craned her head in my direction. She got up, and faced me. Her nose and cheeks were red. She walked toward the door.

Shit, she's going to confront me. I don't have time for this now.

Isabella turned back and sat back down as Sandra leaned over her. Isabella stretched her dress, covering her lap as Sandra moved closer to her. *What's going on?*

Jacob swerved his head toward the offices. "They're coming."

Daniel and Claudia exited Sandra's office and charged down the hall.

I returned to my cubicle and waited. I needed time with Daniel to get information about his friend in the photo. Daniel's friend could have been the last person Jackie dated before she died.

"Claudia, should I reschedule the AleAngels briefing?" I asked as she passed my desk, three strides behind Daniel.

She stopped and called toward Daniel's back. "Shoot. I'll take care of this first, then AleAngels."

"The beer bid?" he asked before reaching the lobby door. "And I'll be seeing this when?"

"Staff haven't briefed me yet," Claudia said. "I can call you later today or tomorrow."

"I'm flying out tomorrow," Daniel snapped. "When's the deadline?"

"Tomorrow, eleven-fifty-nine PM," I interjected.

Claudia started to say something but stopped. She probably suspected we had more time but didn't actually know the deadline because she didn't read the invitation to bid.

"Brief me in the car," Daniel said to me.

Claudia blocked Daniel's view of me to address him. "Maybe she shouldn't go with you since she worked on the website refresh."

"So did you."

"I can call you at any time, day or night."

"I don't want to hear from you at three in the morning." He turned his head in my direction. "Let's go. Rupert is bringing the car out front."

Beside me in the back of the company's *Cadillac XTS*, Daniel hadn't said a word to me. He flipped through the hardcopy proposal while chatting on the phone about his weekend hosting plans in Vegas. Definitely not the Daniel who bought Isabella and I brunch the other week.

Where are we going? Staring at the snow-covered road didn't give an answer, so I prodded at my purple gloves. Claudia said I shouldn't go because I was working on the website. *Maybe we're going to see the client the fiancée works for? Or was Claudia just being Claudia, not wanting me near the higher-ups?*

He ended his call. "When we arrive, stay in the car."

I nodded.

I tried to give him some space to review and turned back to the window, only to find myself staring at his profile reflected in the window. His black-and-white image could have been a high-end designer cologne ad.

"This is pretty good. Why are we pricing so low?" He placed the proposal binder on my lap. His hands were quite large — kind of like my dad's, but only in size. Daniel's didn't have flaked white skin at the base between each finger.

I squeezed my thighs together and gripped the corners of the binder. "Hopefully, low-balling will give us a leg up."

He leaned over, his hand brushing mine, and circled the price with his index finger. The binder spine folded in the crack between my thighs.

"Raise the price by ten percent."

I kept the binder pressed into me in its *V* formation until his phone vibrated. Before bringing the phone to his ear, his eyes sought mine. "Your rate should be higher."

This is a bad idea. Not only do we need to bid low, we need our competition to sit this one out.

He was on the phone again, giving directions to someone about his trip—securing a box for a Golden Knights game.

Who's going to make up the price increase? It wouldn't be him. From what Jackie told me, Daniel spent his time bringing in the business, also known as partying. Seemed accurate. He was rarely at the office.

I sought his reflection again in the window. Everything about him looked new—his phone, suit, haircut, and finger-nails. Even his unbuckled seat belt looked shinier than mine. I wondered what the maintenance cost on him was.

He put his phone down. "What do we know about the president?"

You tell me. Ravi told me Daniel had a connection to Sergei Rustanov, the president of AleAngels. Maybe he was testing me to see if I did my homework.

I flipped a few pages in the binder. "Made his money in Russia in oil and gas, has a stake in a number of energy companies in Saskatchewan, and is now developing liquor products in Ontario. He also owns a few restaurants and bars."

He grinned. "Give me something good."

My back sank further into the leather seat as the car picked up speed. I glanced out the window—we were merging onto the highway. We'd be en-route for a while. *I guess I'll say what we both know.*

I turned to another page in the binder. "More than one harassment case has been brought forward. The claim is he made his employees go hunting. And hunting has nothing to do with the business."

"Those are only allegations. You have apparently determined his guilt. Do you know what this contract would mean?" He flipped the binder, sending it flying off my lap, into the window, and onto the car floor.

I turned towards the window. *Where did Mr. Hyde come from? Daniel knows this about the prospective client. And what harm was done? We're in a car, just the two of us and Rupert.*

Thank God Daniel wasn't behind the wheel. That's probably why they had a driver.

I pinched my eyes closed. *Don't piss off the company owner. Use this time to get on his good side so maybe he tells you something useful.*

"You're right. These are only allegations, nothing more."

I pointed my knees toward him. The movement lifted my loose-fitting black-and-gray tweed skirt, momentarily uncovering what my skirt hid.

I picked up the binder from the floor and used its edge to pull my skirt further up, exposing the mid-thigh lace on my nylons. *Crap.* The binder corner caught the fabric. I was pulling the binder away to release it, but no luck. It was stuck. I was flailing the square object, left then right, trying to free it from my skirt.

Daniel reached over and grasped the binder, one hand on each side. He hovered the binder over my legs and tilted it away from me. He held it there perfectly still as I breathed in the scent of cologne with a hint of bourbon.

I pulled my skirt back in place once I unsnagged the fabric and didn't dare look his way again.

The car pulled into the driveway of a three-story, detached house with two balconies and windows for walls on the street-facing side.

Can't imagine the obscene heating costs on this place.

Rupert and Daniel stepped out of the car, sending stinging cold air my way.

Someone was shovelling snow on the porch. "Daniel, is that you?"

"Jon, buddy, forgive us." Daniel approached the porch, arms open wide.

Scooting over, I placed my hand on the open door, letting Rupert know to keep it open.

Since Daniel was kind of apologizing, this must be the guy from the photo. I couldn't really see his face—it was covered by a mountain of light brown and straw-yellow hair.

"Who's in the car?"

Daniel paused. "A new girl at the firm."

"Don't leave her in there. Rupert, too. Tell them to come in."

Daniel motioned for Rupert and me to join them.

Rupert raised his hand. "Thank you, but there was some debris on the highway, and I want to check the car."

I jumped out of the car, then slowed down. *This guy knew Jackie, but he doesn't know me. Keep it that way.*

Removing my purple glove, I stretched my hand out and introduced myself to this barrel-chested giant wearing a t-shirt when there was snow on the ground.

"Katey Philips. Nice to meet you."

He smiled at me. "Jon Warren. Likewise. Please, come inside."

Yes, this was the guy in the photo. I could tell by the way the corners of his eyes closed when he smiled.

I removed my boots and followed Jon.

This place would have been fit for Jackie. You could do cartwheels in this space. There was minimal furniture, not even a coffee table in the room with the TV.

"We don't want to take up much of your time," Daniel said. "We're here to sincerely apologize for what happened this morning."

Jon's brow furrowed.

"Katey, could you give Jon and me a moment? Old friends like us end up speaking our own language."

"The kitchen is down the hall. Help yourself to anything," Jon said.

"Thanks." I exited and ventured into the kitchen.

I made familiar kitchen noises — ran the water, and opened cabinets. I tested the squeakiness of the hall and kitchen floors, shifting my weight from my right foot to my left. *No sound. Good.*

I was creeping heel-to-toe along the wall back toward the living room and then stopped when voices became clear.

"I'm getting married in a week. Claire is having her final dress fitting today. She said this will be the talk of the wedding. When she walks down the aisle, everyone will be thinking I dated a woman who's now —"

"Sandra is making it up to Claire right now."

"Do you understand?" Jon raised his voice. "You know what Claire's like."

"Shh."

"She left work, went to her mother's. Won't pick up the phone. My next call might be to cancel the caterers."

"She just needs a moment. Pre-wedding stress."

Jon lowered his voice. "What would Sandra say? One night, you promised her the world." His voice cut in and out. "The next morning, she sees what happens when it doesn't work out."

Girlfriend? No way, I would have remembered one of Jackie's boyfriends. He was probably using that term to be respectful. They probably hooked up on a weekend or two, and it had slipped my mind. It was years ago.

"Everything is okay," Daniel said.

The two exchanged whispers. What were they talking about?

"Katey, come in here," Daniel called.

I took my time returning to the living room.

"Jon ghostwrote a memoir for a Québécois politician. You're going to help him with the launch and serve as a personal assistant."

Sounded good to me. "Looking forward to working with you, Jon."

"You won't be disappointed," Daniel told Jon, using a quasi-gloating tone.

This is perfect. "I'll give you my card since we'll see each other shortly."

Jon took my card and studied it. "It's not happening for quite some time. Maybe a year. But I appreciate your enthusiasm."

A year? That's not gonna work for me.

"Do you need help with the wedding?" I offered. "Any loose strings or last-minute items?"

Daniel nodded. *Good.*

"Um. I don't know."

"Anything at all. Transportation, photography?"

"The only thing I can think of is Claire's makeup artist is flaky."

"We will have someone ready," Daniel said glancing at his phone.

"It looks like there's an issue with the car," I told Daniel, looking out the living room.

"I'll check it out," Daniel said with his phone already up to his ear. He exited through the front door.

You're welcome.

Jon slumped into an olive-coloured leather armchair—his massive frame covered the cushions, and he exhaled loudly. "When did you join DMI?"

"A few weeks ago."

"I hope you aren't reconsidering your job. Wait until my wedding is over before answering that," he said, lifting one corner of his mouth and resting his forearms on his knees.

"I'm sorry to see you like this."

The upper portions of his cheeks that weren't covered in facial hair turned pink.

I sat on the arm of the couch and faced him. "I mean, you looked happy in the photo that was posted, and now you're not. You shouldn't feel like this before your wedding. And we did this. I'm so sorry."

"Disasters always come with weddings. But in the end, as long as Claire is happy, that's all that matters."

He was so Jackie's type—the rugby player turned

gentleman.

"And for what it's worth, we're sorry and embarrassed about the insensitivity shown towards a late and, I understand, cherished DMI employee," I said. "Someone who, I understand, cared about you."

He looked straight at me, his face frozen.

That was probably too forward of me.

"We weren't together very long." He got up and approached the fireplace.

Obviously, or we would have met each other.

"Heart break I always hard."

He jolted his back straight and stood taller.

"She left me. The next boyfriend was better than me. And she deserved the best. Can I get another card to give to Claire?"

Jackie had another boyfriend? That doesn't make sense. Now there were two boyfriends I had no recollection of.

"Oh, sure. I'll give you my personal number as well." I grabbed a pen from my purse and scribbled my cell number on the back of the card.

"If I can get yours?" I asked, handing him my pen and a business card.

Cold air gushed from the front of the house. Daniel was still on the phone upgrading his weekend accommodations to include a billiards table.

"Sure." Jon wrote. I examined the number—it didn't resemble the nine-digit number that brought me across the country.

"My apologies." Daniel put away his phone. Turning my back to him, I slid the card into my coat pocket.

"We should get going." Daniel turned to me. "I'm right behind you."

"We'll check in with you on the wedding day," I said to Jon.

Before I reached the car, I searched my phone contacts for

Evelyn.

Something wasn't right. Jackie told me everything, down to the socks she was wearing on any given day. She might not have told me the guy's name if it was a one-night stand, but it didn't look like that was the case.

She definitely told me about Jon. And I forgot. My heart hammered at the thought of losing memories of my sister. I was erasing what I had left of her because I couldn't be bothered to pay enough attention.

Daniel was coming. One hand was in his suit pocket, opening half his trench coat. "Well done. Staff who will go the extra mile for our clients move up my company."

I brushed my hair behind my ears.

He reached behind me, and his arm slid across my wool coat, protecting the small of my back. He opened the car door and offered me entrance to the confined space. "Rupert, our first stop is Katey's home." The dark gleam from the night we met refilled his eyes. "Take the rest of the day off."

CHAPTER ELEVEN

I opened the first e-mail in my DMI account. A proposal was due that night.

I slapped my laptop mouse on the pad. It was already late, and Claudia knew I was looking at condos to rent this afternoon.

Reading the e-mail chain, I noticed the request originated from Sandra with one instruction—*Due ASAP*. I couldn't finish the proposal from home. I needed access to our shared drive. I checked the time on my laptop. It was nearly 8 PM. Everyone should have left the office, including those that started their day in tears because I framed them for company sabotage.

I opened the glass door that connected DMI's office to the elevator lobby and tiptoed toward my cubicle, listening for sounds. *No one will be there.*

Isabella's chair was tucked in—her computer monitor was black.

I exhaled, sat down, and got to work. It would take just a little bit of time—in and out.

It was taking twice as long to write a sentence. I was looking over my shoulder every few seconds as if I was anticipating a serial killer to appear.

The silence was louder than the office's usual buzz. My hands sped up to create keyboard noise.

Isabella's workstation felt like it was growing in size next to me. I turned and faced it.

Jackie wouldn't have approved of what I did to Isabella. And would have been less than proud that I didn't feel bad about it. I would have, over a year ago, but I wasn't who I was then.

But Jackie would have loved my newfound skills. I had never schemed like this before. Never needed to.

I glanced back at my screen—this was good enough. *I'm getting out of there.*

"Hi."

I jumped out of my seat and faced the last voice I wanted to hear. Isabella was standing where the cubicle met the hall.

"Hey."

How did I not hear her? This place had stone floors. I looked down at her feet—she wasn't wearing shoes. "I didn't know you were here."

She pointed to where the offices were. "I was down there."

"I forgot something. Found it. So I was leaving." My chair travelled several feet behind me as I was rising.

"Want to grab a drink?" she asked.

Why does she want to go out with me, unless it's to light a drink on fire and throw it in my face? This wouldn't end well. I was already as anxious as an AA member on day three.

"I'm really tired. Another time."

"It won't be for long. I'm going out later in the evening."

"Sorry, next time." I passed her, eyes downcast. The doors were right ahead.

"Sweetie, I think you owe me one."

I was waiting for Isabella at the bar across the street. She said she would meet me after she got ready.

Fleeing would have been the easy thing to do, but it wasn't like I could avoid her forever—she worked beside me. And if she knew I posted the photo, I needed to know why she hadn't ratted on me.

Maybe she was planning on holding it over my head? I'd

have to move every heavy object in her path, or she'd tattle-tale.

Isabella found me first, even though I'd been watching the entrance for her.

"Hope you weren't waiting long," she said.

"Nope."

She removed her checkered green and white cashmere coat and hung it on a nearby rack. *Wow*, when she mentioned she was changing, I expected something closer to what I was wearing—jeans and a blazer, not a dress that transformed her into a walking hourglass.

"Sam, shots tonight," she said to the waiter.

God damn it, Isabella. Did I tell her I don't drink? No, I didn't, although I don't trust my memory right now. I couldn't let her learn that alcohol would be the perfect way to get back at me. If she knew, she would no longer be that week's screw-up. The new girl who was shaking, sweating, and babbling gibberish after one drink would take the top prize.

I scanned the drink menu for something in a dark bottle. "Tankhouse for me, please."

I met Isabella's eyes for the first time that day. "I haven't eaten since noon. A shot will floor me."

"Lightweight. Margarita and fries with truffle sauce," she said, winking at the waiter.

We stayed seated across from each other. Just the two of us. Each second that passed felt like an hour. No music. No one was seated next to us. No water to sip.

"You look very nice. Do you have a date?" I blurted out.

"I wish. I'm meeting friends for drinks. What about you?"

"What about me?"

"Do you have a date?"

I laughed, and her eyebrows lifted.

"Just quality time with the hotel couch. Give me another week to find someone who won't mind joining me on furniture with heart-shaped stains."

Isabella chuckled, showing off bright white teeth outlined by full red lips.

I wasn't going to question her plans since I'd done enough. But it was already late, and it was a weeknight, and she was already drinking. *Where is she going after this for round two?*

The waiter returned with a tray holding a beer bottle and a margarita. And two shots. *Those shots better be for another table.*

"Don't worry. Snacks are coming. Chase it with beer."

"I can't."

She leaned forward, boobs hiding half the table. "Why are you here right now, Katey?"

On the off chance you tell me what happened to my sister.

"You owe me." She raised her shot glass and waited. *I don't think she hears the word no often.*

It'd been a long time since I drank alcohol. Maybe it was all in my head. Once I got a little in me, it would be fine.

I hoisted the tiny glass. The scent of lime squeezed through an asshole assaulted my nostrils. My hand trembled. I took a deep breath and splashed the drink into my mouth.

"See, that wasn't so bad. It's the good stuff, too."

My eyes watered while my stomach lurched. I grabbed the beer bottle. I was tipping the shaking bottle to my lips, I swished and spat the tequila and beer back into the bottle, but my tongue was left coated with a rancid sour paste.

Breathe. You're gonna be fine. Focus on something else.

"Did you always want to be an event planner?" I asked, struggling to remove my blazer that was sticking to my skin.

"Not exactly. I'm trained in IT. Used to work for *Black-Berry*."

Hold on to something. The underside of the table.

The whites of her eyes were so overpowering. I couldn't look at them anymore. I shifted my gaze to the plain beige wall just above her head. "Why did you leave the IT world?"

"This job pays much better."

Her voice cut in and out.

"I support my family. My dad got sick years ago . . . and my little sister . . ."

I could hear what she was saying, but her mouth wasn't moving. Her lips were sewn shut.

"My mother can't speak English very well."

Stop talking. You need to stop talking.

"Are you okay?"

I took my hands off the underside of the table and focused on her black pearl drop earring. *Stay on it. Focus.* "Yes, I'm fine."

"You seem distracted."

Think. Explain yourself. Take your hands off your forehead. Tell her why you can't drink, and give her a damn good reason.

"The last time I went out with co-workers for drinks, they played a mean joke on me," I said. "They told me they found unprofessional pictures of me on the Internet and that we lost a contract because of it."

"That's horrible. Your old co-workers are dicks. I'm glad you're here." She called her waiter friend over. "Honey, she needs your morning special."

What seemed like seconds later, a tall glass with what looked like paint and tar was set in front of me.

"What is it?"

She said something, but it was like I was hearing her from underwater.

"Is it alcohol?"

She shook her head and the warm smile from the first time we met returned.

I took a large gulp. It tasted like I licked the bottom of a car, but it was better than anything else that was on the table.

Fries in a metal jar appeared in front of me. They might help dilute the taste. I shoved a few into my mouth and took a long drink of this special mixture, suppressing a gag.

Get it together. My eyes snapped back to her black pearl

earring—my hands found each other under the table. "You were talking about your family."

"Yeah, I was."

Isabella took a sip of her marguerita.

My stomach and vision had settled to normal. "I'm already feeling better, thank you."

Isabella took a long drink before she placed the glass back down, creating a noise that could have been heard from outside.

"Allow me to continue and answer your question. My dad worked construction, but a cement block landed on his head, so he couldn't work anymore. So I support my dad, mom, who works minimum wage paying jobs, as well as my little sister."

I bit my bottom lip. I wanted to apologize. I didn't mean to jeopardize her family's livelihood. But I couldn't admit it—it would have risked my existence at the company and the chances of finding out what happened to Jackie.

"So you can imagine how important this job is to me." Her brown doe eyes met mine in a new way. "I know what you did."

I motioned towards my cup. She blocked my reach with her hand and held my eyes. She continued, "I don't know why you posted that photo and pinned it on me. Did you do it because I made you carry the rocks at the Crompton event?"

The sound of my nails that were scratching under my seat took over.

"You were sweating like a pig. Outside in the freezing cold was the only place Sandra would have allowed you to be." Isabella paused. "It's fine. I'm not looking for a confession. I didn't rat you out. If Sandra knew you did it, she would have fired you on the spot this morning."

I was so confused, but I nodded my head.

"I didn't get fired. *I* would have to commit a much bigger

crime before they showed me the door. A lot of people come and go at DMI. I don't care for many. But you, I like." She leaned back. "Maybe we can start again."

Once again, I didn't know what to make of her. She was berated all day and responded by taking the blame for something she didn't do. And now, she was showing off her value at the company. Didn't matter, I needed an ally, and the company prize sounded like a good place to start. "I would love to. But my stay may be short if I don't meet my client recruitment target."

She took a long drink. "There are some proposals coming up that I'll get you on."

Better not be for shot-in-the-dark contracts like Claudia assigned me that day. "Great."

Then I remembered Hillary said Isabella would have to pay for this mistake with a pricey wedding gift. I said, "If there's a financial consequence to this misunderstanding, I'd like to pay for it."

"What are you talking about?"

"Hillary or Christine mentioned —"

"Don't listen to those silly girls. There's nothing you can do." Isabella checked her phone. "Sorry, honey, I have to run." She opened her Chanel wallet, removed a few twenties, dropped them on the table, and kissed me on the cheek. "Glad we did this. See you tomorrow."

I watched her leave and climb into a dark car parked outside. It looked like DMI's Cadillac.

That's weird. Why wouldn't she say she's going to a work function? Probably doesn't want me to feel left out.

I sat back in my chair and examined her half-empty margarita glass stained with red lipstick. She protected me and took the blame when her job, the income, was essential to her. I chewed my thumbnail. And not many people liked me.

Evelyn called on my way home.

"Thanks for calling."

"Of course. How's Toronto?" Hearing her voice was like being wrapped in a velvet blanket.

"I'm having memory lapses."

"Why do you think you're experiencing problems with your memory?"

Evelyn was no fool, but I wasn't going to admit what I was up to.

"What are the odds? I met someone claiming he dated Jackie. I can't remember Jackie mentioning this guy."

"How long ago did they date?"

"Almost two years ago."

"How did he describe the relationship?"

"He said it was brief. I can't remember Jackie dating *anyone* during that time."

"Is it possible Jackie didn't tell you? You've kept certain things from her."

"No, that's not possible," I said.

We paused.

"Give it some thought," she said.

"That's not necessary. I need to know if I'm a thirty-one-year-old with dementia."

"Are you experiencing any other memory issues? For example, are you forgetting routine activities, like brushing your teeth in the morning?"

"No."

"Two years is a long time. If the relationship was brief, he may not have been important to Jackie. If that was the case, you likely picked up on that."

"I really want to remember. I've searched my e-mails, and text messages, can't find anything."

"Write the communication down in one spot, like a whiteboard. Then search your calendar. There may be something that requires the big-picture perspective."

"Thanks. Have a good night." I hung up.

I returned to my hotel room to follow Evelyn's instructions. On a poster pad I bought on the way home, I wrote down Jackie's messages, starting last summer and ending when she died.

Wear a dress and more makeup. It was the last message Jackie sent. Not relevant, but I wrote it down anyway.

I recorded my calendar events in a column beside Jackie's messages. I listed anything odd from my time in Toronto on a separate sheet—Claudia and her reaction to Jackie's photo, Jon, the first boyfriend, and the unknown second boyfriend. To the last item—Isabella's fondness of me—I added a question mark.

It was three AM. My hand was throbbing from all the writing. My thoughts were scrambled, and I couldn't string anything together. But I had just found something related to her love life, so I wasn't going to give up on the night just yet.

In September 2016, I set a reminder in my calendar to call Jackie about watch repairs. One of our chats had been cut short one morning after she scratched some guy's Rolex while he was in the shower. She kept her voice hushed, which was weird because it wasn't like she could hide the damage from him for very long. I assumed she didn't know the guy very well and was dreading explaining how she managed to wreck his expensive watch. So she did tell me about at least one guy from that timeframe, and I was just too focused on helping her. That day, I tracked down one of the few shops in the city that repaired Rolex, and was told that the watches are very durable but that gold could be scratched.

In October, there was another reminder in my calendar—*Call Jackie early. She has a date!* I remembered that, for a while, we would talk earlier on Thursday and Friday evenings. But I couldn't remember why. Again. She must have been going out, partying. Or maybe she was seeing a boyfriend on those days.

I replayed my date with Isabella, wondering about this special relationship with the boss that made her untouchable. She worked hard and was drop-dead gorgeous. That wasn't *that* extraordinary. There must have been something else.

What time was it when she was picked up? Ten o'clock. I closed my eyes and let my head sink into the pillow.

Isabella approached the Cadillac. Her fancy dress was peeking out from the belted checkered trench coat. A woman's figure was inside the car. Shapely legs and high heels appeared when the car door opened. Before Isabella got into the car, she turned around to reveal Jackie's smiling face.

CHAPTER TWELVE: JACKIE

July 2016
"They're working you too hard. You're gonna get sick."

I tried to get out of work so I could go home to Vancouver by licking the mugs of my sick co-workers. But then the stretched-rat caught me and reported me faster than she threw up her lunch.

"It should settle down." A new shipment of dresses came in. They wouldn't sit in the box for a day. "I was going to call. I got home really late."

"Since when has that stopped you?" Katey snapped.

I used to wake her up to tell her about my night and send a picture of what I'd been wearing. The last time, it was a Michael Kors dress—gold lace with capped sleeves and a high neck. She pretended to want to go back to sleep. She loved it, and I needed to know that she would stay up to hear from me.

"It's okay. Make it up to me next weekend," she said.

I put her on speakerphone. I had to continue getting ready. "I know we were supposed to be done with this stupid project by then, but the client is a total diva. You know how they are."

"You're not coming."

I'd hoped she would be used to me cancelling by then. "Kitty, don't be mad at me. It's my job."

She said nothing.

"I'm going to get you one of those audiobook memberships. It can't end up in the landfill," I told her.

"I don't need you to buy me shit."

She didn't, but I did.

We shared the silence on the line as long as it was needed.

"Why don't I come see you?" she asked.

She could have come to me. But I couldn't invite her out. She would be in my condo all alone. "I'm working till three in the morning."

She held her breath.

"Kitty, I suck. I know."

"I have to go."

"C'mon, don't go."

"I have to tell Mom and your dad to cancel the camping reservation. The one *you* suggested."

"*Your* dad? Don't be like that." *It was always her fallback to make it look like she was some victim, some unwanted daughter, and make Dad look like shit. For what? For being a real father and giving her a family.*

I waited out our silent pissiness.

"This was the weekend I was going to ask them," she reminded me.

Oh, right, shit. We were going to ask Dad if we could secure his crew to build a cabin on a lakeside property I was planning to buy.

"I'll ask. Do you wanna video call me?" I suggested.

"You need to be *here*. It will take one word from you."

"They'll say the same thing to you."

"No, they won't. You need to ask once, and by the time you're home, it'll be built."

That was her way of bringing up the stupid tree house. Dad built it for both of us—I just gave the final push.

Give her another minute, I reminded myself. "I'll be home at Thanksgiving. We'll go swimming, hiking on the nudist trail, go to that hippy bookstore with bedbugs. Then we'll burn down the tree house. I promise."

She laughed once.

I wanted to see her and tell her what I had gotten myself into at DMI. I didn't think it would turn out as it had. I didn't understand at the time I signed up. It was too late now.

"I miss you," she said. She never wanted us to part on a shitty note—Dad told us it brought back luck. She would never admit it, but she listened to him.

"I love you."

We never said goodbye. We knew when it was time to end things.

My fingers shook as I was applying Guerlain lipstick and my go-to scent—Gardenia Les Exclusifs de Chanel perfume. The rouge tip broke and rolled onto the table. The oval ring of lightbulbs outlining the make-up station mirror highlighted the oily crimson trail.

And then I wasn't alone anymore. I looked into the mirror and saw the face I wanted to see every day and also never see again. We met in the reflective surface, then she turned away, knowing it was done and I wasn't going anywhere.

And then the image of the ass-kissing rat took over the same space. "Tonight's schedule has been revised," she told me. "You're going to meet clients with Daniel." She tossed a thick roll of bills fastened with a rubber band on the floor next to the make-up table. "Tomorrow night will start in the morning if you even think of using one dollar to go cottaging again."

CHAPTER THIRTEEN

The message from Claudia was useless. *Come in early. San-dra wants to talk.*

Does Sandra want to talk about a project? My performance? Was she interested in adopting me?

I didn't know how to prepare for this meeting, but Isabella told me to look *new* when meeting Sandra. That meant wearing something Sandra hadn't seen before. And a dress, of course.

I was sorting through the closet of my newly rented condo and pulled out a light blue dress with short sleeves. The pleats kinda screamed Church-girl, but I hadn't worn it yet.

Good thing I checked my phone before I had to leave for work. Otherwise, I'd still be lost in my thoughts, figuring out that weird Isabella-turned-Jackie image. Evelyn could help, but then she'd probe about my dreams of Jackie, and I was telling her dick-all about them. During one session, she called them nightmares. I haven't forgiven her for that. Seeing my sister again was not a nightmare — it was the best thing.

That smile Jackie wore when she transformed from Isabella was her persuasion smile. She used it a lot in high school to try to get me to go out drinking with her and her pretty friends. When her friends zoomed up the driveway in the latest SUV, she'd turned around on her way to the car, grinned, and asked, "You sure?" I'd always shake my head, knowing the pack of mean girls would never let me wear pink with them, even if their ringleader was Jackie.

What this all meant wasn't profound — I needed to do what

I came here to do and stop trying to skip to the finish line. If I was going to find out what happened to Jackie, I needed to play in Jackie's old world. Do what Jackie and the DMI girls did, beyond posting narcissism on Instagram. I needed to try harder, and not by working until midnight preparing proposals. I needed to do the things I loathed—partying, going out, socializing, schmoozing. After all, when were my colleagues going to talk—at the office with Claudia sniffing up their skirts or after hours once they'd had a few drinks?

It shouldn't be that hard to score an invite. Isabella said she liked me, so I'd call her on it. Once I was in with the girls, they'd talk about hair, shoes, clothes, and boys. And with a gentle nudge from me, the boys their colleagues had dated. If my sister had met one of these boyfriends through work, then they would fill in my memory gaps.

"Good morning," Sandra rose from behind her office desk. Not a fold appeared in her black pencil skirt or matching suit jacket.

"Good morning,"

No more noise followed. I turned to Claudia and searched her face for a clue of what was going on. Claudia turned towards Sandra, stuck her chin in the air, crossed arms, and stood up straighter.

"We are invited to pitch for the AleAngels contract," Sandra said. "Normally, senior members of the company attend pitches. Given the last-minute notice, we must be ready to answer any questions on the proposal."

"Take cues from us before you speak," Claudia added.

Guess Claudia still hasn't read the proposal. Sandra would have, though. Pretty sure the CEO can BS any question that was thrown at her. They shouldn't need me.

"We're leaving in twenty, no, ten minutes," Claudia said.

Sandra turned to Claudia. "Katey would look lovely in the Tamara Mellon pumps."

"I'm wearing the Tamara Mellon pumps," Claudia said, swinging one foot high in the air.

When Sandra didn't respond, Claudia kicked off one shoe, then the other, losing four inches in height.

"I'll be ready," I said, picking the heels up from the floor. "I just need to change my appointment with Jon and Claire."

"Jon Warren?" Sandra asked, shifting a folder from one hand to the other.

"Yes. I'm helping with the wedding and Jon's book."

Sandra froze into a wax figure like she did. The corner of Claudia's mouth rose.

Crap, I screwed up.

"Your job is here," Sandra said, her tone even. "You can assist with the wedding. That is all."

"Understood," I said.

I thought helping out a client whom we humiliated and her husband's friend would have earned me big points with Sandra. Whatever.

We waited in the car at the security gate to enter the isolated waterfront AleAngels office. Two bulky-shaped men, wearing black beanies and sunglasses, flanked the office entrance. They could've competed with Sandra as live statues.

I took Claudia's lead and followed four paces behind Sandra's left side, forming a mobile triangle.

A young round-faced girl wearing bright blue eyeshadow met us in the lobby.

"They put the Russian mail-order bride to work," Claudia whispered to me.

"Good morning," I said to the girl.

"Come over here," she said, her accent thick. Her chunky six-inch heels and fishnet stockings led the way out of the lobby.

"Mr. Rustinov is coming," she said, sliding the office doors shut. The panoramic lake view was the best I'd seen in the city. Even on a cloudy day, the endless blue-gray water beat the mismatched downtown office towers. This was probably Sergei's office.

I surveyed the room. Animal skin rugs were on the floor, a chandelier was made from antlers, and, *oh God* – a deer's head on the wall. *I'm in Gaston's house.*

"Hello, ladies." A booming voice with a thick Russian accent echoed. "My name is Sergei Rustinov. It is a great pleasure to meet you."

He had a wide smile, dimples in his cheeks, and dark rectangle sideburns reaching the bottom of his face.

Sandra extended her hand. "Sandra Maile, president and chief executive officer of DMI. I am so sorry Daniel couldn't attend. He is out of town."

He bulldozed past her outstretched arm and kissed both her milk-white cheeks, making exaggerated *mwah* sounds.

"Sandra, are you Daniel's sister?"

Sandra cleared her throat. "Wife."

"Ah, yes. My mistake. You look like him."

I love this man.

Sergei made his way over to me. Dark curly chest fur spilled over a white dress shirt with too many buttons undone. "And who are you?"

"Katey Philips. Thank you for inviting us today."

He kissed my cheek. *Ow.* His sideburns might have taken off some skin. When he crossed to my other cheek, his large Roman nose hit mine.

He spun around with the energy you'd get from chugging an energy drink to address the only one remaining. "Hello, princess."

"Mr. Rustinov. I'm Claudia, the General Manager at DMI. It's such an honour to be here."

"Claudia, my dear." He took her hands in both of his. "Do you want some bagels? Muffins? You don't look like you've eaten anything. Ever."

I turned away before my lips retreated into my mouth. *Sergei, stop. You're going to get me fired.*

"I'm fine, thank you," Claudia replied, half-trying to break her hands out of his grip.

Another man entered the room. "Thomas McMarner, director of product development." Not Russian. He wore I-belong-to-a-special-club chunky rings on his fingers. He gave our hands half a shake.

"Have a seat." Sergei waved us to a round, glossy wood table. "What would you like to drink?"

C'mon, alcohol? It's not even noon. Maybe he meant something else. What did Russians drink that was non-alcoholic? Pickle juice.

"I have the best—it's not in stores yet." Sergei made his way over to a minifridge in the corner, took out a square bottle, and poured the clear liquid into five bar glasses.

I kicked my too-big-fitting skinny-heeled pumps onto the floor. That wasn't water he was pouring.

No one spoke. Everyone got a glass. We waited for his lead.

Sergei brought his glass under his nose, inhaled deeply, swirled the vodka twice, and consumed it. Sandra and Claudia followed suit.

My hand crept toward my glass.

"You like?" he asked.

"Yes," Sandra replied. Claudia nodded and speared me with a stare. I hoisted the glass. The vodka lapped at my lips, and I feigned a sip and a swallow. My stomach cramped. *I would do anything to get rid of the pureed garbage stench. I'd take a bite out of the deer's ear on the wall.*

I looked down. My knees were taking turns lifting into the air. I couldn't afford a panic attack. The vodka had to go.

"We will move your product as a leader, both sales and brand recognition," Sandra said. "Let us go over the plan."

Keep talking so I can figure out what to do with this liquid parasite.

As Sandra talked, Claudia rotated, directing her thin-lipped smile between Sergei and Thomas.

"It's the same thing, over and over," Sergei complained. "A rooftop garden, a hangar, those tiny people dangling from the ceiling with the ribbons."

Sandra spoke first. "You are right. We are applying tried and tested methods. They will not work for your unique product. Would you share a sample with us?"

"Camila," Sergei hollered. The girl from the lobby returned. "Bring the new beer."

Damn it.

Thomas leaned into Sergei, whispered something, then turned to us. "The product hasn't received full approvals yet. Next time, we will be more than happy to share the brand."

Sergei held up his hand. "It's fine. I gave it to my nephew. Drank every drop from his sippy cup."

I drained the vodka on the fur rug near my feet. One quick splat. I raised the glass back to my lips and jolted it towards the ceiling for a long drink of air.

Sergei held his glass higher and looked at each of us.

Claudia scrunched her eyes together and downed the remaining contents of her glass.

Sandra didn't flinch as she cleared her cup. She could've been drinking water.

Camila returned with a tray holding five half-pint glasses filled to the brim with an amber fluid. And there was no water for palate cleansing.

They all drank — I wetted my lips.

"You like?" Sergei asked the room. "Katey, what do you think?"

I think my tongue burns with Bambi's blood. "I feel like I inhaled fire," I said.

Claudia's olive skin turned the same colour as Sandra's. "I-it's brilliant. Like nothing I've tasted before," she said quickly.

Sergei got up, picked a loose strand of hair from Claudia's

shoulder, and placed it in her hand. "Sweetheart, when you lie, you blink."

I want to work for him.

"Katey is right," Sandra said. "The bold taste, the colour of flame. It's powerful. Fire is perfect."

"Fire . . ." Sergei contemplated.

"Fire always wins. It consumes everything in its path," Sandra continued.

"Yes! Yes!" Sergei said, his voice rising. "Tell me, where would the fire burn?"

Sandra didn't have an answer — she didn't know. We had to nail the contract now.

Now's the time to choose. Win the contract and Sandra temporarily or lose this opportunity to extend my stay at the company, but Claudia will hate me more.

"Surrounded by its opposite element," I said. "On a yacht." I gestured to the window overlooking the lake.

Sergei stood and slammed his hands on the table. "Yes, yes, a boat!" he roared.

"We will change the perception of beer," Sandra said. "Beer will compete with bourbon and wine."

"Ladies, I need one moment with Sergei. Please excuse us," Thomas said.

The two retreated to the window and spoke in hushed tones.

What's the problem? I jinxed it.

The wait was unbearable. *C'mon, Sergei, you're the boss.* Without this project, I didn't have a chance of staying at DMI.

They returned to the table. "What you proposed is too big for a beer party," Sergei said.

My heart sank.

His hands clasped together, and dimples returned. "But I like what you've come up with." He pointed to Sandra's glass. "You will launch the vodka."

I waited for Sandra's face that came to life to return to its default composed structure. It didn't happen.

Claudia's mouth gaped.

"You are responsible," Sergei told Sandra.

"Yes, Daniel and I will lead. Claudia and Katey will support."

Sergei looked at Claudia. "I don't trust her. She's too skinny."

"As you wish. The rest of my staff will support to ensure the project's success," Sandra confirmed.

"Every man on deck," Sergei said.

Sandra rose like she was bringing the rest of the room up higher with her. In the lobby, she kissed Sergei, leaving red lipstick next to his sideburns. There was something unsettling about her presence. Her energy matched a show-horse, but it was tempered by a flatness her eyes carried. As they chatted, Claudia and I retreated outside to the Cadillac.

"Thank you, have a great day," I told the bodyguards at the door. Not even a head turn. I kinda wanted to stay outside with them. Claudia could have dented the parking area asphalt with her death march.

In the car, Sandra was on the phone, announcing the contract. My name was mentioned several times. *Oh, dear.*

Claudia turned to me. "Do you have any idea what the cost and logistics are to hold an event on a yacht? We can't pull it off with the price we quoted."

We wouldn't be pulling off anything if it weren't for me. And it sounds like we are using Sergei's friend's super yacht anyways.

I kept my eyes on the floor and listened to Sandra. "DMI will be on the map," she said.

"I'll work very hard on this event, anything you need," I told Claudia.

Claudia looked at Sandra, waited until she was speaking, and then turned back to me. "I haven't forgotten your promise from the interview. That'll you do anything in this job."

I expected to work your job and mine.

"Just a reminder, Ravi and I worked on the proposal," Claudia said. "This counts as half a client toward your target."

You didn't even read the damn thing. My idea won the contract.

Sandra ended her call and turned to us. "Ladies, I need to stop off at my home on the way back. I hope you will join me."

"I would love to," I said half a beat after Sandra asked.

CHAPTER FOURTEEN

I'd have been more impressed with the boss's house if we hadn't spent hours running errands in shoes with heels the size of pencils. Two and half hours later, I was about to stuff the shoe heel in Claudia's mouth. *Can I carry your bags, Sandra? That looks delectable on you, Sandra. Bend over, let me wipe your ass, Sandra.*

Sandra unlocked the front door. "Come in, ladies."

The house didn't look like much from the outside, but inside, it was a mini-mansion. The living room and dining room straddled a dark-wood grand staircase. Rubber plants on the landing shielded an oversized picture window.

Why do the two of them need all this space? Jackie told me Sandra and Daniel didn't have children. I wondered why. He seemed like the type to want heirs.

"I'll hang these up," Claudia said, slinging the dry cleaning and shopping bags over her matchstick arms.

Sandra changed into dark brown pumps, said to me, "Come," and headed up the stairs. On the balls of her feet, Claudia followed.

Before the main staircase broke to the right, the landing provided a view of the kitchen and a living space with a large flat-screen TV. The high chairs around the kitchen island were evenly spaced. No food, no junk rested on top of the island, or the nearby kitchen countertops.

Both straddling staircases led to a deep hall with several closed doors on both sides. We took the right one and entered the first door. It looked like the principal bedroom with a king-sized bed so high off the ground that a step stool adorned with gargoyles was needed to climb onto the bed.

Claudia opened another door with a claw knob that led to a bathroom with double sinks and bowls painted with black vines and flower roots springing out of the drains. The mirrors were outlined with carved three-dimensional open-mouthed lion's heads.

At the other end of the bathroom, she opened a second door that led to a dressing room with a closet island about twice the size of the kitchen island.

It looked like one of the show homes my stepdad displayed.

Sandra removed her silver drop earrings. Claudia opened one of the island drawers, and Sandra placed the earrings inside.

"It's like a department store," I said, cowering in the corner.

"Is there anything you like?" Sandra asked.

Is she testing my fashion choices? No, she wouldn't put me on the spot after the AleAngels win.

Pick something. There's no wrong choice. It's all stuff that's hers.

"A pink plastic hair band would go perfectly with your dress. You won't find one here," Claudia said.

"Forgive her," Sandra told me, "Sometimes Claudia forgets she was not raised in a barn."

Claudia opened a drawer, emptied the contents on the island and started folding what appeared to be scarves.

"Go on." Sandra took my arm and led me to the closet. Trying not to touch the fabric, I sifted through clothes that dangled from fabric hangers and were separated by six inches on each side. There were only dresses.

"This one." Sandra pulled out an asymmetrical seafoam-green, capped-sleeve dress.

"Try it on." She draped the dress against me, the hanger pressed into my collarbone.

"That won't fit her," Claudia insisted. "Her rib cage is too wide."

Sandra wrapped the skirt portion of the green dress around my hip, then aligned the seam with the one I was wearing. Her focus was like rain, eyes hitting my chest, waist, and hips at once.

Claudia marched to the closet and took a measuring tape from the shelf. A set of small keys attached to a ring fell to the floor. She scooped up the keys and put them back in the closet.

Sandra, eyes still on me, took a step back to make space. Claudia wrapped the tape around my chest, just below my bra, and pulled the two ends together like tying a bow.

"Almost two inches larger than you," she said to Sandra. "The seams will burst."

Sandra's head swivelled to the left. Claudia's hands retracted. The tape rested around my hips. The two fell silent, in noise and motion.

Loud voices echoed from downstairs. Sandra retreated to the bathroom and exited into the bedroom.

The tape was still strained in Claudia's hand. I felt like a dog on a leash.

When the noise downstairs settled, Claudia released one end of the tape, wound it around her hand and walked back to the closet. "That dress belonged to her mother. You would ruin it."

"Ladies, come downstairs," Sandra called.

I bolted out of the room and whirled down the stairs. Sandra and Daniel were in the kitchen, and two guys with Pillsbury Doughboy builds underneath flannel shirts were settling in with beers in the adjoining TV room.

Hmm. Sandra told Sergei that Daniel was out of town. Odd considering how his aggressive defence of Sergei in the car the other week.

"Katey, welcome." Daniel grabbed a beer bottle from the

fridge, and squared his broad shoulders toward me. "What can I get you?"

You can dump that barn juice you're holding outside.

Sandra, once again, took my arm and led me to the hall. "Katey, my attention is required elsewhere."

"Daniel and his friends must remain here," Claudia barked from behind me.

Why the hell do three adults need a babysitter?

"Sure. I'll tell them to remain here on your behalf," I told Sandra while barely breathing as her face, which was somehow even closer to me, would have felt it.

Sandra released my arm. "A smart girl like you does not need to throw my name around." Her voice carried a tone of warning.

She disappeared with Claudia, leaving me with her husband and two strangers standing around the kitchen island.

Okay, it doesn't matter why these adults need supervision. This is another opportunity to suck up to Sandra.

I've babysat before—kids in the neighbourhood. What did I do? The kids wanted to watch TV.

"Why don't I put on a movie for you." I picked up the TV remote and accessed Netflix, but only Daniel had a profile linked to the account. "How about The Hangover?"

"No time for a movie." Daniel firmly took the TV remote control from me. Images of half-naked, bleeding guys punching each other appeared on the TV screen.

"We're going to the game," one of Daniel's friends said.

"Sorry, Katey, I'd bring you along, but I promised these two hecklers. Next time," Daniel said. "Babysitter's fee."

"All good," I said.

"I had a babysitter," one of the guys said as he settled into a lounger chair. "Ashley. Wore a tennis skirt." He hoisted his beer bottle.

Lovely.

"Come join us." Daniel patted the seat next to him on the

couch. I caught my shrinking shoulders, straightened up and made my way over, but sat farther away from him than where he indicated.

"Your friends," I said to Daniel. "They are?"

He pointed to the guy closer to him, a round-faced, freckled redhead in a blue and green flannel shirt. "Larry." Then he waved at the other beady-eyed guy with ears that wanted to break away from his head. "Franklin."

Neither acknowledged me.

"This is Katey, our new team member," Daniel said.

They mumbled something without breaking their focus away from the screen.

We watched fight highlights in silence. *This isn't so hard.* Until Daniel slid his arm along the couch behind my head. He wasn't touching me, but his wife — and my real boss — was upstairs. I leaned forward.

"How did you meet your friends?" I asked Daniel.

"High school."

"We know too much about your boss," Larry slurred through the beer in his mouth.

"Care to share some memories?" I asked.

"The best stories are from not too long ago," Franklin said. "High school is a blur."

The two saluted each other with their beers.

"She's new," Daniel started. "Don't scare her away."

I needed to hear more. One of these turkeys could know something about Jackie. I doubted either of them was the mystery boyfriend Jon alluded to, but they could know something.

"You know the DMI team?" I asked.

"Yep," Larry said, eyes on the TV.

"Some more than others," Franklin added.

Larry gargled beer and laughed. "Dependent benefits, I'd call it."

Are they serious? I need more.

"We're going to the basement." Daniel got up and took a few steps toward the kitchen.

I moved faster than I planned. I blocked his path and placed my hand on his chest. "Please stay." My hand slid down, catching his shirt buttons between my fingers, before pulling away.

He fastened his eyes on me. "If that's what you want."

"Let me get you another." I opened the fridge, popped the cap, and handed the bottle to Daniel.

"I should be hosting you." Daniel took the bottle, his hand covered mine.

Focus. Jackie. "Who's the most welcoming? I'm still getting to know everyone."

"Are you interested in taking her place?" Franklin asked.

"I was curious whether you're referring to Claudia."

All three laughed.

"Claudia would be like, *Oh, I can't do that. I haven't asked Sandra for her permission,*" Larry mocked in a high-pitched voice.

"They're pulling your leg," Daniel said to me.

Larry focused above my head. *What are you looking at?* I twisted around. The rubber plant leaves on the landing were bobbing. *Someone was there.*

Daniel rose. "We gotta go."

I wasn't sure what to make of their comments. Whether they were kidding. Their assessment of Claudia was spot on.

They got up.

Sandra said to keep them here.

"You got the tickets?" one of them asked.

"They're on your phone."

"No, they're print only."

"I printed them." Daniel searched the compartments of a briefcase near the sliding glass back door. He pulled out a Louis Vuitton sunglasses case and placed it on the glass coffee table.

"I've been looking for those." Franklin grabbed the case.

"They're upstairs." Daniel headed toward the dining room.

"Wait," I said. "I saw tickets in the kitchen."

"Where?"

"Um." I walked around the kitchen island, running my hand along the marble counter.

"They fell on the floor." I circled the island again, alternating between my feet and a crouch.

"The island connects to the floor," Daniel said. "Tickets can't slide underneath."

I heard chuckling intercepted by beer drinking.

"Maybe I saw them in the dining room."

Daniel inspected the dining room table, the wine rack and the buffet.

When he stopped searching, I told him, "I saw them somewhere else."

"Yeah, upstairs."

"I'll get them for you."

"You won't know where to find them." He strode through the dining room toward the stairs.

Jackie was so good at this—she kept our parents' attention once by telling some skiing story when they arrived home early from the Bahamas while I cleared out her party. I'm not doing what she did. *I can't act like a teenager in front of my boss.* Daniel exited the dining room. *Sandra will be pissed if she sees him, if she sees that I failed this stupid nothing-to-do-with-PR task.*

"I had a one-night stand with Bradley Cooper," I blurted out.

Daniel stopped and pivoted. "Congratulations."

"That's probably one of the lighter house secrets," Larry said, holding his belly in place while he laughed.

"That one should be locked up," Franklin added.

The image of Claudia scooping up the fallen keys a little too quickly from Sandra's closet flooded my mind. *Larry's probably talking about Daniel's red-carpet escorts, but maybe not.*

Clicking and clapping sounds were coming from the grand staircase. Sandra and Claudia reached the front foyer.

They looked different. They wore light-coloured, tie-at-the-waist jackets. Their high heels were taller and skinnier. Claudia's chin was up, eye glasses were gone, and her chestnut-coloured dyed hair was piled on her crown with asymmetrical curls spilling out. Sandra's waves were slightly tighter.

They're going out. I need to join them.

"Thank you, Katey," Sandra said. "Why don't you get started on the project? It's going to be a lot of work." She passed three blue-and-white tickets to Daniel without looking at him.

Get started? How about you celebrate with the one who scored the contract.

Claudia opened the front door. The Cadillac was parked in the wraparound driveway. Someone got out of the car. It was Isabella.

"Being new to the city, I don't have a bustling social schedule," I said to Sandra. "Could I join you tonight?"

She faced the wall mirror and adjusted the collar of her jacket.

Isabella stepped one foot into the front foyer, and I tried again. "I thought we could celebrate the AleAngels contract."

She barely paused. "Bravo, honey. This is a big win for us." But then the outside corners of her eyes dipped.

I wanted to slap that cheerleader voice out of her throat.

"But not much longer. You'll join us soon enough," Claudia added, glancing at the mirror.

My skin burned. *What's going on? How's Claudia on my side while Isabella abandons me? And this is Sandra's decision. Why is she letting her minions answer for her?*

"Great work today." Sandra kissed me on the cheek—she smelled like roses. "Your ride will be here shortly."

No, roses that turned into something more bitter at the end.

Almost like sulphur.

"Bye, honey," Daniel called to Sandra's back. "Let's go," he said to his friends.

My night isn't over. "My purse is upstairs," I told Daniel.

"Go get it."

I ran through the principal bedroom and bathroom and halted in front of the closet. Ripping open the closet doors, I felt along the shelf walls for the keys.

There they were. The key ring rested on a nail protruding from the inner shelf wall. I grabbed it.

Okay, what do these keys unlock? There isn't enough time to search the house. Pick a room.

One by one, I opened the shallow closet island drawers. None were locked. Slide, scan, shut. Jewelry, ties, clutches, belts, scarves, thongs—*do these belong to Sandra or Daniel? Gross.*

I heard footsteps on the stairs. "We gotta go." It was Daniel.

"In the bathroom," I yelled. "Might take some time. Can you leave a key for me?"

"I'm not leaving you a key."

I made a painful, groaning noise.

"Rupert will come back and get you," he conceded.

I waited until it was quiet and then returned to the hall. *Secrets are locked in this house. There's probably nothing here related to Jackie, but I'm here alone with a set of keys.*

Following the hall deeper into the house, I came to a study. The furniture looked like Sandra—a redwood desk and matching accent table in the corner.

And there was a floor-to-ceiling cedar bookshelf. A full bookshelf. Not a space of the back showed. It was so tempting, but I resisted and pulled open each of the desk's three drawers and found only neatly piled books.

Next, I checked the accent table. It was locked. I bent down and tried to unlock it with the first key—it wouldn't go into the hole. The second key entered, wouldn't turn. The third key clicked and turned. I licked my lips and bent over to get closer to what was hiding in the drawer.

"What are you doing?"

I dropped the keys on the floor and whipped around.

Daniel stood at the entrance with the anticipation of a hunter finding fresh tracks. He approached, squatted down, and picked the keys up. "Tsk, tsk. What am I going to do about you?" He shook his head and dangled the keys by the ring with one finger. "Sandra wouldn't appreciate you snooping around our home."

Shit. I should have come up with a story in case I was caught like this. Idiot.

He rose, inches from me. "Tell you what. This can be our little secret. Heck, I'll let you look through anything here. I need one small thing in return."

"What?"

Heat pooled between us as his hands travelled to frame my face and then held my jaw. I flinched, and he moved closer. I blocked the shadows that lurked in his eyes and let his lips lock mine. Firm and greedy.

This time, I didn't pull away.

This is the only way.

I shifted my weight, standing on tiptoe.

He brought me in from the curve of my back—our bodies pressed together.

The only way.

He broke away with hands still on me. "That's all I wanted." He led me closer to the end table and opened the drawer that I had unlocked. "See? Nothing here."

My eyes widened as I looked into the open drawer.

Daniel, nothing to you means everything to me.

CHAPTER FIFTEEN

The book, *The Mouse and the Turtle*, wasn't easy to find. It wasn't available in Toronto bookstores or on Amazon, but I found a copy on Kijiji.

Reading the children's picture book over and over only fed a guilty pleasure. There was no hidden subtext in a story about a mouse lost in a meadow that would tell me what had happened to Jackie.

Everything I needed to know was in the drawer — the first page of the book was torn out and contained a handwritten message from Sandra to Jackie. It was written by someone who practiced handwriting — the words were evenly spaced, and the lines ran straight across the page.

Dear Jackie,

My mother gave me this book when I was a little girl. I read it to this day. May it teach you the lessons it taught me.

Sandra

I had no idea Sandra liked anyone besides . . . well, no one. The whole thing was weird — just one page was ripped from the book. If this cherished book was from Sandra's mother, you'd think she'd want to keep it intact.

Now, what to make of this snuggly relationship between Jackie and Sandra. There was only one person who would have had a problem with it — Claudia.

But that wasn't for probing tonight — or any night in the foreseeable future since my colleagues kept turning down my pleas to go out with them. Tonight, for once, I was invited out, but by clients. Jon and Claire offered me a ticket to a concert as a thank-you for helping them with their wedding. Tonight would be about Jackie's ex.

I arrived at a giant dome sized for tens of thousands of people and made my way down many stairs to the third row.

"Hi, great seats," I said, taking the seat next to Jon.

"You made it," he said.

"This is very generous of you," I said, trying to connect with Claire, sitting on the other side of Jon. Even seated, Jon's giant stature dwarfed Claire.

She brushed her chocolate-brown curtain bangs away from her face. "It's the least we could do." She leaned forward and rested her hand on Jon's lap and twisted her fingers, showing her oversized oval diamond ring at different angles. "You'll understand when you get married one day. It's the only day you need to look flawless."

On the day of the wedding, Claire's makeup artist split in the afternoon. The ceremony wasn't until the evening, but the bride's day had started at five AM and had included a photo session in a humid green room. From what I heard, Claire was so livid with the temperature that her bridesmaids called in a backup dress in case Claire lost it and shredded the dress she was wearing. So I got a text from the bridesmaid and then contacted a well-known makeup artist who was on call. She arrived at Claire's home half an hour later.

I owed Christine for coaxing a high-in-demand makeup artist to cancel her plans and wait by the phone for the day, for a handsome fee, of course, paid by DMI.

"To be honest, we asked Sandra first," Jon said. "She's busy."

Claire nudged him on the shoulder, and her ring was angled my way.

Jackie would have twisted his arm for that remark. She could have pissed on his leg, and he would have been grateful. He knows it. Claire knows it.

"Do you have your wedding photos yet?" I asked. "I'd love to see them."

"Soon," Claire said. "My photographer is compiling preview photos. I'll send them to you when they're ready."

"Heard you looked stunning," I said.

I slung my jacket and purse onto the aisle seat next to me. I doubted that anyone would come to the *Fifty Shades of Grey* soundtrack concert by themselves.

Jon leaned over me and tapped the seat with my purse and coat. "He'll be here soon."

"Who?" I asked, squishing myself back into my seat. His oversized frame, so close to me, was a bit intimidating.

Cheers erupted when multi-coloured lights danced through the darkness of the dome. Jon couldn't hear me over the screaming crowd. He was on his feet, his attention focused on the stage.

I got up and stuffed my jacket and purse into my chair. As I was adjusting the jacket belt so that it didn't drag on the ground, and felt something graze my side.

Daniel! What are you doing here? You touched me in front of 20,000 people.

Heart racing, I glanced over at Jon and Claire. Their arms were wrapped around each other. It was like no one else was there. Good, someone needed to set a good example.

Keeping his eyes on stage, Daniel was holding the small of my back. In front of me, Daniel handed Jon and Claire two drinks from the drink tray he was carrying.

My mind raced back to his house and the study room. My boss' house. *This is a bad idea. I should leave.*

I had successfully avoided thinking about my interactions with Daniel, more specially the *why*. He had the tall, handsome, taken, position of authority and rich appeal, but that was never my type. I liked the idea of wreaking havoc at the company my sister worked at when she died, but doing so before I solved what had happened to her, well, I couldn't reconcile that. At least, not yet.

"Thanks for sending Katey our way," Jon told Daniel, and glanced back at Claire. "We're lucky she's with us for the book launch."

I guess Daniel didn't pass on the memo from Sandra about me not working on the book. Or she did, and it wasn't well received.

"We're lucky to have her at the firm. She won't disappoint you," Daniel said.

I smiled weakly at Jon as the crowd exploded into cheers again.

Sandra probably hadn't gotten around to it. It would look bad if I failed to mention it. That, among other things. I sent Daniel an e-mail — *Sandra axed book help. Sry.*

He checked his phone, typed.

I checked mine. The reply e-mail said, *Take my direction.*

I couldn't tell if that was a threat or an offer of help. I looked down at his hand resting by his side and mine.

Daniel plucked one of the two remaining drinks from the tray — red wine in a plastic-covered glass and offered it to me. "Don't feel obliged," he said. "I didn't want you to think I forgot about you."

I stuttered, brushing my hair away from my face.

"It's all right," he said and lowered the drink tray to the floor.

Dancers wearing black shorts, suspenders and white crop tops began their routine. Flesh peeked out from the bottom of their shorts.

Fog created by dry ice rolled into the third row. I could feel him drawing closer.

He found the back of my neck underneath my hair. I jolted. He massaged the collar of my shirt into my skin until my quivering subsided. When my breath reached a steadier, yet quicker beat, he ran his fingertips downward over my spine. My back straightened. He stopped where my shirt met my jeans.

I could hear my breath over the music.

He grasped the back loop of my jeans and threaded his fingers through. I jerked him away. He let go.

More smoky grey steam was building up quickly. We couldn't see an inch in front of us.

He found my jeans' loop again and pulled me towards him, until the armrest blocked me from moving closer.

Just let him flirt. It didn't hurt to have someone who wanted me around as the company clock ticked. No one could see us. It was just me, him, and the music.

He pressed my back, where my jeans met my bare skin. Grabbing the same place on my front, he held me in place and slowly slid his hand down the back of my pants. He found my underwear — the fabric strained between my legs. I let my head fall back to watch the colours from the stage turn in the dark while he alternated the pressure using the fabric strewn between my legs — light tension to a controlling ache. Lifting away, two of his fingers slowly traced the inside waist seam of my jeans. His hand was warm, welcoming against my cool skin.

The smoke dropped off. The stage was visible again. I didn't move. I stopped myself from directing his touch further down, wanting to feel him spread the pooling moisture.

When the fog lifted, Daniel retreated, stood up and clapped. I followed and checked Jon and Claire for reactions. Especially Claire's. The new wife might have thrown Tantrum 2.0 over a straying husband. But they weren't looking at us. They were focused on each other.

My gaze fixed on the stage without paying attention to the dancers while my body tensed in preparation for my boss's husband to return. I waited for him like the crowd screamed for the next song to start.

Jon and Claire sat in their seats. The smoke was gone, the music was paused, but the dark remained. And I was sure

Daniel just noted that. He took his seat, and I did, too.

I turned to Jon and Claire to ask them their favourite number and shifted forward to the front of my chair for a clearer view of Claire. "What's your —"

Hands found the back of my thigh and didn't waste any time. His thick, steady fingers drew, caressed and longed to reach my flesh.

I threw my jacket over my lap and turned towards Jon and Claire, blocking Daniel.

"Sorry?" Jon said.

I squeezed my thighs together.

The dry ice spilled from the stage.

"Your favourite song?" I asked. Daniel flipped his hand to the top of my lap and buried it between my legs, separating my thighs.

I slightly lifted my outer hip and didn't catch a word of what Jon was continuing to say while Daniel massaged me over my jeans, using his whole strong hand. As Jon's face disappeared with the smoke, I covered my hand over Daniel's and pushed down. I led his fingers further down to the square seam of my jeans, marking entry. He pushed the firm fabric into me hard and I moved forward, pressure mounted, and further as far as I could go until my knees collided with the chair in front of mine.

I didn't know what had gotten into me. This didn't come close to anything I'd done before, ever. Not on a date or at a party, let alone with a married man.

It was so hot in there. I couldn't tell if anything was dry. I felt my pants expand.

And then it changed. The sharp pain stabbed my lower abdomen — the same one I felt when I woke up from my dream with Jackie. I felt exposed suddenly, like my skin was undone with my jean zipper.

I jumped back to my feet, holding my stomach before the

ominous image of Jackie appeared.

Head down, I rose, did up my zipper and tried to move past Daniel, but he wasn't budging.

I faced him. His fingers pressed his white dress shirt. He turned around, facing the row behind us.

A guy in ripped black jeans behind Daniel held a clear plastic glass. Red liquid dripped down his hand. He apologized to Daniel. "Dude, I'm sorry. It was an accident."

The venue should know better than to provide one-use plastic cups.

"Asshole, that's gonna stain." Daniel snarled and tugged his shirt away from his chest to inspect the damage. Then he grabbed the cup from the guy, ripped off the clear plastic lid, and threw the remaining red liquid in his face.

Oh dear.

The guy wiped his face with his sleeve. "What the hell." He advanced toward Daniel, and his knees hit the chair beside me.

Daniel collided into his chair.

As I retreated a step, my arm was gently pulled away from the scuffle. Jon pivoted in front of me, and he didn't let go until he saw I was balanced on my feet.

Jon placed himself between the sopping guy and Daniel. After some protest, he steered Daniel up the aisle.

"Daniel. There he goes again," Claire said.

"Is this normal?" I asked.

"Yeah, Jon's always saving Daniel."

I recalled the ride in the company car where Daniel lost it fast. *Spoiled brat.* He never needed to control his temper. What consequences did a guy like Daniel ever face? A downgrade to a lower-end Benz if he didn't eat his peas? If I or any other DMI employee acted like that, we'd be fired. Except Isabella, apparently.

I couldn't look at Claire. I should have been seeking the type of man who protected his wife and friends—a man like

Jackie and Claire chose — not the petulant child who freaked out over a wet shirt.

Jon stayed next to Daniel, and I next to Claire. *Would things be different if Jackie chose Jon? Would we all be here tonight?*

When the bright yellow lights turned on, Daniel chatted with Jon, and to my relief, arms dangled at their sides.

Alone, I followed the crowd to the exit. My phone buzzed. *Meet us for drinks.*

If I do what he says, maybe he'll be a secret weapon if I can't meet my client target. He did, after all, override Sandra on my helping with Jon's book launch. But will a night starting with drinks get me what I truly need from him?

I messaged him back.

CHAPTER SIXTEEN

"Someone had a night out." Isabella tugged a lock of my unwashed hair as I walked by her desk.

"My alarm didn't go off," I told her.

"Claudia wants to know where you're at with the vodka party permits." She smiled. It was too early for that blinding mouth. "Don't rush. She can wait for you."

"Not far. I'm working on a bid."

"Do you need help?"

"Um, sure. Can you review it?"

"I'm on it. Speaking of AleAngels, throw yourself at it like Henry Cavill walked through the door. Don't focus too much on other stuff."

I'd love to make AleAngels my priority, but I can't do that if I need to recruit clients so I can stay employed here. "AleAngels is only counting as a half-client."

Isabella pushed her chair away from her desk and swivelled to face me. "What? You nailed the contract."

"Claudia seems to think otherwise."

"That's bullshit. I'm talking to Sandra."

"Not today."

"Why not?"

"I was out with clients last night. The concert. Remember?"

"Yeah, so?"

I turned to my monitor. "The guy is friends with Daniel. Daniel came out, too. But not Sandra."

Isabella rolled her chair over to my workstation. She lowered her voice. "Honey, stay away from Daniel. Because he

110

won't. He does what he wants."

"Don't scold me. I didn't invite him. I did nothing wrong."

She rolled closer, levelled her eyes with mine, and placed a concerned hand on my lap, silver bracelets jangling. "That's why you can't look at me right now."

I inhaled her mint-scented breath, looked down at her silverware, then back up at her.

Nothing happened between us after the concert. I messaged him, asked where we should meet for drinks. He didn't write back for hours until I was asleep. "I'm helping his friend's business."

"This is the guy from the photo refresh?"

You know this. I nodded.

"I thought Sandra cut off anything after the wedding."

"She did." I logged in to my DMI account on my desktop.

Isabella had put me in this position. If she didn't want me near Daniel, now was her chance to put her money where her mouth was.

Isabella cupped my knee, and her bracelet snagged my knit skirt. "Listen to Sandra. And Daniel, I've been here long enough to know it won't end well. Trust me."

I turned back to her. "Should I trust you? You said you would help me recruit clients."

"You're working on a bid."

"A dead-end bid. We don't have the skills or experience the company's requesting. I don't know why we're making a submission."

"You're right, I haven't given you what I promised. We get bonuses if our bids win contracts. I needed the money. I'm sorry."

Not good enough. I don't have time to wait for your delegated work couched as charity.

"Or trust you to include me on a night out with the team?" I pressed. "When you rat on Claudia for awarding me half a client, I wonder how quickly Sandra will run to my defence—

her employee who's unworthy of celebrating the contract with the team."

Isabella started to say something, then cut herself off.

"I need to get to work now. I have less than two months left here."

We spent the rest of the day in silence, facing the solid beige wall in front of us.

CHAPTER SEVENTEEN

*W*here *is she? Not at her desk.* "Has anyone seen Joan?" I called out.

No one replied. Everyone had probably left for the day.

I glanced at her screen. *Looks like I'm just in time.* Joan was processing the AleAngels invoice. She could combine this new one with the old one, making Camila's life easier.

I positioned myself directly in front of Joan's screen to minimize the screen protector's blackout effect and took a closer look.

What the heck is this? That's way off. I didn't submit $317,000 as the total. AleAngels is going to freak when they see an invoice for that amount.

Joan was coming. *Good. We'll clear this up.*

"What are you doing on my computer?" Joan hurried past me and tilted the screen away from my view.

Chill, I didn't find your accounting porn. "I wasn't on your computer."

"What are you doing here?"

"As requested, I'm dropping off the AleAngels invoice. I noticed an error." I motioned to her screen.

She dropped into her chair, adjusted her thick glasses that magnified the size of her eyes and positioned her face inches from the screen. Her tone was clipped. "You shouldn't lurk. This is confidential."

Lady, I found your mistake. We're trying to build a relationship with a new high-profile client. Not that I really give a crap, but I need to look like I do.

"I've got it under control," she said, her voice raspy.

Am I losing my memory? Is this right amount? Evelyn's gonna get a call.

"Is there a problem?" Sandra appeared at the entrance of the cubicle, holding a yellow folder. She looked like the faux mom from one of those sexy vampire movies.

Perfect timing. She'll appreciate my eagle eyes. Another opportunity to impress. Just don't look like her husband wants you.

I glanced at Joan. *Go ahead. Explain.* Her eyes, enlarged by thick lenses on her glasses, didn't leave the screen.

Silence.

"There was a miscommunication with the AleAngels invoice," I told Sandra. "We're working it out."

"What is the issue?"

I turned to the accountant.

Joan looked at Sandra, tapping her leathery finger on the computer screen.

Wow, she didn't just respond that way. Sandra's going to tear a strip off of her.

But no. Sandra passed me, and Joan swivelled out of the way, giving Sandra the prime spot in front of the screen.

Joan removed the screen protector and landed her finger on the other screen. They examined both screens, back and forth, on Joan's direction. No talking, but they were communicating. *What is going on?*

Sandra half turned to me. Her words were harsh, but her delivery was the same — composed and pure. "It was my understanding you were instructed to negotiate a price increase to manage the revised scope."

I was just told to do that. Unless Claudia reported that she told me days ago. Of course, she did.

"Not yet. Sorry. I'll let you know as soon as it's done."

"A disappointment." Sandra looked past me and walked away. Her thick wavy hair seemed to exit several seconds after the rest of her.

How did I get in trouble for the accountant's financial screw-up?
I shot Joan a that-wasn't-cool look.

Maybe she found out about Daniel and me. I understood, even if she was the type to turn a blind eye, she didn't want his fun parading around the office.

It shouldn't have bothered me. I was there, and that's all that mattered. And I didn't come there to earn the employee of the month award. But I couldn't completely rid myself of who I was. I'd never half-assed anything — school . . . two Bs, music . . . principal saxophone, cooking . . . took a class on chopping because I didn't like seeing uneven pieces in my crock pot.

Back at my desk, I looked up Camila's number so she could give Sergei a heads-up about the inflated invoice. Maybe I'd call later? Less likely that she'd be at the office, and I could break the news on voicemail.

"Hi, Katey." Isabella and Claudia formed a wall around my cubicle. More like a blossoming fruit tree in spring and a birch tree in a haunted forest.

This was the first time since our Daniel blow-up that Isabella had engaged with me.

There was nothing to talk about. Isabella wasn't helping me. She reviewed my proposal, we submitted, haven't been invited to pitch. Nothing else had come my way.

Isabella gathered the fabric at the side of her dress. Claudia was looking at me the same way she did during my interview — sizing up what's in front of her, but her interest came and went.

"Whatcha doing?" Isabella squeaked.

"I'm connecting with AleAngels."

"We're meeting with prospective clients. Has Isabella filled you in?" Claudia asked, her tone flat.

Isabella widened her eyes and stared at me.

Okay, guess I do. "Yeah, she did. The, um . . ."

Isabella mouthed something.

"The, uh, cremation clients."

"Autocorrect sent the wrong message," Isabella said quickly. "I meant to say aviation clients."

"Right," I added. "You told me. I forgot."

"Then you know what to do," Claudia said.

Not a clue. I nodded.

"I don't think I told you the date," Isabella said. "This is super last-minute. If you have plans, don't worry about it."

I can't read this doll. She could be trying to redeem herself and genuinely forgot to tell me about the plans.

Claudia moved a hand on her hip, nearly engulfing it. "Cancel whatever plans you have to sit on the couch. Come now, we're getting ready."

I'm confused. Claudia wants me to meet clients. Isabella knows I need the exposure, lied to Claudia about informing me of these plans, and continues to fight it.

Whatever. This doesn't need to make sense if it means going out with girls. Especially Claudia, the most likely candidate to have had it in for Jackie.

Even if I don't learn anything about Jackie, maybe I'll recruit a client. Or whatever fraction of a client Claudia deems appropriate.

I followed Claudia and Isabella down the hall, and we entered Sandra's office. There was a lot of open space — the room had just a desk and table with clean surfaces and chairs.

Claudia moved aside an unused coat rack near a wall, took a key out of her dress pocket, and inserted it into the wall.

I'd never noticed a door. Probably because it was blended and looked like a continuation of the charcoal-grey painted wall.

Claudia gave the key a twist, the wall shifted inward, and she disappeared into a dark opening.

Isabella pushed the door a slice wider, gave me a reassuring smile and waved me through.

In the dark, I followed the sound of footsteps toward a sweet scent. Like cake batter.

Lights turned on. Another door at the end of the hall led to a windowless rectangular room. We entered.

Two walls were covered by purple fabric wallpaper. Rolling racks were filled with clothes resting on plush pink fabric hangers.

The room must've been where they stashed those designer clothes. Still, seemed like an overly high-security location for dresses and shoes.

We moved deeper inside. There were two makeup stations with oval mirrors outlined by bright incandescent lights. And on a high round table covered in purple fabric, two hourglass-shaped jewelry stands held sparkling earrings and bracelets.

This is taking presentation very seriously. Even for a PR firm.

Isabella typed on her phone. A song sang by someone drunk about a girl called Valerie played.

Isabella pulled small—no, tiny—dresses from a rolling rack and balanced them on her arm. The dresses were similar in style to the one Isabella wore that night she met me at the bar.

One by one, Isabella draped the dresses against me and then looked to Claudia for approval. With each dress, Claudia nodded or shook her head.

Claudia took the okayed dresses and hung them on the wall by a full-length mirror at the back of the room. She pulled a curtain connected to the ceiling into a semicircle surrounding the dresses. "Put these on." She handed me a package of black stay-up nylons with a single opaque line running along the backs.

The curtain closed. The doll clothes stared at me. I took off my faded brown faux suede skirt and loosely tucked-in cotton blouse. *Ugh, these won't fit.* I pulled opposite ends of a black lace dress, stretching it at the waist. The fabric barely moved.

I sighed and decided to start with the nylons. I tried to turn in a circle, but there was no room in there. I needed to sit down to put these things on. Leaning on one foot, crap, I stumbled into the curtain.

I got back up and pressed against the wall for balance. *Hmm.* The wall sounded different over here behind the clothes. Hollow. Peeling purple wallpaper revealed lines crisscrossing up and down the wall.

I tapped on the wall closer to the ground. The echo sounded deeper.

Placing both palms on the wall, I pushed.

It was a façade. Swinging the door open, I saw a safe the size of a banker's box.

A safe in an office building. Odd. Why not use a bank safe-deposit box?

I ran my hand over the safe, and the circular protruding dial locked. Then I turned the dial. *Click. Click. Click.*

Shit. It sounded like a winch on a construction site.

I stopped. It was too loud, even with music playing.

"Everything okay in there?" Isabella called.

I stepped out of the changing room with the zipper running up my spine undone.

Isabella rolled a platform in front of the full-length mirror. "Step up."

I looked ridiculous. The black dress barely covered my bottom, and the neckline dipped further down than my bra. I'd never worn anything like that before.

She grunted, pulled the fabric together, and tugged the zipper up. It wasn't moving, but I was being thrown around the platform like a surfer dodging monster waves.

She tried again. "Oh, ah. Almost there."

The zipper hadn't moved.

"It doesn't fit."

"There isn't a larger one," Claudia contributed.

"Exhale," Isabella said.

"What?"

"Take a deep breath in. Exhale for as long as you can."

As I emptied my lungs, Isabella pulled the zipper up my

spine. It stopped at my shoulder blades.

My chest broke out in a rash when I inhaled. "Let's try another one."

"You'll get used to it, honey. Short breaths."

Her hands combed over my waist and hips, smoothing the fabric. A wrinkle wouldn't survive a minute with me inhabiting this dress.

"Fix that," Claudia snapped.

Yes, this whole situation needs fixing, starting with ripping off this neck warmer that's being passed for a dress.

Isabella gently lifted and rolled the lace dress from the bottom. I flinched when my dress bunched, and the tension created a strap below my bum. She dipped her long red-painted fingernails under the nylon adhesive, sending a ring of heat around my thigh. She pulled the nylon gingerly upwards, then moved to the other. She grabbed my inner thigh and squeezed firmly, five nails pinching, to steady me with one hand. My knee slightly buckled as she used her free hand to massage the nylon adhesive, blending the fabric and my skin together. When both legs were done, she carefully pulled the dress back down.

"That did nothing. I can see the bulges from here," Claudia called from the makeup station without looking our way. "Try on the butter drape dress."

I retreated to the changing room, shut the curtain, and kept the fabric in my fists. *Eye on the prize, eye on the prize.*

I cast my eyes to the vault. *I'll come back to you.*

I pulled on the silk dress. *Thank goodness, I can breathe again.* I stepped out, jumped on the platform, and completed a three-hundred and sixty-degree spin, showing off the knee-length, open back, thick straps, with a modest cinch at the waist.

"Love this dress. Can I borrow it? I'm attending meetings with Sandra. I need to wear something new."

"You look like you gained fifteen pounds. In your face," Claudia spat out. "Put the Gucci back on. After we do the rest of you."

Pretty sure the dress tag said Dolce.

She's jealous all right. But I don't know if she's capable of acting more territorial than a girl guide selling cookies. Her emotions lead her, not methodical forethought.

Isabella offered her hand. I took it and stepped off the platform. "You're going to put us all to shame when your makeup is done," Isabella said.

On my way to the changing room, I grabbed a satin robe from the rolling rack.

I changed and rejoined them.

"Sit here," Claudia said to me, pointing to a low stool by a makeup station.

From behind me, Claudia gathered my hair in front of my shoulders and pulled down until her knuckles met my bra.

Starting at the crown, she ran her long plum-coloured fingernails sharply against my skull, collecting hair at the nape of my neck. A wood comb scraped my scalp, long after the tangles were gone.

Changed into a short, low-cut red dress, Isabella pulled up a stool until her knees were touching mine. Her doe eyes ping-ponged over my face.

She opened a drawer, shuffled its contents, and pulled out an eye shadow palette. She dipped the brush in a shimmery dark grey powder, leaned forward, straddling my legs and dabbed at my eyelid. I parted my lips when I felt her mint-scented breath.

Claudia separated my hair into segments. She then clamped, coiled, and pulled the sections of my hair with a hot curling iron with a surprising amount of strength. The iron was getting closer and closer to my scalp—as was the hot steam. I tried to shrink away. No use, she got closer. As did the perfect opportunity.

"My hair looks perfect," I told Claudia. "You must practice."

"Sandra taught me." Claudia's swan-neck wrists sharply twisted around my head.

"Makes sense. My hair looks like Sandra's. I'll ask her to teach me a few styling tricks when I go back to her house. Ouch!"

She burned me. My hand flew to the back of my neck.

"Are you all right?" Isabella asked, narrowing her eyes at Claudia.

"Oops. You're fine." Claudia grinned and continued.

"All good." I took my hand off my neck. That was gonna leave a mark.

She's definitely petty and insecure. And she proved my instinct — this is normal behaviour for Claudia. Real damage is done in the dark, plotted carefully. Not a spur-of-the-moment reaction in front of a crowd.

"Give me the lip palette," Claudia said. "She's too pale for that tone."

Claudia jerked and spun my stool. She met me with a makeup brush covered in a creamy pink substance.

She took hold of my jaw and stretched my lips between her thumb and index finger.

Ow. Ow.

Stop it. My lips were about to split into four. My neck shot back, breaking her grip.

Her claw reclaimed my face as a thick unsharpened pencil scraped too far from my natural lip line. *I've had it.* A scream reached my throat when she released my face with discard.

"Gorgeous." Isabella beamed, twisting the stool so I faced the mirror.

Smoky eyes, rosy cheeks, lips twice as big. Hair, there was a lot more of it.

Is this where I lost Jackie?

Isabella smiled at me through the mirror, like it was my first day of school.

When Claudia turned her back, I mouthed, "What's going

on?"

Isabella looked back at Claudia and held up her finger.

I should have realized earlier that I needed to brace for a bar and booze. We weren't dressed like this to play Monopoly.

"Can't wait to *drink*," I told her.

She got it. "I've got just the thing." Isabella disappeared down the hall and returned with an unmarked bottle of dark liquid. It looked like the paint drink from the bar, only darker.

She poured me a tall glass. "Down this."

I drank the mystery substance in one gulp and banged the glass on the table when I was done. And then coughed. *Blech.* Same car paint and oil taste from the bar.

"Get changed," Claudia ordered me. "And don't eat anything. That dress costs four grand. You're on the hook for any damage."

A song about breaking up in November was blaring, and I headed back into the changing room dancing, even though I couldn't find the beat and looked like a drunk pigeon.

I went to the safe and entered the mysterious nine-digit number.

Pull. Wouldn't open. *Damn.*

Back into the asphyxiation costume, I went.

When I was ready, Claudia told me, "Almost forgot. Sit back down."

I did. She twirled around and headed for the changing room.

Isabella nodded at me. I returned to the stool at the makeup station.

Slam.

What was that metal clanking noise? Must be the vault.

Claudia returned, one hand behind her back. She spun me to face the mirror. Admiring her reflection, she collected my stiff waves with her free hand, and piled them behind my shoulders, exposing my neck.

My head turned, looking for reassurance from Isabella. *Where is she? This doesn't feel right.* She wasn't there.

Claudia turned my head back in place. She moved her hands behind me, where I couldn't see them.

She smiled wolfishly.

My rash returned, red blotches marking my collarbone.

Snap. Claudia wrapped a diamond necklace around my neck.

"Now you're ready," she said to the mirror.

CHAPTER EIGHTEEN

I couldn't stop checking the rear-view mirror of the car from the back seat. It wasn't because I liked my reflection. I needed confirmation that it was actually happening. That I was going out with the girls, the girls Jackie went out with. And clients that could be my lifeline would be there.

Just like AleAngels — listen, impress them, and seal the deal. I can do this again.

Isabella and Claudia led the way inside the bar, bypassing the long line-up. Security guys in black leather jackets nodded at them.

It was dark, busy, and noisy. The space was deep and the ceilings were high and unfinished, like an old garage.

We moved in further — the crowd of suits and cocktail dresses thickened. Isabella grabbed my hand and heads turned to follow her. She was the only one not wearing black, although she could have sported corduroy overalls and still received offers to do her laundry.

Claudia led us to the far end of the room. With her perfect hair arranged in long, thick waves, Sandra was huddled at a table, chatting with two tall dark-haired guys in suits.

Claudia whispered into Isabella's ear and took off. Isabella claimed a spot at the bar and leaned over, chest spilling over the countertop. More gazes shifted her way.

Just when I was feeling pretty.

Who else is here? I scanned the bar. Behind Sandra was a string of half-moon booths. *I think that's Hillary and Christine in one of them.* It was so dark that it was hard to tell. I didn't recognize the guys they were with. Now I was just staring.

"Is that Hillary and Christine?" I asked Isabella.

"Hillstine. That's them." She didn't glance in their direction.

"Should we say hi?"

"Let's check in with Sandra first."

I eyed Sandra and company.

The bartender placed two vodka martinis in front of us.

I veered backward.

She handed me one. "Just hold it in your hand."

"You gonna tell me what's going on since Claudia thinks I know?"

"We're trying to recruit clients," she said.

"Shocking," I replied.

"I'll lead. And stick with me, okay?"

"Okay."

"Hiya." Hillary pawed at my lower back.

"I wanted to wear the Dolce dress. Hold my drink." Christine shoved her fingers under my dress shoulder strap and brought her face up close to it.

I must be wearing a Fondle Me sign that only DMI employees can read.

"It's mine next," Hillary whined. "Is this your debut? Cheers!"

They clicked their drinks to my stationary martini glass.

"We're going." Isabella grabbed my hand.

"Don't forget the tradition," Christine said.

"Dare I ask?"

"On your way out" — Christine swiped her crotch with her thumb, and pressed it into Hillary's purse — "make a thumbprint."

"What does that mean?"

"Goodbye." Isabella yanked me the other way.

"Ladies." Sandra greeted us with a double-cheek kiss. Daniel's scent — expensive cologne with a hint of bourbon — hit me when Sandra's baby-smooth skin touched mine.

Focus.

"I would like you to meet Ian Thomson, CEO, and Chris Deri, vice president of marketing, of the North Pass," Sandra announced. "They're launching an airline."

They looked alike—both were clean-shaven, tall, short brown hair gelled straight up. Ian had a fit physique, but Chris did not.

Grinning like the Cheshire cat, they shook our hands.

"That's exciting," Isabella said.

"Are you considering a launch event?" I asked.

Isabella pinched the back of my arm. *Ouch. What was that for?*

"You don't waste any time," Ian said, exchanging laughs with Chris.

"How about a drink first?" Chris asked. Before we could remind him that we already had drinks, Chris ran his eyes down the waitress wearing a dress that ended at the crease separating her bum and thighs. He ordered more beverages.

"Excuse me for a moment, gentlemen," Sandra said. "Isabella, can you assist me?"

Isabella hesitated and stared at me. "I'll be right back," she said.

"I love to fly. What are your routes?" Claudia asked.

"Nowhere near here," Ian said. "The far north." He made zigzaggy motions in the air with his finger. "Calgary to Whitehorse, Fort McMurray, Prince Rupert, Anchorage, Churchill, Baffin Island."

Claudia clutched his finger and swept her tongue over her lips. "You may as well point to outer space. Use this." She unbuttoned his jacket and ran her erect hand over his perfectly vertical chest and stomach. His chest jutted forward, straining his white dress shirt. "Now, if Calgary is here"—she pressed his lower right rib—"where is Baffin Island?"

"To the far left," Chris said, licking his finger and tracing a wet line down Ian's chest.

Claudia ignored Chris and dragged her fingernail up to Ian's collarbone.

All my work with Evelyn on my PTSD has been eliminated in one night.

"And Anchorage?" Claudia twirled her finger around the point of his shirt collar.

"The other side and lower," Ian said, widening his stance. Claudia's fingers walked to the other side of his chest as she was humming, Itsy Bitsy Spider. She finished the line by dotting his nipple.

I brought the martini glass in front of my mouth, but not quickly enough to hide my laugh.

Claudia saw me—her expression flipped away from one that sang a lullaby.

"Gentlemen, Katey is new to DMI. Not only is she beautiful, she has many great ideas . . . for the company and our clients. In fact, there isn't anything she isn't good at. She would be honoured to show you her talents."

Three pairs of eyes turned to me.

I felt like I was naked on a stage. I didn't know what to do.

"C'mon," Claudia pressed. "Don't be shy."

Just go with it. You need to recruit clients. "I c-can tell a j-joke," I stammered.

Claudia's lips curled.

I shuffled backward and bumped into someone. *Shoot.* Beer spilled on my shoulder, down my arm, onto my dress—the four-thousand-dollar dress.

As I wiped the black lace with my forearm, my martini spilled on the floor. *No.* My clutch dropped into the mess on the floor while I inspected the damage.

"You all right?" Ian asked.

Breathe and visualize. Spiders are on the floor. They crawl up Claudia's leg, dress, into her underwear—

"She's being modest," Claudia said. "She needs the

spotlight. Chris, help her onto the table."

The giant trucked toward me. In one motion, he hoisted me by my armpits and planted my feet on the glass table of our booth.

I squatted, wobbled, and tried to use my fingertips to balance myself in my high heels.

Claudia grabbed my wrist and used her height to pull me into a standing position.

Chris dusted off his hands and moved back with Claudia. They created a half-ring of empty space around me.

The pot lights above the booth didn't help. More eyes turned my way.

Stay calm.

Shouts from the crowd got louder. There must have been hundreds of people staring at me. *Don't look at them.*

Someone shouted, "Take it off!"

Boos and hisses drowned out the music.

I reached for Ian's outstretched hand, but Claudia took his arm and wrapped it around her waist.

"Dance," she called. "Then you can come down."

Unbelievable.

A lime wedge hit my torso.

If it gets me off of here, I'll move a little. Do that dance on YouTube. *What's it called? Twalking? Never tried it before—no one wants to see two-hundred pounds of quivering flesh. But my current, normal size but too-big-for-DMI, should be able to handle it.* I tried to widen my stance, but the lace hugging my knees stopped my feet from extending past hip width. The sound of tearing fabric ensued when I bent my knees. *Forget that.* My hips broke into a fast swirl-pop combination, not sure if I was in sync with the music.

"Yeah, like that," Chris called, pumping his fist in the air.

Oh, okay. I must be doing something right. Sync to the beat of Chris's clapping hands.

Ow. Ice had hit me. *What the?*

Scanning the crowd, my only cheerleaders were bending at the waist in laughter.

A lemon garnish hit my face, and straws littered the table at my feet.

I dodged another flying ice cube and kicked a saltshaker off the table. A woman standing well over six feet with Chris' build squared herself towards me and held her hand to her eye. "That hit me, bitch."

"I didn't mean to. I'm sorry."

Claudia was in hysterics, stomping her foot on the floor.

More taunts came from the crowd, "Get an Ass."

The one-eyed woman charged toward me. I backed up — she shouted and flailed her free arm. She was saying something, but I couldn't hear over the yelling. I moved further back and hit the wall. *Shit. Where's Ben when I need him?*

And then red fingernails gripped the woman's arm. Isabella's fingernails.

The raged woman stopped advancing.

There was no way to hear what they were saying over the crowd.

Isabella grabbed a drink off a waitress's tray. She pointed to Claudia — the waitress nodded. Isabella handed the drink to the woman, who accepted, released her hand from her face and left.

Thank you, Isabella.

Isabella didn't let go of me, not even when I was stable on the ground. "Are you all right?"

I repeated her words in my head several times before I understood the question. "I'm fine."

Claudia handed me a tall glass with a yellowy-coloured drink that reminded me of bile. "Good work."

I took it. "Do you know where the bathroom is?"

"I'll go with you." Isabella found my hand and led the way.

In the bathroom, she cornered me in front of the sink and mirror. "I'm so sorry. I didn't think that would happen when

I left."

I stayed quiet, still processing what exactly did happen.

"Are you all right? Say something or start drinking."

"I'm fine. Thanks for saving me."

"Do you want to go home? I'll take you home."

I want to go home, but home can't help me. "No."

"You don't look okay."

I searched her face for a moment. "It's been a while since someone had my back."

"Your former co-workers set a low bar." She hung her head, tight curls falling over her face. "I'm not doing a great job raising it."

No, you're not. But you're all I've got.

"Don't ask our guests what DMI services they are seeking, okay?"

I nodded.

Isabella grabbed the neckline of my dress from the center of my chest and aligned it with my matching black bra. "Let's go. This time, I'm not leaving your side." Isabella stepped back and bumped into someone with the same frame as Claudia.

"Sorry, honey," Isabella said.

The woman's eyelids chomped—she crossed her arms.

"Hey, nice dress," Isabella said.

She didn't respond.

Isabella stepped beside her. "We have the same dress."

"I couldn't tell. The dress is supposed to fall below the knees."

Two other women in the bathroom line-up were bursting into laughter.

Isabella rolled her eyes, but her face turned red before she hurried into a bathroom stall.

Swirling the drink in my glass, I walked over to the stall where the lamppost-figured woman retreated. The toilet flushed. I covered the glass with my hand and let the liquid spill through my fingers onto the floor.

Isabella washed her hands in record pace.

On the way out, I took my time to hear the sound of heels desperately trying to grip the tile floor. Muffled high-pitched yelps penetrated the swinging door.

When we returned, a new suit with shiny dark hair forming a widow's peak joined the group. I slid onto the bench, followed by Isabella and then the new guy.

"Hello, ladies. I'm Faris, the chief pilot."

"I'm Isabella" — she touched my shoulder — "and this is my colleague, Katey."

Planting her palms on the table, Isabella hoisted herself onto his lap, giggled, and landed on his other side. His eyeballs nearly popped out of his head. As did mine.

"The pleasure is mine," he said.

Faris and I were beside each other now and so close that shaking hands was awkward.

Isabella blabbed about how great DMI was. Faris lifted his pelvis much higher than necessary, knocking the table, and reached into his back pocket. He fished out his phone and started typing. A photo appeared on his screen, and he brought the phone close to his face. "Please excuse me. I may need to take a call. This business doesn't sleep."

"Didn't know the aviation industry replaced radio with nude photos to communicate," I said.

Isabella kicked me under the table.

Faris let out a tight laugh, flipped his phone, and placed it facedown.

"Or is that the uniform your airline wears?" I asked.

He forced a smile, displaying two big shiny front teeth. "Sure you ladies don't work in interrogation?"

"What are you up to during your stay in Toronto?" Isabella asked in her cheerleader's voice.

"We're here for a mix of business and pleasure."

Surprise.

"Chris is getting married. It's his last hurrah."

"Bachelor party!" Isabella shrieked. "Chris, come here."

Chris moved in and smothered me with his sweat-stained arm. Then he rested it across my shoulders.

I shuffled forward.

"Bachelor Party Part one it is," he said.

"We'll help get you ready for the big event," Isabella said, and whispered something to Faris.

We will do nothing of the sort.

"Four tequila shots," Faris said to the waitress. "Wait, make that six shots."

Wonderful.

"Ian, get over here," Faris yelled. "What's your colleague's name again?"

"Claudia," Isabella replied, winking at me.

Faris called to Claudia, who's face had re-inhabited a scowled librarian. Ian joined us but remained standing at the head of the table.

The waitress arrived with a tray of shot glasses, salt shakers and lemon slices. "Cheers," she said.

"Chris, I'm sure one of these lovely ladies will help you with that," Ian said.

Chris looked at me, "I would be honoured."

I'm not happy to help him with anything, except directing him to a shower. And I don't understand what that means. Am I supposed to feed him the shot?

I picked up the shot glass and examined it as if I was waiting for it to come up with an answer.

"Me first," Isabella said. Faris lifted her back onto his lap. She giggled and splayed her wrist.

"Lame," Faris said. "C'mon, it's his last chance to enjoy life."

Isabella gathered her hair into a pile over one shoulder, exposing her neck as if she was feeding a vampire.

Leaning over me, Chris buried his face into Isabella's chest, leaving a saliva trail that followed a bikini tan line from the top of her dress to her collarbone.

Isabella squealed as Faris sprinkled salt on her chest — most of it dropped inside her dress.

To a chorus of cheers, Chris leaned in further. The sweat on his neck made my dress wet. He rested his arm on Isabella's shoulders, shoved his head against her skin, moved up, and snapped his head upright. Isabella's hand gripped Faris' belt buckle as Chris sucked a lemon slice.

What the hell is going on here? Jackie never mentioned this crap, and I know she went out with clients. Sandra would flip if she knew what was going on here.

Claudia landed her eyes on me. My eyes found the ceiling. "It's Katey's turn to congratulate the groom-to-be. Chris, take off your jacket."

How bout I send him flowers and deodorant instead.

Chris wrestled his arms out of his jacket. His shirt was soaked — armpit sweat stains ran down to his waist.

You have to stay in the game. It's only a neck.

I screwed my eyes shut and took a breath like I was going underwater for a long time. A warm salty-rotten egg mix taste violated my tongue. My head recoiled. "Sorry, you feel like sandpaper," I said between coughs.

"Ouch." Chris pushed out his tongue, licking his lips. "Let's try again."

"If things are too rough," Claudia said, "find another spot."

"I can think of a few spots." Chris looked down, leaned back, and placed his arms behind his head.

I pressed my knuckles down hard against the bench to keep them from landing on his face.

"I'm good." Like a lizard, I collected the salt with my tongue, following a dotted line. Chris quivered, then pushed closer.

Now put the tequila in your mouth for a second, then spit it out. You can do it.

Here I go. And pour. No, I can't. The shot drained from my mouth onto Chris' lap.

Claudia tossed the straw and chugged the rest of her drink.

The night continued in threes. Three more rounds of shots. Three stains on the fabric bench, absorbing my liquor. Holding my breath, counting to three, as Chris whisper-spat into my ear that we had made his night and wanted to do this again.

I rather have three live rats sewn under my skin than spend another minute with him.

And at least three times Claudia got turned down by Ian.

When Claudia settled the several-thousand-dollar tab, she paid with fifty-dollar bills, then told me to join her in the bathroom. I did.

"Glad you and Chris got along," Claudia said, leaning into the bathroom mirror and applying lip liner.

"Um, I guess I didn't vomit for a second time on him."

"You can have the morning off."

Take the morning off to what? To throw up my memories of tonight?

The door swung open. Isabella walked in and planted herself between me and Claudia. "It's late. We're going home."

"What are you doing leaving them out there?" Claudia barked. She didn't wait for an answer and turned back to me. "How many clients have you recruited?"

She can't be serious.

"You may as well offer a sad clown," Isabella said.

Hey. Okay, fair.

Isabella grabbed my arm. "Let's go." She turned to me outside the bathroom. "Get in a cab now. Go."

"What?"

Claudia, hands on hips, blocked our path. "You don't decide when the night is over," she told Isabella.

"Ladies, hope you enjoyed yourselves tonight." Sandra rejoined us as if she'd been gone for five minutes.

Where was she all this time? I thought she'd gone home. It must be two AM, and she looks camera-ready.

Claudia dropped her arms to her sides. "We hadda great time. I was explainin' to Katey that the night isn't ova."

Stress always brings out what we know best. Claudia may not have worn Prada as a baby.

"I need one moment with Claudia and Isabella," Sandra said to me.

Isabella's lips brushed my ear. "Go now," she told me.

Not arguing.

I flew outside, even though part of me wanted to watch Sandra rip into Claudia for her appalling behaviour.

I climbed into a cab, then told the driver to wait. *Something isn't right.* Claudia admitted to Sandra that craziness she said to me about the night continuing *privately.* Sandra didn't flinch. She never did, but this was her business' reputation that Claudia was threatening.

My eyes scaled tonight's work—four-inch pumps, shrink-wrapped body, wavy hair.

Of course. This is how DMI recruits clients.

CHAPTER NINETEEN

"Where to?" the driver asked.

"One moment." I needed to look up my address.

My phone rattled in my hand—I undid one window to defog it. Outside, Isabella said something to Faris, then ran to the other side of my cab and got in.

"Drive. Now," she said, looking back.

We were stopped. Car horns honked.

"Go," Isabella repeated, her face was between the driver and passenger headrests.

The driver shrugged. "Traffic, miss."

Sandra exited the bar with her regal glide and approached another cab with Chris and Claudia inside. On my knees, I peered out the back window as we inched forward.

"Put your seat belt on." Isabella tugged the belt of my jacket.

I wiped the back window for a clearer view. Chris handed Sandra a small white envelope.

"What the hell is going on?"

"What?" she asked, as we pulled away from the bar.

"In what format were you consuming shots tonight? Why did Claudia casually tell me to continue my night with that buffoon as if we were going to have tea? And what the hell was Sandra taking from Chris back there?"

Isabella glanced out the window. She leaned over me, pulled down my seat belt, and secured it.

"A one-night stand between two adults is one thing. The boss getting paid for it is another," I told her.

She remained facing the window.

"*Isabella!*"

"DMI has a unique business model."

That's one way to put it.

"Are DMI employees required to interact with clients *that* way?"

"No, it's not like that." She rested her fingertips on my shoulder. "It's your choice. You don't have to do anything you don't want to."

"Does anyone meet their client recruitment targets without earning a handful of padded envelopes?"

The cab sped up.

She sighed. "They're hard to meet by winning bids alone. I'm sorry, sweetie."

Jackie never mentioned any of this. I'd remember that detail with Alzheimer's.

"What does this company even do? PR or this other service?"

"No. It's not like that. You can't sign up for only the fun stuff. It comes with a promise to do business with DMI, PR business. And Sandra vets everyone."

She vetted that douchebag trio? Don't want to know what characters she blocks.

"What's in it for you?"

Her voice quieted. "How do you think I put food on the table for my family? Keep the bank from seizing their house? Pay for my sister's dance . . . the lessons, competitions, costumes, makeup? These are my choices. The reward is steep. It has to be. I keep the cash from *my* work."

"Then what did Chris give Sandra?"

"She collects, takes her cut. He gave a deposit, too, for upcoming *legit*" —she curled her index and middle fingers on her coat—"business."

Chris, or the other two, could have counted toward my target. "I'm six weeks and two and a half clients away from getting fired. You know this."

"Oh, please." She looked at me. "You were a rabbit in its hole at best just sitting beside him."

True, but she doesn't know I wouldn't have felt otherwise if I knew what was going on and a client that could count towards my target was on the line.

"There were two others. I need this job," I told her.

She looked out the window. "You're right. You need to recruit to stay. It's not negotiable."

"You didn't even give me a chance. I had no idea what the hell was going on, and you made sure it stayed that way. That was my opportunity."

She said nothing.

"*You* invited me out tonight. You set me up to fail."

"Claudia invited you. Sweetie, no offence, but after tonight, I'm voting to pull the plug on you."

"I'm going to lose my job. You said you wanted to help me."

"I'm going to lose many jobs if you tag along." Isabella turned to look at me. "Even if we fix you up some, can you handle getting paid by strangers for this type of work? Do the weird, dehumanizing things they want? That's why they pay the big bucks. How much experience do you have? Forget the money."

"I skipped most of the escort training courses at university."

"Uh-huh. They were prerequisites for my Master of Computer Science at the most prestigious tech school in North America."

"Okay, fine. I'm rusty," I said. "Tell me how to be like you. If I fail, then I'm done."

"No, sorry."

"If I can do half of what you did tonight, I'll be golden."

We stopped at traffic lights I recognized near my home. I was getting nowhere fast. *Think.*

"You need to understand," she said, putting a lot of space between each word. "It's this job, then nothing comes next. We have confidentiality agreements, but word gets around."

"Then I'll move back home, to the other side of the country. Work in forestry. There are no standards in that industry."

She crossed her legs and shook her head while looking at the back of the driver's seat.

Why won't she give me a damn chance? Try harder.

I leaned forward into her peripheral space. "See what you did to me? This is the best I've ever looked. I know what I am. It's not this. Stupid of me to think I could move and turn into someone I've always wanted to be."

She twisted in her seat. "Honey, you're beautiful without the dressing. Stop it."

"I assume other girls at DMI participate?"

She said nothing.

"It's fine. I'll be the odd one out. Like I said, I know what I am."

"You're better off that way."

"I'm better off employed."

She went back to looking out the foggy window.

Okay, you made me go here. "Claudia wants me to participate. I'll talk to her."

"Honey, don't do that. She wants to pawn you off on the guys she doesn't want. She might have got her way if I didn't intervene. Or, from your perspective, ruin your golden opportunity."

So that's why she hired me. To sleep with the Chrises of the world. "How did Claudia get stuck with Chris and not you?"

"Like I said, it would take a lot to get me fired. I can afford to choose."

How nice for you.

"And my night isn't over. I'll be able to buy my whole family the newest *iPhones* with tonight's payment. I just wanted to make sure you got home safe." She bunched her jacket in her fist. "This is the last time you come out. Hooking up with married sweat stains is not the worst thing that can happen."

"What do you mean?" I asked.

Isabella lowered her voice. "This line of work isn't always safe. There has only been one incident that I know of, but it's enough."

"If you really think I'm better off staying away, then tell me."

"I barely know anything. Really."

"Please."

Isabella sighed way too long. "One night, a co-worker and I arrived home at the same time, but separately from our second shift. We lived in the same building. She wasn't okay." She paused.

"What was wrong with her?"

She bit her lip. "She looked like she'd been in a car accident. There was blood and—" She stopped. "I insisted we call the police. She refused. I convinced her to go to the hospital, but only if I swore to never speak of what I saw."

"I thought Sandra screened everyone," I said softly.

"She does. But she was out of town with Claudia when this happened. Daniel was in charge. And he broadened the definition of acceptable services."

"What does that mean?"

"Some of our clients have particular tastes. Some just plain weird. Others . . . dark stuff. Doesn't matter. I want you to know that I didn't let it go. I told Sandra what I saw, even though I was sworn to secrecy. But I should have done more."

I rubbed my palms together. "Was your co-worker all right?"

"She was away for weeks, wouldn't see anyone. When she came back to work, she was different. She told me Sandra took care of it. And didn't want to talk about it."

"The-this took place recently?"

"More than a year ago." As the cab turned the corner, Isabella said, "This is where I saw her that night."

I swallowed hard and lowered my head.

"That's why I don't want you coming out," Isabella said.

The car pulled over. Slowly, I turned my head and recognized the unsheltered metal buzzer and plants between the first and second double-glass doors.

It was Jackie's condo.

CHAPTER TWENTY

Endless darkness. Nothing to see, nothing to touch, nothing to hear. The air was cold.

The white bathtub came into focus. It's far away.

I walked with bare feet. Stopped.

Jackie stood at the side of the bathtub, no clothes. Her stomach and lips were white like paint.

She stepped into the tub, one foot at a time. She sat down, looked my way. Disappeared.

I ran to the tub. The water was murky and still. My arms plunged into the water. It was thick and coated my hand. I pulled back, and drops formed on my fingers, and hit the water. No splash, no ripples. I got down on my knees and let my arms sink back into the water, feeling for her.

I pulled her head out of the water. She was weightless. I wiped a dark substance as thick as wet flour from her eyelids, mouth cheeks.

Her eyelids flipped open. Black holes stared back at me. I let go. No splash.

She rose — stiff, like a stone figure. Her head turned to me. Clumps of snow fell out of her eyes in waves like blood from an open artery. The snow collected on top of the bathwater, creating a white layer. It built, and the water disappeared. The snow pile grew taller and was spilling over the rim.

I cradled my stomach with both hands. That's enough.

CHAPTER TWENTY-ONE: JACKIE

August 2016
I was covering for Hillary and Christine while they inhaled half the city's drug supply in the bathroom. But my company was far more than the suits deserved. I'd been up for forty bloody hours and just got off a plane. The two goons and their suburban cologne were an insult, even though I was only keeping them company for a few minutes.

I flipped back my hair. Their eyes zoomed in on my neckline, complete with a diamond drop necklace.

The two were crowding me. I walked backward until the railing of the VIP section stopped me. More eyes drifted my way. I spread my arms over the railing. "I'm not assigned to your project," I told them, but not loudly enough so they could hear over the music. I was being honest—I didn't give a fuck about what they had to say. And they felt the same way about me.

I thought about my last clients in New York. I slept until one PM every day. Woke up, hot stone massage, cleansing wrap, nails, then dinner at restaurants that only accepted reservations made in person. Then, to work. Only *I* was invited on the trip. Isabella whined when I reported my earnings upon my return. Claudia somehow was also vacationing in New York at the same time and just happened to stay at the same hotel as us. It didn't matter. The rat cut for overalls didn't spoil the purpose of the trip. New York was my chance to flaunt to Sandra what I brought to her company. She needed to experience me for her herself, so she would keep me to herself.

For a while, I enjoyed the dynamic I introduced between Sandra and Daniel. She used me to remind him that she was the CEO of the company—and he used me to remind her that he was the owner. I'd spend a night with his clients—he would pull into work the next day with an updagraded Benz. And then I'd spend next week with her clients, and a Range Rover would occupy Daniel's DMI parking spot by the end of the week. That was their arrangement. They alternated first dibs on their rosters every weekend.

And then it changed. Daniel stopped giving me white envelopes, but Daniel didn't stop flying first class, nor did he cancel his trips to the Swiss Alps. I told Sandra I wasn't working for free—I told her after our time together in New York. The timing had to be perfect. An HR complaint alone—as fucked up as that was—wasn't going to free me from Daniel. She said she'd take care of it. *So far, so good.*

One of the clients under my watch signalled to the VIP area waitress. My drink didn't need a top-up.

I scanned the room for the horse-tailed idiots. I said I'd keep their clients occupied for five minutes.

Normally, I would have told them to call Claudia to enforce Sandra's stupid rule—never leave clients alone. Claudia wasn't there tonight, but I enjoyed knowing she was at home ready and waiting by the phone. Waiting to be wanted.

The truckers in suits planted themselves on either side of me, all three of us leaning our backs against the VIP rail barrier.

"You should work on our project," the one on my right screamed into my ear.

"Product placement isn't my specialty." I couldn't help myself. I arched my back, and so many stares made their way to me, I couldn't count.

"Why don't we teach you more?" He cocked his head

toward the private room Sandra and Daniel rented for client business.

"Hillary and Christine will be back any moment," I told them.

"They can join us." He clamped his hand on my wrist, but I pulled it free.

I felt them exchanging looks behind my back. The one on the other side of me wrapped his arm around my waist—I picked it off like it was garbage.

Like a line of cockroaches, his hand travelled down my back and over my ass to where the dress ended. He went under the fabric.

I grabbed his hand, held it in mine and made the eyes he sought. "I'll meet you back there."

The other one grabbed my silk Prada dress strap and brought it up to his face, and breathed in.

And I had it. I grabbed my clutch and ground the round metal clasp between the tendons on the back of his hand.

"Bitch," he yelled, knocking the purse out of my hand. The contents—lipstick, phone, mascara, eye and lip liner, and rolled-up cash—spilled to the floor.

The other one cackled, bent down, and scooped up my phone. "Is this your madam calling?"

I snatched it back. On my feet, I checked the screen. *Why is Katey calling me at this time? Shit, she already called twice. It wasn't like her.*

I swiped right. "Kitty?"

They choked with laughter. "Go make your master purr."

I needed to get out of there—I couldn't hear her. "Get the hell out of my way." I ploughed through them.

Then I stopped. Daniel had entered the VIP area. Tall and proud. I wanted to smack that frat-boy smirk off his face with my phone, but I blew it. I'd just given him permission to do what he'd been waiting for.

But not yet. I needed to check on my sister before dealing

with Daniel.

"Gentlemen, will you join me in the back room for Cohibas and Macallan 18?" Daniel led them out of the VIP area and promised another hostess would take good care of them.

I jumped off the raised VIP area and pushed through the crowd. I hit the green phone symbol on my cell. It rang. It was so hard to hear over the music. *C'mon, Kitty, pick up, pick up.*

It would be quiet outside. *Move it, people.* I pushed, pulled, rammed, and used my elbows—whatever it took to move forward.

My call went to voice mail. *Shit.* I called again and kept pushing. I was almost there. I just had to get past ten or so assholes.

My cell was taken right from my hand. "What the fuck." I whipped around.

"I'll take care of your phone tonight." Daniel tapped the phone once on his palm and placed it in his back pocket.

"I'm going to Sandra," I told him.

He tilted his head down, smiled, and I knew no help was coming.

"Let's get a drink." He grabbed my hand and led me, not to the bar, but towards the back room. "Tell me what went wrong with our transportation clients. Claudia told me everything was splendid in New York. What changed in such a short time?"

"I have to go," I told him.

He put his arm around my waist, hooked me against him. I couldn't move an inch.

"Let's go back to our guests," he told me. "Offer them what you gave my wife in New York. On the house."

Chapter Twenty-Two

I should have called in sick, but I was already there. How would I have described my illness to Claudia? I knew what DMI did to my sister. Thinking of what she went through and preparing my statement for the police—both had left my toilet filled with vomit.

At the office, my stomach cried again and I wished I'd saved a bag of puke to spill on DMI's spotless floors. I wouldn't be there long—I was getting the company car and driving to the florist to buy flowers for the vodka launch party.

Isabella said the company car keys were in Daniel's office. *Get them, and go before you see anyone.*

I used the forbidden curved hall that directly connected the offices to the entrance to avoid office traffic.

I entered Daniel's office.

Get the keys and leave. Do it fast.

Standing in an executive office at DMI, my stomach set off and reminded me what I was never ready to learn. Jackie was never in a bike accident. She'd sustained the concussion from a client—Daniel's client. The damage was done. All it took was a slip and fall in the bathtub. Daniel profited from that night—the night that secured her death. And I was working for him, funding the designer leather chair and cedar blinds in his office.

Get the keys, then figure out how you're going to send them behind bars.

I found his desk, but the keys were not in the metal box. It was a disgusting desk by DMI standards — pen left open lying on top of the wooden desk, an empty paper coffee cup, the chair pulled out from behind the desk.

Check the top drawer Isabella told me to check if the keys weren't in the box. I opened it. *So this is who he is when Sandra doesn't see the mess that needs cleaning.* The drawer represented him perfectly — a small space shoved full of garbage. I sifted through the contents — cologne, a razor, a tie, mouthwash, deodorant, a Zippo lighter, a fidget spinner, paper, and more paper. Touching his things reminded me of Jackie's boyfriend in the eleventh grade. It shouldn't, or, I wish it didn't. It was so long ago, and things that happened in high school didn't matter. He was handsome, playful and had the lead part in the school play. She dumped him by our pool. He left his towel. He came back to get it, And I was there. Then he came back again, never when Jackie was home.

Next drawer. More crap. I took out a stack of loose paper and shook it to see if keys were stuck in the pile. A set of keys on a Ford key chain fell to the ground. This was them. *With all their money, they should get an electric car.*

As I was putting the paper back into the drawer, I stopped. Under more paper, the bottom half of a black box caught my eye. I dropped the paper on the desk and picked up the box. A large-faced gold watch rested on the velvety bottom. I scooped it up by the band and inspected it. It was heavy, expensive. Of course it was. It had gold hands, diamonds for numbers, and a crown symbol for twelve. It appeared to work. The time was right.

It's a Rolex. What the heck is this doing in a drawer full of garbage? It probably cost a fortune. It should be locked up in that vault in the pre-sex-work room.

I flipped the watch over. The back was scratched. I ran my fingertip along a rough hairline-thin diagonal line. *It can't be.*

The sound of chatter grew in the hallway. I shoved the watch into my purse and the papers into the drawer.

Isabella entered Daniel's office. "Hey." She eyed the desk. "Did you find the keys?"

I dangled the key chain. "On my way."

"Sandra told me to go with you. You know, the flowers need to align with everything, down to the blush for her cleavage."

I don't want your damn cheer around right now. "I'm doing a few other errands. I don't want to drag you along."

"It's never a drag when you're there, honeybun."

CHAPTER TWENTY-THREE

I told Isabella my condo was too messy for anyone but me and asked her to wait in the car.

I don't care if she waits all day and night. I'm not leaving my condo until I piece this together. I made my way over to the poster-sized calendars pinned to the wall that mapped out a timeline to Jackie's death.

From left to right, one calendar with Post-it note-sized boxes were coloured and marked with handwritten notes.

Jon said they dated in the summer. The summer boxes were shaded in blue.

They broke up, and she moved on to another guy. The calendar squares after the break-up were orange — some blue and orange overlapped. Sandra was out of the country in October, and Daniel was in charge. October was black. Jackie told me on October 21, she was in a cycling accident and sustained a concussion. Last night, I scratched out *cycling accident* and replaced it with *murderer-slash-client*. She called me on November 26 and told me to come visit her. Her party was on December 2. She died in the early hours of December 3.

The adjacent calendar pinned to the wall documented my communication with Jackie.

I ran my fingers over the rows separating the weeks. Rolex . . . *where is it? Here — October 14*, when Jackie told me she'd damaged some guy's watch. One week before she'd told me about the accident. There were only text messages from her between October 14 and October 21. All her messages said she'd call later.

Only one person would lose it over a scratched watch. My eyes darted back and forth between the October 14 and October 21 squares.

A scream tore through my throat. I brought my nails to the paper and scraped the paper and the beige-coloured paint underneath on the wall.

CHAPTER TWENTY-FOUR

"Honey, we have plenty of time," Isabella said, looking up from her phone. "Slow down, sweet stuff."

My knuckles turned white on the steering wheel. "Isn't this the speed limit?"

"The speed limit, plus thirty clicks. Chill. You made me write *dick* instead of *deck*."

I didn't know whose neck I was pretending was the steering wheel—the one who killed my sister or my sister.

This pain was different. When Jackie died, I felt as if my heart was cut out, and I'd been forced to carry it around with me. Now, a piece of my heart had been sliced off, but I didn't want it back.

How could Jackie have kept what her boss did to her a secret? She suffered alone and went to the hospital alone. I would have dropped everything to take care of her. She waited a week—told me it was nothing. She said she ran over a fallen tree branch, fell off her bike, landed awkwardly on her ankle, and hit her head. It could have been much worse if she hadn't been wearing a helmet, she said.

I should have known. She didn't talk to me for a week, which neve happened before. I pushed those thoughts away and buried myself in the comforting lie of her text messages that said she was busy with work.

She didn't tell me because she knew I would have gone straight to the police. Too bloody bad if it all came out— screwing her boss's husband, working as an escort. Daniel, Sandra, and anyone who knew and covered it up would have faced criminal charges.

Daniel probably didn't know what to do after Jackie was lying at his feet unconscious. So he did what he always did — got someone else to deal with it.

I could picture it — he called his wife while she was out of town. Sandra didn't question what he was doing alone with one of their most attractive employees. She explained to him, like she was explaining to a toddler, that you can't hit someone if they break your toy. She came home, only pissed over the lost business.

Sandra probably blackmailed or threatened Jackie into silence. Isabella said Jackie told her everything was fine, taken care of.

They didn't deserve to breathe fresh air, shop, party in Vegas or run a PR firm. They deserved one thing — to live the rest of their lives behind bars.

That's what she wanted to tell me that night. The night I arrived two minutes too late.

My foot hit the gas pedal.

No, Jackie wasn't going to tell me. This was more wishful and pathetic thinking to protect what I thought we had. There were so many other things she kept from me. How long had she been in the second business? If it took them over a month to give me a shot, then Jackie was probably participating from day one. Was there a second boyfriend, or had she left Jon to spend more time with clients? She was conveniently unavailable on Thursday, Friday, and Saturday nights. And I thought nothing of it — she was out entertaining clients, I told myself. *Uh-huh.*

I thought Jackie and I were different, not like the other sisters we knew. We were never jealous of each other, or became more involved in each other's lives when one of us hit rock bottom. Maybe she was just my half-sister after all.

Isabella tapped on the window. "Take this exit."

I jerked the steering wheel to the right and veered two

lanes over.

"I'm driving on the way back," she said. "No more coffee for you."

We were the only customers in the tiny flower shop. Flower petals were scattered on the floor, tables and window displays. The mess was probably there to provide a distraction from the chipped mint-green walls.

A woman with a messy raven-black braid slung over her shoulder and corduroy blue overalls approached us from behind the cash counter.

"Are you Katey for the boat party?"

"Yes." I cleared my throat. "And this is my colleague, Isabella."

"Wonderful. I'm Helen." She pushed the bridge of her round glasses closer to her face and rolled up her baggy sweater sleeves. "Right this way. They're waiting for you."

Isabella and I exchanged glances. Who are *they*?

She led us a few steps deeper into the store to a woodworkers' table. On top were a handful of flower arrangements standing in tall, clear, straight vases. Green stems and petals coloured pink, purple, yellow, red, and white littered the table and floor.

"Do you hear that?" Helen asked, bringing her hands to the back of her ears.

"I don't hear anything," Isabella responded.

"The flowers. They know you're here."

Isabella looked my way. I ignored her.

"Can you walk us through what you prepared?" Isabella asked.

"The theme is fire. You'll see gold, yellow, amber, red, scarlet, and maroon accents in each sample."

The carnations in one vase reminded me of the flowers on Jackie's casket. An arrangement of red carnations on the chestnut surface. The one I placed stayed right in place when the casket was lowered into the ground.

"Did you bring the table linen?" Helen asked.

They're both staring at me. "Yes." I pulled out a dining tablecloth, one hand after the other, from my shoulder bag. Helen rested her veiny hand by her side as the never-ending trail of fabric unspooled from my bag.

Smack.

Shoot. My phone had hit the floor. I picked it up and examined the screen for cracks.

"Everything okay?" Isabella asked me.

"Please continue," I said, keeping my head down.

Helen's finger landed on her mouth. "No loud noises. It disrupts the aura."

"Then I'll give the flowers some space." I stepped back.

What are you going to do? Play some mind game by buying the flowers used for Jackie's funeral to decorate her killers' party? That'll show them. Think. How are you going to nail these monsters? You need to bring evidence to the police.

What proof did I have that Daniel hurt Jackie? A scratched watch. It wasn't enough.

Helen droned on. "Tulips are popular, especially in the spring. They're also fine for an event in July. Beyond the elegant colour and symmetry, they're low-fragrance and hypoallergenic. They were very expensive in seventeenth-century Europe . . ."

What else do you have on Daniel? He smacked a binder into a car window. He flipped out at a concert when a guy spilled wine on his shirt.

Police will say, one, those events are unrelated, and two, who cares, no one was hurt. And would Jon, Claire, or Rupert speak honestly about Daniel's temper? No, they wouldn't. He's their friend or employer. It would be my word against his.

The police would be right to question my allegation. It's one thing to throw a drink at someone and another to put a woman in the hospital. I can't prove it. The only people who know for sure are the two people who were there. The one who survived isn't that stupid. I don't need criminal prosecution experience to know how this is going to play out.

I could still go to the police. I have enough to make them poke around, make DMI visible. Rumours will circulate.

But what good will rumours do? The allegations will damage DMI's reputation, but only temporarily. I'll be demonized as the unstable, grief-stricken sister, looking to blame someone for an unfortunate accidental death. DMI specializes in crisis management. They'll bounce right back.

" . . . Other tall arrangements that don't take up a lot of table space are roses. Like tulips, they can match your colour scheme. Roses are my personal favourite. Did you know that you can make jam and jelly, and even boil the petals and treat yourself to a facial? Not only are they stunning, they give off a fragrance making anyone fall in love. Wouldn't that be amazing? You come out of this event as matchmakers. A new line of business."

"No roses," Isabella said. "We're selling hard liquor. No references to love, cuddles, or snuggles."

You don't have enough evidence. Daniel needs to talk. What will get him talking? Maybe bourbon. If he's drunk enough, maybe something will come out besides his dick.

" . . . perfect for a summer event, a mix of carnations, delphiniums, fuji mums, hypericum berries, pom mums. Carnations have a bad reputation, but they're very useful. They flavour beer and wine. Would you like some? I've made my own . . ."

No, Daniel won't talk. Sandra has trained him well. And they'll get rid of you as soon as you ask.

" . . . the lilies are not just for weddings. Did you know —"

"Katey, what do you think?" Isabella asked.

I don't care. "The lilies," I muttered.

Helen started again. "Wonderful, let me tell you about

lilies. You're going to love this—"

"Helen," I started. "My mother is an avid gardener. Save the tall tales for your green-thumb cult meeting."

Isabella gawked.

My phone vibrated. "I have to take this."

I exited the shop and found shelter from the sun next to the floral window display. Tears welled in my eyes as I checked the screen. A picture of my mom flashed above the dancing green phone symbol. The phone shook in my hand. I wanted to tell her everything those demons did to her daughter.

It rang to voice mail.

I turned to the window and used it as a canvas to imagine what had happened to Jackie that day. Daniel came out of the shower, towel wrapped around his waist. Jackie, hands clasped, profusely apologized for damaging his watch and insisted she was on her way to get it fixed. He grabbed the watch and saw the scratch. He knocked over the blue bottle of perfume on her dresser and then screamed at her. She ran to the door, but he grabbed her by the hair and—stop. *Stop it.*

I shut my eyes and felt my wet mascara spread on my cheeks. I hit my hand against my head to rid my mind of these images, but instead, I was back in Jackie's condo and saw blood smeared to the pattern of her hair on the floor.

My eyes opened, and my throat held back a scream.

Isabella stepped out of the shop. "What's going on?"

"Nothing." I wiped my face with my sleeve. "All good."

"You're not okay. Honey, come here." She wrapped her arms around me tightly, rubbing my back. "It's okay."

I let her hold me.

"You can talk to me. Or say nothing at all," she whispered.

I broke away from her hold. "I'm lonely, that's all. Sorry, I was rude in there."

"Whatever. I was two seconds from decapitating those roses, but wasn't convinced that would shut her up."

I tried to smile.

"I placed the order. Sandra will be pleased. I'll tell her it was your recommendation."

I searched my purse for a tissue.

"We're done for today. And I have some time before my night begins." She moved my hair away from my face. "Why don't we go to my house? We can watch a movie. You can tell me about those sad thinking books you read while I give you a manicure." She took my clean-at-best hands into hers that looked ready to model engagement rings.

I'm not taking one step into that building. I pulled my hands back to my sides. "No thanks."

"How about the spa? Warm salt water will make you feel like new."

I prefer the cold. "I don't know." I didn't expect that to come out.

"C'mon, we can drink those non-alcoholic detox vegan shakes. Well, you can. I need a real drink."

"Sandra would be okay with this?"

"Clients and potential clients hang out there."

Of course. I wiped away the last of my tears and let her look at me. She raised an eyebrow.

I'm going to need help. There isn't enough evidence against Daniel to bring him to justice for what he did to Jackie. He needs to do it again.

"Okay," I said to Isabella. "But only if you show me some tricks. I'm tired of being alone in this massive city. I need a man in my life to replace my couch."

Isabella clapped her hands. "I can show you how to get a guy's attention. And keep it."

I wondered what Isabella would disapprove of more—teaching me to entice Daniel or teaching me her second business tricks? Luckily, they were one and the same.

"Deal," I said.

CHAPTER TWENTY-FIVE

"My grandma's bathing suit is more daring."
"Forgot my thong bikini at home." I descended the steps of the shallow saltwater pool wearing a one-piece black and purple striped bathing suit that covered my back entirely. I didn't pack this swimsuit. Mom snuck it in. She hoped I'd take up swimming again.

And I'd rather sport this garbage bag over one of Isabella's string bikinis. I couldn't pull off that number — she looked like a character out of Baywatch. Red triangles half covered her boobs and a string forming the back of her bottoms disappeared into her smooth bum. There wasn't a blemish or unsightly mark anywhere on her body.

"I've seen worse than my suit," I said.

"Ah." She giggle-chirped. "Yeah. Joan's lingerie."

Speaking of Joan, the odd one out at DMI, by 30 years. "She's different. Seems like a lost opportunity for DMI business growth."

"She's family."

"Joan's related to whom?"

"Daniel's cousin or something."

That sort of explains Sandra's reaction when Joan screwed up the invoices. It still feels off. Sandra doesn't tolerate any mistakes when it comes to her company. I put that thought aside for now.

"Tell me more about getting a guy's attention," I asked, before swimming over to the soapstone waterfall.

Isabella floated on her back, two red mounds peeked out of the water and didn't fall anywhere close to her armpits.

"Tell me about the last book you read."

Don't avoid our purpose. "Salem's Lot. I'm not much of a go-ing-out-to-the-bar person."

"Could have fooled me." Her head sank deeper into the water, covering her ears before disappearing under the water.

I lifted myself onto my tippy toes to check on her while she was underneath. My ankles wobbled.

She sprung out of the water like a mermaid and stared at me. Her brown doe eyes were pronounced with her curly hair slicked back. Water up to her hips, she glided closer to me, locking gazes, and stopped, her chest, rising and falling, an inch from mine.

"What are you doing?" I asked.

"Making eyes."

"You look like you want to wear my skin."

"This is your hook." She slapped the water. "Your verbal flirting skills are non-existent. You have to shut your mouth and use your other tools."

"Can I just offer to buy him coffee?"

"You buy coffee for colleagues."

"Okay. Say we go on a date, or two. I'm not the type to, you know, dive into things."

"Now you sound like my grandmother. The WASP ver-sion."

"I need to keep him interested."

"Try that place where people gather and sing on Sunday morning. They'll wait for you." She winked.

"I take a little longer and guys get bored and leave."

"Um." She waved her arms on the water's surface. "You could send pics of what's under the granny suit."

My fingers ran over my midriff. "I can't do that."

"Yes, you can."

I lifted one side of my bathing suit, showing the squiggly white worm stripes—my stretchmarks.

Isabella lowered herself so she was at eye level with my scars and ran her thick fingernails under my bathing suit, and brushed away the water droplets from the area that made me wear a one-piece. "You just need the right shot," she said.

I pulled down my bathing suit, covering my marks and goosebumps. "So, there is this guy," I said.

"I knew it! Who is it?"

Now think of someone real so that she's invested. And someone who won't talk. "The AleAngels security guard."

Her tone dipped. "Wait until the launch event is over. Okay?"

I nodded.

"Come with me."

Following her, I climbed the pool stairs.

Isabella grabbed her phone from the side of the pool, and we made our way to the sauna. "I'm wondering about the second business at DMI," I said. "How did it get started?"

"Not through crowdfunding." She opened the sauna door. "That's a story for another day, sweetie pie. Go in."

I entered. The thick steam made my eyes water. My lungs felt like they were carrying weights.

"Take off your bathing suit. Sit over there." She pointed to the highest bench, barely visible in the haunted hot box. "We're taking photos."

I pulled the towel up to my armpits and kept it in place while I rolled off my bathing suit.

Isabella snorted. "We're not doing an ad campaign for hotel towels. Drop it."

I pulled the towel tighter around me.

"For the love of God, stop dawdling. Someone's going to come in."

I shrieked as she ripped the towel off of me.

I jumped onto the elevated sauna bench and crossed my arms. Sweaty wrists covered my nipples.

"Now, think of a time when you did something badass.

When you won the AleAngels contract."

She took my ankle in one hand and the back of my knee in the other and crossed one leg over the other. Peeling my arms off my chest, she directed me backward with her palm on my chest. "Perfect."

Standing over me, she leaned to one side, then the other. The phone was clicking away.

"Please delete these after you send them to me."

"I'm sending them already. Remember what I said about timing."

Good. I need to get Daniel's attention tonight. "Thanks."

CHAPTER TWENTY-SIX

"Camila, so sorry to bother you at this time."
"What do you want?" she responded, her accent thicker over the phone.

"I'm calling to verify that you received the correct invoice. There was some miscommunication with our accounting department. They asked me to contact you."

"I have to find it. Wait."

I wish she worked at DMI. She's going to give me what I want. No questions asked.

"Invoice is for three hundred and seventeen thousand dollars."

"Perfect. Thank you for checking."

"Goodbye."

"Hold on. I need to ask you something else."

"What?"

"Your security guard at the door. We hit it off."

"Which one?"

They were clones. "The guy with the thicker waist."

"Vlad. The fat one."

"Yes. Could you give me his phone number?"

"I'll give him yours."

"Sure, but I have a Vlad in my phone already. Total asshole. Dumped me by bringing his new girlfriend to the same party."

No reaction from Camila.

"Could you give me his full name so I don't mix it up with my jerk ex?"

"Vladimir Lebedev."

"Can you spell that?"

"L-E-B-E-D-E-V.

"Thank you, Camila. I'm so nervous. It's been a while."

"Goodbye." She hung up.

Google was already open on my computer. *Let's see if you are who I think you are.*

I typed *Vladimir Lebedev* in the search box.

Soviet painter, born 1891. *No.* Russian Olympic skier, footballer. *Not likely.*

I went to the news search tool, entered *Vladimir Lebedev,* and the word *charge.*

Here's something. I scanned an article listing several Russian names besides Lebedev — Aleksandr Vasiliev, Artem Rabinovich, and Ivan Mikhailov. It also cited the charges against them. *Bribery, don't care. Fraud, closer.*

Yes! I slammed my mouse on the pad. Laundering money from the proceeds of crime.

I shouldn't have been that happy that a criminal was expecting a call from me.

Now, it made sense. The invoice was correct. A small firm like DMI would never land the AleAngel's vodka launch contract based on its merit. Didn't matter how many girls you threw in the deal.

It's a good cover, I'll give Sandra that. She overcharged illegitimate clients through inflated invoices. The dirty money from organized crime was hidden by paying business expenses in cash. The bar tabs, the girls. That's why the girls didn't collect the money. Sandra mixed the clean and the dirty cash, then paid the girls. They were happy — instant cash, no hard trail. And it was out of Sandra's hands.

Money laundering was a common practice in Vancouver. Half the homes there were bought with dirty funds.

But if this information got into the wrong hands, it would rattle more than one cage.

I only need it to shake up one.

CHAPTER TWENTY-SEVEN

Isabella would forgive me for sending the photos she took of me to Daniel before she forgave me for scheming with Claudia.

Guilt drove Isabella to protect me, not my failure to flirt. She still hadn't admitted that the girl she let suffer in silence — my sister — was dead. I imagined she didn't want to be reminded of the heavy weight she carried. *Try living with arriving a few minutes too late.*

It would take her some time to forgive me for my plans with Daniel.

Ideally, if Daniel and I met in private, Isabella would never find out. But that was not how Daniel operated. He needed the chase and an audience.

I sent him the photos at the beginning of the week. And no response. Then, on Thursday, he sent me a text back, *Baseball game, Friday.*

The only way to score an invite to a box seat game was to be a client, a prospective client, or one of the girls recruiting clients.

It had to happen today. I wouldn't be invited back by Claudia when I failed to comply with her condition of participation — taking her discards. Then I'd have a few weeks of employment left at DMI.

If it worked, it'd be the last time I saw them all. *Thank God.*

Isabella, I would see again. She actually took a night off and, of course, would only do so to spend time with her family. She sent me a picture of herself dressed up as the Queen in Frozen for her little sister's birthday party with the caption, *Not that different from what we wear.* She went all out — the blue Elsa dress with a slit to the hip, white braid wig to her waist and gloves reaching her elbows. Someone should enjoy their night.

Upper deck.

The fans in the stadium box were no different from the unruly crowd dressed in blue at the gates one floor beneath. There were maybe forty people, overwhelmingly guys, squeezed onto two decks — a lower deck with seating and an upper deck with a bar, high tables and standing room.

Where are you?

Sandra made a beeline for me. Her silky rose cheeks brushed against mine. I squeezed my hands together tightly behind my back as she finished her second kiss.

"Come join us. These gentlemen represent an oil company and are quietly shopping for help with their image. They don't want to talk about work."

Neither do I. I nodded.

Sandra led the way, waiting between pitches to make introductions. "Steven, Adam, meet Katey Philips, a valuable member of my team."

One of them, probably in his mid-forties, took a long swig of beer from a pint glass and held out his hand after wiping it on his jersey. "Steven Sanfield." The scent of beer and chicken wings wafted into my face as a glob of orange sauce slid down his jersey, rounding his belly. He pointed to a massive pile of chicken wing bones. "You should try these."

My eyes returned to scan the room. *Where is Daniel?*

The other guy, wearing the same blue baseball cap, looked around my age. He placed a tall beer can on a nearby standing table. "Adam Doles. Nice to meet you." He gripped my hand comfortably. Either his teeth had been whitened like Ben's, or those weren't his teeth at all.

There was a bar to my right, but Daniel was not there.

Claudia, full pink drink in hand, blocked my line of sight. She wormed her way back into the circle of carnivores, touching Adam's arm. That was her not-so-subtle instruction for me to migrate to the guy who was probably more interested in eating me whole. And then use Claudia to pick his teeth.

The crowd booed and hissed.

"What's going on?" I asked Adam.

"The manager is about to get thrown out for arguing with the ump," Adam replied.

"Forever?" Claudia shuffled closer to Adam.

"For the game."

"Ump, you suck," the big one yelled, beer spilling onto his black nest of a beard. He beat his chest once with a half fist.

"Our bad," I said. "We don't know much about baseball. This is my first game."

Jackie had dragged me to Seattle every summer to see the Mariners. She drank a lot. Once, we were held at the border after she complimented the border guard on the bulge in his pants.

"Look at me, wrong colours." I outlined my frame with my hands, exaggerating hip and bust curves.

Adam followed my hands, his pupils surrounded by ice-blue rings widened. "I'll teach you."

Claudia crossed her arms and opened her mouth, but I spoke first. "Let's get a drink." I led the young one to the bar.

Tonight calls for the burning of a few bridges. And it can't be with Sandra. I have much bigger plans for her.

Daniel was not at the bar. Back to the lower deck. Wasn't there, either. He might have ditched the evening and didn't care to tell me.

"What would you like?" Adam asked, leaning on the top of the bar.

"Tonic water, please."

I scanned the lower and upper decks again.

"What's going on?" I asked Adam, facing the field.

Adam pointed to the batter, his shoulder touching mine. "The other team is at bat."

"Couldn't have guessed that."

"Sorry. Okay, there are no outs." He pointed to the field. "Watch the runner on first. He's gonna steal second in three, two . . . there he goes."

"Well done," I said when the player got off his dirty stomach at second base. "You must play."

"Played my whole life."

"Not anymore?"

He shrugged. "No time."

I leaned closer. The top of my head was parallel to his chin. "Don't you miss it?"

"Every day."

"There's probably batting cages around here. Is that fun?"

"Hell, yeah." He edged closer, padding from one foot to the other. "Do you want to come with me?"

"Don't know how to swing a bat. Maybe you can show me?" I took my phone out of my purse to search for the location.

"Of course. It's easy."

Sandra stepped beside Adam. "Are you enjoying the game?"

"Yes, turns out Adam plays baseball," I said.

"How long are you in town for?" Sandra asked.

"Three days."

"The company tickets for those days are yours."

My phone vibrated. It was a text message from Daniel. *Go to the single bathroom. Knock once.*

He's here. Don't look around. She'll notice. But me and him can't happen here. There's no way he'll go that far in a public place.

Tonight, my place, I texted back.

Sandra and Adam continued to chat. She flashed me

warning glances to put down the phone. If only she knew.

Another message from Daniel arrived. An image. I tapped the thumbnail. It was a photo of the torn page from the children's book Sandra gave Jackie. The caption read, *Now.*

We can still go to my apartment. The plan will have to wait until then. It had better wait until then.

"I have to use the restroom," I said, trying not to sound rushed.

Outside the box, down the hall, there were men's and women's bathrooms with swinging doors. Farther down, there was a single stand-alone bathroom.

My heart pounded as I gripped the door handle and hit the *Record* button on my phone.

I took a deep breath and knocked. The door opened just enough for me to slip inside.

Before I was in, the door slammed behind, but I wasn't shocked. His scent filled the room — the trail of what I'd come for.

I didn't see him until I was pinned against the opposite wall. My hair clip scrapped the cold concrete behind me.

"Did anyone see you?" he asked.

"No."

His pupils grew so wide they took over the grey outer colour layer. His rock-hard body slammed against mine. My spine curled into the concrete. He yanked the neckline of my dress, landed his mouth beneath my collarbone, and took my skin between his teeth.

"Ow," I told him. He came up, took my jaw in his hand, angled my head to the side, and breathed on my neck. He retracted but held me in place. Pressed against the wall like a painting, I saw him for the first time. His chest bounced, belt buckle waved, and eyes feasted. I didn't want him to feel pain, pleasure, or triumph. I wished much worse for him — to feel nothing at all.

His hand slid between my legs, bunching my dress around

my hips. He lowered himself to the floor—hot heavy breaths seeped through my mesh thong and pulsed under my skin. My back arched and separated from the concrete wall as the heat built. I shifted my weight back and forth, ramming my heels into the ground. It was too much—I shuffled to the side, but he slid me back into position and took the barrier separating him from me in his teeth and pulled. I shoved the sides resting on my hips down and rammed my exposed flesh into his mouth. His teeth and tongue competed for the inside of my skin. The heat fighting the cold concrete wall against my back sent my body quivering. His tongue travelled upward and rammed into my navel before moving back down to where he started. I slammed my heel into the ground. *I can't stand it.*

A voice inside my head, not mine, reminded me, *"Not here."*

I tried to break away to the side. Hands grasped my hips, his hold unbreakable. I tried again to push him away. He wouldn't move.

"Later." I shoved the side of his head with my thigh.

He rose fast. "Later?" His palm smacked the wall beside my ear. "You have another job tonight."

"No, I don't."

"The blond dotard."

I shook my head.

"How's your target coming along?"

"I think Sandra has got this one."

Daniel picked me up by the waist, carried me to the other side of the room and dropped me on the sink counter. He shoved his way between my legs as two massive hands gripped my face, and his dark eyes moved like thunderclouds. "Careful."

I pulled his hands away from my face. "Am I far behind? How many did the other girls bring in after a couple months?"

He laughed, a hard grunt.

"It's not happening with that client. He's not interested in me."

He moved one hand to the wall behind me, his face an inch away from mine. "Really?"

"Yes."

"Didn't look that way."

"He doesn't want me. Come to my condo after the game."

He moved away from me. "We're having a party after the game. Then we're going to L.A."

His house will have to do, then. Not ideal. "Then I'll be at your party."

"You're stealing from Sandra if that yuppie rejects you."

What she thinks of me isn't your concern. What matters is what you think of me. And you think enough of me to pick this up later.

I grabbed his loose belt and brought my lips to meet his. His hands found their way through my dress, beneath my bra. Fingers, strong and stiff, scissored my nipples. I let out a soft cry and bit my tongue.

I brought my lips to his ear and let him hear the heavy air escape me. His hands clamped my thighs and left a red handprint as they moved to gather new flesh.

My thighs trapped his sturdy waist and closed in on him.

His hand reached behind my neck, and his fingers shaped my throat. I slammed my eyes shut. Abruptly, he let go when a mobile ring tone set off. He reached into his pocket and answered, leaving me dishevelled on a public sink. I lowered myself, straightened my dress and exited while he continued talking on the phone.

In the women's bathroom next door, I swiped and wiped at my dress like insects had inhabited it. *It's just one night. One night, and he'll pay for what he's done.*

I soaked my face with cold water and looked up. New creases and lines had formed on the outer corners of my eyes.

I would inject bleach into my face if it meant having one more minute with Jackie. Just one. I wouldn't ask her what happened, what I should do. I wouldn't say anything. No need. She'd know what I want to tell her.

But not yet, because I don't want to hear what she would have to say right now.

Sandra and Adam were still at the bar.

"Apologies for my absence," I told them.

Sandra smiled, closed-mouthed as always, never showing displeasure in front of clients. She left.

"Sorry about that." I tugged at the sleeve of Adam's jersey. "Lady stuff."

Adam looked away, grabbing the tonic water on the table. "Here. I saved your drink."

The clear liquid nearly overflowed from the glass now that the ice had melted.

"How many innings are there in a game?" I asked.

"Nine, unless it's tied. Then we go into extra innings." He was bouncing to the music, snapping his fingers. *Not good.*

"And we're in what inning?"

"Bottom of the seventh."

I needed to get rid of Buffoon Junior. "Tell me more about you and baseball."

"I played Triple-A in my hometown."

"You're kidding. So did my little brother. You remind me of him so much." I pinched his right cheek. "Same pudgy face." My fingertips brushed his eyelashes. He flinched. "Same gorgeous long eyelashes. Wish I had yours."

He wrinkled his nose. I repositioned myself so Sandra could see him more clearly.

"Are you wearing mascara?"

His lips peeled back, showing shiny white. "No."

"I'll put some on you. I do it all the time to my brother."

Lips retreated into his mouth. "I'm going to check on Steven."

"Okay. See you soon." I kept the smile plastered on my face

while Sandra was watching.

Lower deck.

I found myself with a group of people who worked in advertising. They claimed to be friends of Sandra's. I think they meant acquaintances. Business contacts. Sandra spent her time with work. She didn't have any friends.

She was surprisingly reasonable when I explained Adam's sudden disinterest in me. She said my comfort was her priority. *Liar.* That meant there was something else she wanted.

Claudia was exactly where I left her—on the upper deck, stinking of Steven.

She texted me—*You have no idea what you did.*

Whatever. I have bigger fish to fry.

Claudia had expended her use. She brought me to Daniel tonight. Now, the priority was taking down Daniel for what he did to my sister as well as Sandra for covering it up. I'd figure out what to do with the accomplices, but one step at a time.

I glanced over at Daniel, the unsuspecting fool, leaning too comfortably far over the railing.

Don't stare now. I turned around. *Wait, what did I just see?* I whipped around. Isabella. *What in the hell is Isabella doing here in Steven's armpit-stained hold?*

Swollen eyes, red cheeks—I'd seen that look before. It was her little sister's birthday party. She should be at home celebrating with her family. Claudia pinned me with a stare and mouthed, "Back off."

Then I understood. I was out—a replacement was needed. That was what Claudia's text message meant. I ruined things for Isabella.

This isn't right. I should intervene. Isabella should not have left her little sister's birthday party to satisfy this meathead and bolster Sandra's shady revenue stream.

Intervene and do what? I stared at the baseball field, the vast unoccupied green space. *Are you really going to walk up there and offer to take her place? No. You won't do anything but stay here and wish you felt guilty.*

Two years ago, I would have done something. And it would have made Jackie proud. But tonight, I couldn't make her proud. She took that part of me when she left — and I didn't care to bring it back.

CHAPTER TWENTY-EIGHT

The odd time I went to a house party, I stood at the entrance and waited for the door to slam in my face.

I pulled the alcohol-blocker drink Isabella made for me weeks ago from my purse, took a long gulp, and entered Sandra and Daniel's home for the second time.

There were probably more than a hundred people crowded onto the main level. Music blared, but no dancing. Everyone was posing with drinks along the walls and scrambling from room to room, looking for the more important person. Plenty of turned backs, but none with that perfect *V* shape.

I completed a lap of the main floor. He wasn't there.

"Hey, Hot Stuff." I turned around. Hillary peeked through a doorway in the hall that connected the front rooms with the kitchen. "Come chill with us."

I joined her, banking she could tell me where to find Daniel.

The bathroom reeked of cigarette smoke. Hillstine and two other girls with white-blonde hair extensions down to their waists crowded the dark, grey-walled small space. The non-DMI girls leaned against the wall, their heads hung to the side like turkeys with snapped necks.

"You look a little stiff," Hillary said with hair draped like curtains over her face, like the girl from The Ring. She hunched over the cream-coloured vanity and used a credit card to divide white powder into five lines.

"I'm still new. Have to be on my best behaviour."

Hillary rolled a hundred-dollar bill into a tube. "The Red Queen never attends her own parties."

"Why not?" I asked.

She inhaled the top line with one ugly snort and passed the tube to one of the non-DMI girls.

"Probably doesn't want a reminder of her youth, getting hammered with D&D," Hillary said.

"What's D&D?"

"Daniel and douches." Hillary and Christine cackled, pierced tongues flashing.

I waited until they calmed down. "What makes you think that?"

"Intel like this doesn't come for free."

"To get this juice, she couldn't sit for a week," Christine said, patting Hillary's bum.

"One of *those* clients," Hillary slurred.

"How about you share this intel, and I take your next unwanted client off your hands," I offered.

An easy deal to make, considering my exit from DMI is hours away.

"Deal," Hillary squealed. She turned to her twin and grabbed her shoulders, her eyes bulging. "I'm gonna give her the guy that makes me dress up like his dead mother."

Hillary flipped her hair behind her shoulder. "In high school, Daniel had a party with his friends. Brought his shiny new ginger maid. First, they tried to make her wear a uniform—a feather duster. No dice."

"But these aren't the type that are used to hearing *no*," Christine said, her pupils large.

"Didn't stop their . . . fantasy." Hillary's hand closed, then sprung open, like she was performing magic. "They offered her money to, you know, clean the dirt down there. She said no, again. They got pissed off, upped the ante, twenty thousand. I don't know what happened after that. I couldn't go on with McFreak screaming for Mommy."

"Daniel was okay with all of this?"

"If it meant impressing his friends, ya."

I turned on the tap. "And how is the thoughtless company owner enjoying himself tonight?" I asked.

"Probably funnelling bourbon out back."

Thank you.

It was Christine's turn. She bent over, her black strapless dress rode up and revealed marks on her bum. Looked like she sat on a snapping turtle.

The fourth line of powder disappeared. Christine turned to me. "Your turn."

I lingered over the remaining white trail. "Ladies, can you see my underwear line?" My hair fell in front of my face forming a shield over the vanity. I swiped the powder into the sink.

Still turned around, a fingernail traced a diagonal line across my bum. "Yeah, take off the granny panties," someone said.

I flinched at the suggestion. "Things might get a bit cold."

One of the strangers straightened her neck. "I need some. Give me yours."

Is she serious? "I don't think they'll fit you. Maybe someone else can help." I glanced at the others.

"We don't wear underwear," they stated in unison.

Of course not.

"Be a good sport," Hillary said.

Hillary leaned into the mirror and applied bright red-orange lipstick. "You'll never fit in if you're the only person wearing such things."

They did give me some useful information. My hands slid under my dress. Light black fabric, already spoiled from this evening, fell to my feet, catching on my stilettos with high ankle straps. I picked up the scrunched-up ball of between my legs and handed it over.

"Thanks, ladies." I unlocked the bathroom door and left.

In the kitchen, I hauled open the island drawer and took

out a wine opener with a folding corkscrew. I hooked it onto the center of my bra, between the cups.

Another two hundred people were clustered on the grass and the concrete surrounding the pool.

I moved along the perimeter of one of the tallest cedar hedges I'd ever seen.

I heard familiar voices coming from the back of the lot. Annoying voices. Larry and Franklin were playing table tennis. They moved as gracefully as drunk ducks in their oversized and wrinkled checkered shirts.

No Daniel.

"Look who it is," one of them slurred.

"You must be looking for the Danhole," Franklin said. He threw his head back, gulping down some beer. Beer overflowed from the side of his mouth.

"He wants me to get the *Château Mouton Rothschild*," I said. "I can't find it. And now I can't find him. Where should I look?"

Their paddles were swatting the air. The ball landed on the grass.

"We know," Franklin said.

"We definitely do," Larry said.

"I'd appreciate if you told me."

"We'd appreciate something, too." Larry threw half his pudgy ass on the table. "Tell you what, show us the picture. The one you sent Daniel. Then we'll tell you where to find him and the wine."

"Tell me first, then I'll show you."

Franklin dropped the paddle, joining me and Larry on our side of the table.

"Wine is in the basement cellar," Larry said, getting closer. "Daniel comes after." His nod made me shudder.

I took out my phone from my purse and swiped through the sauna photo collection, landing on the least risqué shot—

me seated, towel draped over my chest, and hung between my legs.

I flipped the phone around and waved the screen in their faces.

"Slow down," Larry said. "We can't see."

The freckles on Larry's face came into closer view. Suddenly, my phone was lifted out of my hand. "Give it back!" I lunged at my phone, but the other clown blocked me.

"Whoa. Daniel didn't mention this one." Larry flashed the screen with an image of me in the sauna sans towel.

Tears pricked the back of my eyes.

"Photo sent," Larry said.

"What are you doing? That's illegal." I wrestled out of Franklin's hold.

"Report it to Sandra," Larry said.

People are looking at me. No, I don't need the attention.

I stood still.

"Here you go, sweetheart." Larry held my phone out. "And we have no idea where Daniel is."

I retrieved my phone and knocked the beer out of his hand. The bottle fell to the ground. Beer poured out into the ground in rhythmic chugs.

"You ruined my shoes," a voice called to my back.

I wish Jackie was here. They wouldn't have even thought of this shit with her present.

With my chin down, I re-entered the house.

I held back tears and told myself the photos, now public, were a small price to pay to send Daniel and Sandra to prison for the rest of their lives.

I took my compact out of my purse and fumbled to open it. I'd go upstairs where it was quiet, just for a moment, to recharge.

From the landing on the stairs, I peered out the window. Everyone was having a good time. Jackie should be out there. None of these assholes would ever give the world what she gave. It wasn't right.

"Katey."

I spun around. Sandra was at the top of the staircase, illuminous with one hand gripping the railing, like a noble figure in a Renaissance painting.

"Sorry, the bathroom line-up is long downstairs."

"You are welcome to venture anywhere in my house."

If only you knew.

"I want to share something with you," she said, in her usual steady and composed tone that reminded me who I was to her.

She turned around, her jumpsuit completely exposed her back, revealing defined shoulder blade muscles. She disappeared into the dark hallway.

I glanced downstairs, then checked my phone. Eleven-thirty-seven PM. It wasn't like Daniel was waiting for me. Or ready to call it a night.

I twisted my hair through my fingers. *Act normal.*

Whatever she wanted to show me, it should be quick. We'd never interreacted for very long before. She had always told me what DMI needed, then left.

The hallway lights were out. The floor squeaked when I walked. It was silent for her. The house didn't like me. A dim light spilled from one of the rooms at the other end of the hall. I headed for it.

I entered and saw a wooden ottoman, a red wooden desk, a bookcase, and an accent table. We were in the study. My eyes flicked to the grey-and-white patterned rug where the keys dropped.

Why did she bring me here? Does she know?

From behind the desk with her back turned to me, she opened a bottle of bourbon and filled two glasses.

Shit. Doubt that tar drink is going to cut through that.

Circling the desk, she handed me a glass, rolling hers. "Congratulations on the AleAngels contract."

We clinked glasses. She waited, magnetized her gaze on me.

I brought it to my lips and held my breath. She covered the top of my glass with her hand — my lips brushed her porcelain skin and black gemstone ring.

"You don't like to drink. Still, we must celebrate properly." She took a sip from my glass — her hunter-green eyes stayed on me. "Last time you were here, I erred. Offered you a dress from my collection."

She searched for a reaction from me. I didn't give her one.

"I didn't know you yet."

You still don't.

She turned, sauntered over to the bookshelf that spanned the length of the wall and laid her palm out flat like she was holding a tray. "Choose one."

The book she gave Jackie might be there to trap me into confessing about Daniel. I should probably leave, yet I find myself by her side before I can finish my thought.

Her scent tonight was different, roses and something else sweet, something edible.

I looked at her.

"Take your time."

The books were mostly hardcovers. They looked worn, old. I didn't see the one she gave to Jackie.

But I did see Oryx and Crake, Lord of the Flies, Crime and Punishment, IT, a Ulysses S. Grant memoir, Angela's Ashes. I wanted them all. My hands jumped from spine to spine. I couldn't choose just one. Maybe she'd let me come back for another one later.

Stop. Look at yourself. Don't gawk at a book collection. Idiot.

I travelled to the other end of the shelf, "This is you?" and pointed to a mirror-framed black-and-white photo.

She glided over to my side. "I was seventeen."

The grainy image showed mother and daughter hand-in-hand on the sidewalk outside a decrepit apartment building.

Her mother looked like Sandra — thick waves piled over her shoulders, generous curves. I squinted. Her mother's eyes looked cloudy.

"She had some vision left at that point."

Her mother ran a cleaning business blind? That's impressive. "Is this where you lived?"

"We came to Toronto with nothing. Lived in a small apartment with strangers. Shared a single bed." She paused. "It was still above sleeping with the rats."

I took one step further away. "She must be proud of her daughter."

Sandra spoke to the photo. "She was. But she was a product of her time. Taught me how to survive. And stopped there."

No one would argue that you've done more than survive. "If you could talk to your seventeen-year-old self now, what would you tell her?"

Her tone stayed the same, like she was sharing an old memory. "Dreams are not for sharing. When you use every breath to pursue your dreams and can't claim it as yours . . ."

She stopped and fixed on the dated image in silence.

I can't believe she just revealed that Daniel is her biggest regret.

I turned toward the books, away from her.

I don't feel bad for you. You let your husband do the same to Jackie as Daniel's friends did to you. But much worse. You chose to protect him. You chose to be weak.

"Have you made your choice?" she asked, focus re-gained on me.

"James and the Giant Peach."

I yanked the book from the shelf, nodded, and exited. I pulled out my phone and messaged Daniel to meet me in the cellar.

CHAPTER TWENTY-NINE

I flipped on the light switch outside of the cellar. I gave the door a push with my hip, and it opened. Three wooden wine racks reached the ceiling. Hundreds of bottles lay horizontally in each rack. There were no windows in the room.

The cold concrete penetrated the thin soles of my high heels, sending a chill up my spine.

I took a long gulp of the alcohol-blocker drink and pulled out a wine bottle from a rack, then the corkscrew from my bra. I uncorked the bottle, stuffed the cork back in and placed the bottle back on the rack.

I heard the door slam shut.

The lights went out.

"Someone is in here," I called.

It was pitch-black. The light from the bottom of the door dimmed. "Hello," I called. "I'm in here," and ran to the exit.

Shit. The door wouldn't open.

"Shouldn't have ruined my shoes," a familiar voice said from the other side.

"Come back here," I screamed. The feeling of presence on the other side of the wall faded. I couldn't believe I fell for it. Daniel said he'd be waiting. He didn't wait for anyone.

And all for spilling beer on Tweedledum's shoe.

I rubbed my arms and shoulders and paced around the dark room.

Will he come once his side-schmuck stops crying? Maybe Sandra will come down. Then this won't work. Don't go there. It has to work.

My hand fumbled through my clutch, searching for my phone. *I'll send him a reminder.*

Shit. No reception.

I kicked my leg into the black air. It hit something.

Crash. Oh dear. Glass smashed on the floor.

Liquid pooled around my feet.

I took a step. *Crunch.*

I activated the flashlight app on my phone and found another bottle. I put the phone in my mouth, with the light shining down.

I downed the remainder of the tar drink and brought myself closer to the ground to inspect the damage. Looked like two bottles broke. I didn't even know there were bottles stored outside of the racks. I couldn't clean the mess in the dark.

I stuck my hands under my armpits and flinched, but not from the cold. I wasn't ready to be left alone with my thoughts.

Did they torment Jackie like this? She wouldn't have let them. She didn't put up with anything – or anyone. She didn't need the money. Mom and David would sell their organs before suggesting this career path. She's not Isabella, responsible for her family.

The why doesn't matter. All that matters is what I'm going to do about it.

Another hour passed. The music softened. Footsteps above me faded and grew on the same floor.

I turned my phone on *Record* and grabbed the bottle I uncorked from the rack by the neck and waited beside the door.

The light came on and the door swung open.

It was Daniel. Rage shot out of me like a firehose – I swung my arm at his face.

He caught it. "Take it easy."

My other arm lifted the bottle behind me. Before the bottle could come down, he pulled me in and took it from my grasp.

"Knock it off." He let go of me, shut the door, looked

around the room. "See you found plenty to do."

My breath was harsh. "What the hell is the matter with you?"

"The matter with *me*? My blonde squirrely employee was begging for me all night like a lost puppy." His eyes dropped. "What did you do in here?"

He brought the bottle he took from me to his face. "France nineteen-fifty-five. Let's not waste it." Removing the cork with his teeth, he took a drink. Breathed. Then another.

He kicked the glass pieces on the floor. "This will be fun to explain to Sandra."

He smiled and held up the bottle. "You can have some if you promise to behave."

"I was cold, alone in the dark."

He handed me the bottle.

Holding the bottle by the neck, I took a deep breath and rehearsed the motions in my head.

I'm ready. I brought the bottle to my lips, snapped it backward, then forward. Blood-red liquid flooding his white dress shirt.

CHAPTER THIRTY

Daniel looked down at his shirt and then at me. I backed away toward the wine racks.

His eyes burned a trail on me from top to bottom. He advanced, then he pulled me by the arm towards the wine rack. Now facing the rack, he raised my arms above my head and weaved his fingers into mine, then shoved my palms over the stacked horizontal bottles.

A belt jingled, and a zipper was undone. I let my arms fall to my side, but he placed them back up. "Stay," he told me and sunk his lips into my neck. The wet heat rippled down my back. He moved in.

I watched the corkscrew fall from my bra and hit the concrete floor. And I looked away.

Every inch of him was pressed against me. Hard pulsing torso didn't leave my backside. Strong arms, wrapped around me, wouldn't leave a piece of me unstirred. Grasping, under my dress, under my unhooked bra, he didn't fumble, knew exactly how to handle me. Each touch, full and firm, served its purpose.

He ran his hands to my thighs, and I quivered again. My dress rode up, and I sank into him. The bottles in front pushed back as he ground his weight into me.

I pushed my hips into him, felt his blood surging, ready for me. He slammed back, held me against him, kept me there, kept me waiting for what was to come. Hard lips kissed my neck when his teeth no longer scraped my skin.

My breath was loud, fast. I pressed the back of his neck into mine, wanting to feel him command my body to his will again.

He drove his lips, his tongue into my shoulder, to my neck, came up to breathe, went back down to leave his mark.

He pulled my hips up and back, and entered me. I cried out.

His hands travelled between my chest and hips, pulling me in, squeezing hard for leverage with each thrust.

My eyes slammed shut. The sound of hot breath and the unsteady rhythm took turns pounding the floor and the rack.

When he came to me, I drove back harder, building the heat we shared in the cold cellar. My chest was burning. I wrapped his hands over my breasts, my nipples between his fingers, and he closed them hard. I screamed louder. He filled me deeper, pulsing and prolonging with each thrust. He broke the fast-beat pace, pulled away and paused. Lingering outside of me, he forced me to feel every inch of what I wanted inside of me. He enjoyed my struggle, my aching hips thrown back to wait.

A hand enclosed over my mouth. "Shhh." His deep hot breath penetrated my ear. His grip strengthened, and he shoved further into me. I clutched the wine rack, sweat from my palms coated the panels, and we rocked in sync. We were breathing together. His heart pounded into my back, setting the rhythm for mine.

His hand swiped my inner thigh. Soaked, he rubbed the moisture on my breasts in circular motions, increasing the pressure from his palm.

He brought my arm over his head to rest on his shoulder to make room for his mouth to clamp on the side of my breast. I gasped and twisted to bury him further into me. I wanted him to have me deep down his throat. My breast was now beet red and throbbing as I massaged his neck and watched his jawline pulsing for more. Trapping both his hands with mine on one side of my chest, I shoved his face into my other side and didn't let go until his front teeth clamoured hard on my nipple.

He came up, took desperate breaths, and repositioned himself behind me. A hand pushed up my spine and bent me over from the waist. We separated. A cold draft hit my exposed back. Uninvitingly cold. Not like having a warm blanket ripped off, but more like being slapped.

And the cold reminded me. Reminded me of that night. How I waited in the cold. Waited for my phone to ring. Waited to enter the bathroom. And arrived a few moments too late.

And I finally focused.

I reached toward the opened bottle I stashed, lying on its side. It was too far away. My fingertips barely touched the rack panel.

Sensing my lean, he seized my hips and surged into me at a faster and harder pace. The butt of his hand pressed my spine, and he bent me over further, creating more distance between us.

I grabbed another bottle and gripped it hard.

Wait . . . wait . . . now!

My hips drove back, knocking him backward. I flung the bottle, but with a tomahawk-throwing motion. It shattered and defiled the bottom of his pants and leather shoes.

He charged, but I stepped out of his path.

"Not too close. I don't need to be stained," I told him.

He reached me, wound my hair around his fist, and squeezed. My scalp rose. Yanking my head backward, parallel to his mouth, he covered the side of my head with his forearm, crushing my cheek into his. "Dirty brat."

"I told you I would make it," I groaned. "Your wife took care of the client herself."

He let go of my hair and placed his thick fingers on my shoulders where they met my neck. He turned me around, bent me over in half. The only thing that kept my forehead from colliding with concrete was my grip on the wine rack.

Feeling each brutal thrust one after the other, I knew this interaction wouldn't do. There probably wasn't a mark on me that would last till dawn. I pushed again. "Does she take care of your friends like she takes care of your clients?"

The timbre of his voice changed to the one at the concert and in the car. "What did you say?"

He grabbed my shoulders and snapped me upright. It was too fast.

The room waved, split in half.

His grip tightened, and I slid further into his hold.

I reached for the wine rack, and I couldn't get there. The room spun, and I surrendered to his rhythm. A pace was fast or slow, I couldn't tell.

The sound of my wheezing breath took over. My breath. *No.* I was going to pass out.

I tried to refocus. Closed my eyes and thought of her. No use. All my attention was on his bear grip. I moved my hand on top of his, curled my fingers, and pressed my nails into his skin. He didn't let up. My fingernails dug into the back of his hand. He knocked my hand away, took both my arms, held them together behind my back with one hand and splayed his fingers over my collarbone.

Everything moved in slow motion, and I shut my eyes again. *This is it. I'd pass out with nothing more than a hickey on my body. Then it would be my word against his.*

But I may not wake up. What then? The cops would piece it together. They don't need me to get him. But no one will be after them if I go. No one else wants what's right. Daniel and Sandra will do what they do best — cover everything up. I'll still be here, six feet under this cellar.

Fuck this bastard.

With one quick motion, I stomped my stiletto into his foot.

I grabbed onto the wine rack for support and wheezed

until my vision was restored.

He moved toward me, his eyes forming narrow slits. The wine rack prevented me from moving back any farther.

It's either you or him. I scooped up the corkscrew that fell to the floor and gripped it tightly. He came closer. I wound up, thrusted my arm forward, and hit him on the side of the head.

Daniel stumbled to the side. He pressed his palm to his head, pulled it away, and examined it.

Blood.

He turned. "Forget this shit."

No, no, this isn't supposed to happen. Threaten him, tell him you know. If he's going to react, it's going to be now.

I shoved my hand into my clutch and grabbed the Rolex. I ran to the door and shoved the watch in his face. "The scratch on your watch. I know." My voice was hoarse.

"What the fuck are you talking about?"

"I know how it got there," I screamed. "You thought you could run." I whipped the band through the air.

He grabbed my wrist, ripping the watch from my hand. He flipped it around and dangled it by the band.

The son of a bitch is remembering.

Our eyes locked.

"This isn't my watch."

CHAPTER THIRTY-ONE: JACKIE

September 2016
Plunging V-neck. No bra, no need. There was no chance of him keeping his eyes off me.

In the full-length mirror, I saw that I was wearing more money than my sister made. Not just her. I out-earned all my friends from home—the lawyers, consultants, doctors, engineers. Everyone who bet against me.

And I promised myself, again, that I wasn't giving any of it up.

Finally, I knew what had to be done to rid my life of DMI. It was never a choice between Sandra and Daniel. They came together and always would as long as they both treasured the same things—wealth, success, and that image that went with it.

I stepped onto the platform for the full view. *My date doesn't stand a chance. We won't make it through cocktails.*

Sandra's rule—no dating clients—was meant to be broken. Her rationale was simple—if you dated clients, they wouldn't be clients anymore.

She made that rule yet put us right into clients' laps. Literally. She always told us to keep them wanting more. So I did.

What did she think was going to happen when she dangled boys who showered us with things we never of owning?

I remembered when my date first used DMI's services. He kept checking that his wallet was still in his pants—afraid of walking around with that much cash. By the end of the night, the whereabouts of his wallet was the last thing on his mind.

It was that easy.

We had scheduled many dates since—only a few had worked out. That's how Sandra made sure we stayed available for clients. Changed the schedule last-minute. That way, we could never be reliable or committed to anyone else but her.

He was about to give up. I promised him I was worth the wait. And I've lived up to my word—every time.

That evening, I thought about what Kitty would think. She would have killed me if she knew my plan for reuniting us. She didn't need to know. All that mattered was the forthcoming day she would move to Toronto and live with me and the pool I would build for her. *For once, I was going to take care of her.*

It wouldn't be long from now. He told me he wanted to settle down.

I was getting out of DMI, but the things I wanted, were going with me. There'd still be travel to Miami, ski trips to Colorado, spa days, and weekend shopping in NYC.

Daniel and Sandra would lose their shit when I resign. But in time, they'd realize it was for the best. That I'd made a client very happy. And that was all that ever mattered.

And I'd see to it that my fiancé still pumped business their way. Didn't matter which services he bought. I owed it to Sandra.

I leaned into the mirror and caught the perfect light. *Lipstick should match my nipples.* He would be able see through the fabric. Every detail counted.

I heard footsteps. *Finally.* I almost left without Isabella's clutch. I'd get Isabella out, too, after I left DMI. Then we could both make our sisters happy. My date had more than enough rich friends looking to fill a few hours. I checked my reflection one last time, even though I swore the last time was the last.

"What do you think?" I said, fanning the multilayer tulle skirt.

"Adorable."

I whipped around. "What the hell are you doing here?"

Claudia locked the door, leaned against the wall, and slowly tapped the brass key to the dressing room on her wrist. "It was my day off. Got called in."

By who? Sandra wasn't in town.

"Something urgent came up." Six feet of stick in a military-style suit marched over to me, stopping an inch away from my skirt that parachuted around me. "Your dress came in."

Isabella told you. She told you. Coward.

Claudia fluffed the tulle. My chest broke out into red splotches like bubbling lava. "Sandra ordered it for you. Looks like you're in a rush to put it to work." She circled me. "But not for the job you planned tonight."

Her limp-noodle lips brushed against my cheek. "Daniel found out long before Plastic Tits leaked."

I pulled away. "Get on with it. Tell me to take another turn. With *those* clients."

She shook her head. "I'm not here to stop you. Go on your date." She grinned.

She swayed, behind, to the side, reminding me where I belonged. "You're almost ready. Just need the finishing touch."

She held up the metal undergarment—I had heard rumors of it and didn't believe them. It was from Sandra's former *professional* cleaning days. Clients made her wear it—enjoyed watching her groan in pain while she bent down and scrubbed the floor. And the sickest part—the client held the key and decided when it would be over.

"Turn around," she commanded.

I turned to face her, looking up. "You're welcome." She lifted an eyebrow. "I just gave you an extension. Your next day off, the only thing they'll call you for is to collect your phone and security pass."

Her nostrils flared.

We both knew she was about to expire at DMI and would

be tossed like a four-month-old pair of shoes. They did it to the girl Claudia replaced when she worked half a day past her prime. And when Claudia was relieved of her DMI duties, that meant back to the junkyard strip club for her. Where tips came in toonies left at the bottom of beer glasses with tobacco spit. Right where they found her.

I let that thought sink in as long as I could.

Her gear switched. "Turn around." Not waiting, Claudia spun me around by my shoulders.

I swatted her hands away from my arms, but she maintained her hold.

Our reflections met in the mirror, and she pressed her cheekbone against mine and let the farmgirl accent she worked so hard to suppress come out. "Either I do it, or Daniel does. Pick."

When I said nothing, she got down low, held the loops open in front of my feet.

I decided I'd rather wear that thing for the rest of my life than spend another night with Daniel's clients.

My right foot went in, followed by my left foot in the left loop.

Bumps on my skin flared as she dragged the cold metal garment over my skin from my ankles to my hips.

I pressed my forearms against the wall. She moved to my right hip. I sucked in my breath. She tightened one side and snapped it in place. The dull-spiked surface of the metal plate bore between my legs.

I bit my lip.

She took out a key and locked that side, then moved to the other side. My cheek rammed the wall, my fingernails clawed the purple wallpaper.

"It's too tight," I yelled.

She fastened the other side and locked it.

My jaw clamped, and salty liquid filled my mouth.

"Loosen it," I screamed and clawed at the sides, trying to get it off.

Claudia grasped the back of the contraption—a curved metal stick connecting the top to the bottom like a thong. She jerked the undergarment upward. "Fits fine."

Pain scissored me from all directions—from my hips holding the chain link straps and between my legs that were pricked whenever I moved.

I took a step and my body screamed. I hit the wall, folded at the waist.

The tone of her voice almost acknowledged what was happening. "This comes off when you get back to work."

I pushed off the wall, stood as straight as she did. I spat on the floor. We both saw red on purple.

She told me, "Daniel's expecting you. Tell him you'll never dream it again."

CHAPTER THIRTY-TWO

I'd been sitting at my desk with the watch ticking in my lap for two hours, and I still hadn't been fired.

This must have meant that Sandra hadn't been to her basement yet, and rumours of me leaving her house in the state I was in hadn't reached her. Or she had more important things to do than fire me.

I still needed this job to figure out who the Rolex belonged to. Daniel said the watch didn't belong to him. I didn't think he was lying. If it was something he needed to hide, he would have taken it with him. But the watch was still with me. And I was still there.

Jackie was with someone that morning when she called me, freaking out about a little scratch. Whoever hurt her, owns this watch. Daniel knew the watch owner — the watch was in his office.

I raked my hands through my hair, lifting my scalp. *Think it through. Again.* One of Daniel's turkey wingmen reclaimed his Louis Vuitton sunglasses when I babysat. Daniel and his friends borrowed each other's things, so the watch belonged to someone Daniel was buddy enough with to swap things. Isabella said Daniel was in charge that night because Sandra was out of town. He could easily had tossed Jackie to one of his douchebag friends.

How am I going to figure this out? I only had weeks left at DMI, and I was even more on my own. There was no way Isabella would help me after the baseball game fiasco.

I dug my heel into the floor, trying to create a dent in the stone tile. *I was so sure about Daniel.*

I looked over at Isabella's empty chair, then the bobby pins carefully placed between the rows on her keyboard.

I was ready for Isabella to throw a steaming cup of coffee in my face. I deserved it. But she wouldn't do that. She would offer me her coffee.

My phone rang. I checked the screen. *Go away.* I answered. "Hi, Claudia."

"I'm going to cut out, so write this down," Claudia instructed. "We're running late to the Titan interview and might miss prep time. Print two copies of the briefing package. Go to the studio and rehearse with the client, Walter Kovac. The client goes off script. The interviewer is some psycho. Thinks she's someone she's not. It's imperative that you rehearse. And don't let the interview start until we arrive. Do you understand?"

"Understood."

"Message me when you get there."

The CEO of a women's undergarment shapewear company was exactly what I pictured—fat, bald, short, and old. So fat that the rolls in his neck spilled over his jacket collar when he twisted on a stool that squeaked a sad noise. He looked as if he'd been running—red-faced and panting. Pink skin flared from beneath the pale foundation the makeup artist applied to his bulbous nose.

At the door, I positioned myself so he could see my reflection in the mirror. "Mr. Kovac? Hi, I'm Katey Philips, with DMI."

"Where's the redhead?" he said gruffly.

"Sandra's on her way." The spiral-bound briefing package that was prepared and delivered in advance was covered by white cream sauce and a sandwich wrapper. "Why don't we go over the key messages?" I handed him the loose paper version I brought.

The makeup artist put her brush in a clear plastic container and left the room.

"Yeah, I read the Q and A, key messages, the crap about expanding the business while keeping it local." He dropped the paper to his side.

"Let's review the tough questions."

"That bullshit on gifting consumers choices?"

I paused. Without knowing my next move, I got up and closed the door. "Why don't we work on a more honest approach? You're the founder of the company. You know better than anyone."

I pulled up a chair close enough to smell his salted meat breath.

We got started.

About twenty minutes later, a woman with a black crew shirt and an earpiece interrupted us. "Ready in five?"

I looked at the now fired-up CEO and raised my eyebrows.

"Ready," he replied.

Once our client nestled into a cushioned chair opposite the interviewer, who had too many shades of blonde in her hair and wore a turtleneck that reached too high up her neck, I knew there was no going back.

I couldn't fully recall what happened in the dressing room. I was the conduit for something I couldn't explain.

"Mr. Kovac, thank you for sitting down with me today."

"It's my pleasure, Felicity."

"We have all heard the story of how quickly your company, Titan, grew. Can you share the story of its birth?"

Sandra and Claudia rushed into the dark studio room, trying to minimize the noise their heels made. Sandra eyed the client, then me.

I looked to the stage.

"My wife complained that undergarments felt like another

layer of clothes, like wearing pants over pants," Kovac said, twisting his torso. "They move and bunch, make you sweat. She sent me to the basement with a sewing machine. I tested prototype after prototype until it was perfect. You know, the product felt good and hid everything that made her feel not so good."

C'mon, Felicity, you're not catching up with a college buddy.

She pulled her smile and went on. "And what happens today when your wife is looking for something that isn't fitting the bill?" Her lips tightened. "I assume she's involved in the company, given her role in its creation."

His voice lifted. "Nothing has changed. When my wife wants something, I go back to the sewing machine in the basement. Our talented team decides what products best meet our customer needs."

Claudia nodded and looked at Sandra. Sandra was focused on the two on stage.

"What role do women play in your company that designs products only for women? I understand you have two-hundred employees at your corporate office in Toronto. And hundreds of employees in factories overseas. How many women work at the corporate headquarters?"

"Half of our employees are women. As we grow, the proportion of women who make up the company grows, a testament to the success of this organization."

Most female employees are overseas working in factories. Only a fraction work at headquarters.

"And how many women make up senior or executive roles?"

"Those numbers are evolving as we speak" — he leaned forward, slapped his hands on his thighs — "once we complete our strategic organizational alignment in response to our customer demand, we will provide the updated information."

He continued, stressing syllables as if the journalist couldn't understand English. "Our growth strat-e-gy aims to re-cruit wo-men in exec-ut-ive pos-i-tions."

Before he could finish, Felicity picked up some loose fabric next to her. "I'm holding one of your midsection products." She held up a large hot pink tag connected to the product. "The description says the product starts below the bust and ends at the lower abdomen."

She stretched the skin-coloured fabric. It looked more like a neck warmer than something designed to cover a torso. "Could you confirm it's called the BoaCon?"

He nodded. "Yes, the BoaCon is our most popular product."

From the corner of my eye, either Sandra or Claudia swayed back and forth.

"Your products have been criticized for their tight fit causing distressing discomfort. Have you made adjustments to your products in response to this feedback?"

He crossed his arms causing his belly to poke through his jacket buttons like jelly seeping from a donut. "We offer free one-on-one consultations at our retail distributors to any customer interested in or dissatisfied with our product."

Felicity's eyes formed thin slits.

"Some criticize the product as encouraging negative and outdated notions of female beauty," she said. "Parallels to girdles in the nineteenth century have been made — creating tiny waists that your hands can wrap around." She created a circle using her hands, connecting her fingertips and neutral-coloured painted fingernails.

He took her hands into his, overlapping her thumbs and fingers, creating a smaller circle.

Damn, I didn't teach him that one.

Sandra's facial muscles twitched like a snake was slithering under her skin.

"BoaCon provides another option for women."

Felicity smiled. "I don't mean to belabour the point. However, this *option* draws a comparison to a time when women's ribs and organs were warped to achieve a dangerous standard of beauty."

His fingers curled into fists.

"Mr. Kovac, there are reports of women seeking medical attention after using your product. Do you think it's responsible to present your products as an option for women?"

He cleared his throat. The TV screen showed sweat beading along his hairline. "Felicity, no one is forced to use our product." He took the stick of gum I gave him from his jacket pocket, removed the silver wrapper and chomped on it like a cow chewing its cud. "There are other avenues to achieve our look that are much more dangerous. Women can get liposuction."

Sandra stopped blinking. Claudia's arms straightened like a mime.

I bit my tongue to keep myself from laughing. I shouldn't have felt this way — so much as a smirk would put me in shit far deeper than I could get out of. But I couldn't stop myself from watching Sandra, who was paler than milk. This was better than the time I helped put the oil dumpers behind bars.

Felicity folded her hands in her lap. "As an individual who works in fashion, you are recommending cosmetic surgery — major surgery — as a plausible alternative for women?"

Kovac looked like one of those birds on nature shows that tripled its size when it was threatened. "We care about our customers and all women. I recommend women use our product so they do not turn to dangerous surgical procedures."

This is your house, Felicity.

"As mentioned, women are seeking medical attention after using your products," she said. "You have not suggested your company is addressing this issue beyond encouraging customers to meet with a consultant to purchase another product of yours. How does this demonstrate care for your customers?"

"I do care. And I care about you." He picked up a small black cloth bag from the floor, just as we had rehearsed. "If you don't own our product, this will change your mind."

He pulled out an extra-small BoaCon from a cloth bag and handed it to Felicity. She held up the garment that looked like a tube sock next to her torso.

The camera zoomed in on her. She looked down, then straight into the camera.

CHAPTER THIRTY-THREE

This bar was crowded, just like last time. I didn't recognize anyone.

I pushed ahead. I lost count of the number of white cotton dress shirts and leather belts I rammed into by the time I made it to the bar. And when I did, I collapsed my arms over the bar counter as if reaching the pool deck after sprinting through laps. The sights and smell of booze were hitting me at once. I cleared my throat and held my breath.

I pulled out my phone to message Hillary. She told me Daniel would be there tonight. The trip to L.A. was cancelled because of the Titan interview.

A text message from Claudia awaited. *What are you doing here?*

Where is she? My eyes followed the U-shape of the dark bar. There she was, in the corner at a standing table. She was with some suits clutching to bourbon. Clients. *Good stay, there.*

And she's coming over.

When she reached me, she stood straighter than usual and slammed her hands on hips. "What the hell are you doing here?" she barked. "Does Sandra know?"

"I need *that* drink," was all I could say.

"What drink?" she spat.

"The relaxing one that cancels alcohol. Please, tell me what's in it."

"Look over there." She tipped her head to where she came from. "Do you see them?"

I did. Guys with caterpillar eyebrows and sweat-stained

shirts bobbing around their bro circle like apples in a bucket of water.

"I need a whole lot of calm before taking that on. By myself."

"Tell me what's in the drink."

"How about this, you take on fat bastard, like I hired you to do, and I tell you what's in that drink." She took a step back and looked me up and down. "I forgot, you have standards. You only fuck married men over garbage."

"Screw you." Without thinking, I shoved her. She moved backward as easily as a sapling branch. She huffed, pushed off some guy's shoulder and came at me.

"Ladies, what's going on here?" Daniel appeared. His tone was like giving a speech at a pricey fundraiser and separated us. He held us apart, one hand on my arm, the other on hers.

"Go back to your gentlemen," Daniel said to Claudia.

Claudia straightened her tomato-red silk dress and retreated to her former circle. But what she said had sunk in. She knew about me and Daniel. If she knew, Sandra knew, or was about to find out.

"What did you do this time?" Daniel asked with a wry grin.

"Nothing."

"This isn't the place for a fight."

"That's not why I came. I need to talk to you about the watch." I fumbled through my purse for it.

He tucked a wisp of my hair behind my ears. "You're doing a lot of talking these days. You weren't even in the interview chair."

He was right, kind of. I was talking out of character. When I was alone with Kovac, I wasn't in control. Words poured out of my mouth like a broken faucet. Everything I said to him, no matter how ridiculous, he soaked it up like a sponge.

I tried not to look away. "Mr. Kovac has a mind of his own."

"Borrowed from you."

I opened my hand, revealing the Rolex. "Who does it belong to?"

That smile returned. The smile he wore when he found me snooping around his house.

"Let's get a drink." He took my hand and led me to the bar.

The bartender took his order immediately.

Every moment that passed screamed that I was making a big mistake by being there tonight.

The drinks arrived.

"Drink up," he said. Without looking his way, I felt his command closing in on me.

The amber liquid glared at me from the bottom of the glass, followed by the scent of rancid beef and oil, hitting me like someone had spit in my face. *When he isn't looking, I'll spill it.*

I brought the glass to my face. It trembled at my lips. *I can't.* I placed it on the bar.

"The watch," I said, "then we'll celebrate."

He leaned against the bar, elbows on top. "You're the one holding this up." He lifted his chin at my drink.

I picked up the glass with one hand and gripped the top edge of the bar with the other. One of my fingernails broke on the bar countertop as I took a long sip. I turned my back to Daniel, grabbed an empty glass and brought it to my mouth. *No.* As I was about to spit out the vile fluid, Daniel reached around me and grabbed the empty glass.

He turned me around to face him — the grey in his eyes was gone. "Swallow it."

A hole burned through my tongue.

"Finish it."

I forced the drink down until only ice remained in the glass.

"Good girl." He took my wrist and led me to the dance floor.

I coughed. *Focus.* "You promised. Tell me who owns the watch."

He faced me, weaved his fingers in mine. "Let's dance first."

He moved me, closer and away, broken by twirls and twists. I let his hands settle on my hips and waist. We touched. We broke away from each other. He pressed my lower back. His other hand was intertwined with mine. We were moving fast. I wanted to slow down, but I kept following his lead and trusting him in the dark with strobes of coloured lights blurring into each other.

We stopped, but we were still moving together. We migrated to a smaller room with fewer people. Another bar ran along the wall.

We separated, and I felt cold. He started dancing with a girl with long, straight brown hair. I watched them while I listened to my breath over the music. As I leaned into the wall, Daniel caught my arm and brought me back to him.

His voice echoed, "Guess you're not interested in the watch."

The other girl was between us, facing Daniel. Her long hair was whipping back and forth in front of me. I felt his hands on my thighs as the girl pressed into me.

Daniel wrapped one arm around my waist, brought me, the girl, and him together. His other hand slid inside the slit at the front of my dress. I reached for him — he coiled my arm around the girl's waist. He found the thin straps securing my panties on my hips, reached down the middle and pushed the fabric held by the straps out of his way. At the same moment, his fingers slid into me.

The three of us moved together as he added more of himself inside of me. I moved to my tippy-toes, and watched the blue, green, pink, and purple light colours take turns streaking above my head like a broken rainbow. Another finger shoved its way in to meet the others. Now, fastened inside of me, he wrapped his arm around my neck and pulled me down until my feet were flat on the floor, my knees were shaking, ready to buckle. The weight, the pressure from inside, mounted me to paralysis.

He turned the girl around to face me — her eyes were half open, half covered by her hair. He released me, enclosed the girl with his strong arms, cleared her hair from her face and placed his fingers inside her mouth.

Still in his hold, he faced the girl towards me and locked my focus. While her tongue caressed the fingers that tasted of me, Daniel stroked the girl's hair, then dismissed her with one gentle pat. He took me back and led me to the small bar.

Larry and Franklin were behind the bar. I saw my reflection — multiple reflections — in the mirror behind them.

I turned to leave. Daniel put his arm around me and pulled me back.

"Boys, give Katey a drink for being such a good sport."

"I don't want anything," I whispered.

Franklin poured ice into a glass.

"Daniel, no more," I pleaded.

"Pushy girl. First, she destroyed your home, then refuses your generosity," Franklin said.

"She wants information." Daniel turned to me. "And she will get it. Show it to them."

He held me tighter as I fumbled through my purse for the Rolex. I found it and dropped it on the bar.

They were bursting into laughter.

"I know who that belongs to," Franklin said, pouring beer from the tap into a pint glass.

"Me, too," Larry said, bouncing the watch in his palm. "She owes me one for ruining my shoes."

I tried to step back. Daniel held me in place.

My clothes felt like they were shrinking.

Larry continued, "I don't think she cares. Daniel fucked her on a cold, filthy floor. You know Sandra won't allow Daniel to touch her unless—"

"That's enough," Daniel said, holding up his hand.

"You promised," I said through shallow breaths. I tapped the watch's gold band.

"Drink up."

The ice knocked against the sides of the tall glass in front of me. I couldn't smell the alcohol anymore.

"She's just pretending," Franklin said.

"What will we get this time?" Franklin brought out his phone, face-up on the bar countertop. The screen showed the photos Isabella took at the spa. "Daniel said he was going to take the next series. With you and the porn star that works there."

I turned again. I was going to throw up.

Daniel brought me back with one hard pull. "All right, that's enough. Katey, make it up to Larry."

"He can have my drink." I slid it across the bar.

Larry started to say something, but Daniel waved him off. "Give him a taste."

I took the straw between my shaking fingers and held it up to Larry's mouth.

"Not like that." Daniel took the glass and set it back down.

"Promise you'll tell me right away," I begged, holding onto the edge of the bar.

"I promise. For real this time."

Daniel took my arm, gripping it firmly by my side.

Using the straw, I filled my mouth with vodka and orange juice. *Swallow it.* The clown leaned over the bar counter, and I tried to move towards Daniel. *Swallow it, swallow it.*

My chest, throat, and tongue heaved. Too late, as soon as his mouth met mine, orange liquid sprayed on his face.

Daniel briefly let me go to clap and snort with his other

stooge.

"Okay, okay," Daniel said. "You've earned it. As I said, that's not my watch. It doesn't belong to Larry or Franklin, either."

Daniel slid the heavy watch onto my wrist and clicked the band.

Oh my God, I'm so stupid.

"You see, it would take a small dude to wear it."

But he, he wears prettier things than the girls do. I ripped my eyes away, then back to the dull warm gold wrapping my arm. He was right—this wouldn't fit him or any guy.

"It's not for me, like these." Daniel picked up the silver necklace around my neck, then the bracelet around my wrist. "But I own them."

It was part of the jewelry stash in the DMI dressing room.

I peeled the watch from my wrist and dropped it on the bar.

They were laughing uncontrollably. Daniel let go of me.

The room was closing around me. The air was hot and still.

I fled for the wall and grasped it to fight my way through the crowd.

I reached the bathroom.

The ceiling pot lights were as bright as a spotlight. My eyes were shut.

The air was heavy.

I splashed water on my face. When I looked up, my stomach lurched at my reflection—a reflection that wouldn't come into focus. Black spots flashed in my peripheral vision. My fingertips dug into the porcelain sink. My head hung over the tap.

"Are you okay?" a voice asked.

I opened my eyes. The ceiling moved toward the floor. The side walls closed in.

My knees buckled, and I sank to the ground. My head was between my knees. My forehead felt both cold and hot. Blood surged through my ears.

High heels crowded around me.

My vision narrowed to a single point. I screwed my eyes shut. She was there. I didn't want to see her.

"Help me up."

Hands clasped my arms, hoisting me to my feet.

"Let go," I shrieked.

I was at the front door. The bouncer said something to me. He came closer. I ran straight onto the street.

I saw bright yellow lights and heard a horn honk.

Brakes screeched.

CHAPTER THIRTY-FOUR

M y phone went off at six AM. It was a message from Claudia. I
let the phone slip from my fingers, and it dropped to the floor
beside the bed.

I pulled the covers over my head to block the screaming morning
light. Time passed, and the light seeped through the covers. I got up
and drew the blackout curtains.

Dark again.

The curtain fabric had five waves, four creases and six rings. I
counted them, left to right, then right to left. I tapped my finger on
the bed for every ring and wave.

My eyes closed.

She was standing, facing a bare white wall in an empty room. I
could see the dimples on her lower back. My feet moved, but I
stopped at the threshold. She was close.

I didn't want to go farther.

Her head turned to reveal her symmetrical profile. She was wearing a white pearl necklace. Her black hair was pulled back in curls
spilling from the crown of her head. She faced me. She was wearing
heavy makeup on her face, as if she was getting ready to go somewhere important.

Her face faded into a black-and-white image.

She tried to say something. The corners of her eyes sagged. Her
lips moved like they were being sped up.

I covered my ears.

She was pleading, arms outstretched.

Stop it. Shut up.

I slammed the bathroom door.

CHAPTER THIRTY-FIVE

"Clients are cancelling contracts," Sandra informed me.

I stuffed my hands between my thighs until I could feel the chair in Sandra's office.

"You cannot make up the lost revenue."

My chin dropped to my chest. I thought I could convince her this was all a misunderstanding, but I crumbled like dry clay as soon as I entered her office.

My head stayed down as I listened. Her voice was flatter than usual. Her rose scent came and then went when the smell of my perspiration took over.

"Your response might make a difference in what happens next." Sandra rose to her feet on the other side of the oakwood desk. "Why did you take Mr. Kovac in a new direction?"

There wasn't an explanation for what I did before the interview. I had no idea what took hold of me and spat out the words that weren't mine.

And I had no explanation for myself on how I came to Toronto to find out what happened to my sister, but instead learned how to be the willing rag doll of my boss' husband. I couldn't make sense of it—he represented everything that I'd lost, and yet, when I was near him, I became a zombie. The answers I was looking for were all within reach—but I let stupidity and fear of the unknown win.

"I didn't," my voice broke. "I didn't rewrite the script."

"The man made his fortune convincing women they look like shit. Reminding the public—who made him rich—seemed like a great idea?"

I started to look up and sank my head before we made eye contact. "Mr. Kovac was displeased with our messaging. I told him he shouldn't feel uncomfortable because the audience would pick up on it. I didn't think *that* would happen. It isn't the first time he's gone rogue."

I sensed her rising.

Sandra dropped a piece of paper folded into four squares on the desk in front me. "Open it."

I unfolded the paper and focused on the black ink, but not the words. It was only a matter of time before it caught up.

"You will have me believe you're as reliable as these references?"

My eyes started to sting.

"Claudia called them again. They all told her *wrong number*."

I clasped my hands and placed them on her desk, eyes down. "I really want the job," I said. "Let me stay until the end of my contract. I'll make up the lost revenue. I promise."

"You will pay me half a million plus twenty-five thousand in spilled wine?"

I didn't have a response.

She took her seat back.

"Do you have anything to return to the dressing room?"

"No."

"What about the dress you're wearing?"

I looked down at the mauve-rucked, high-waisted dress. She was right. I forgot. "I'll get it dry-cleaned and return it."

"You're going to leave in two minutes. Nothing of mine is going with you."

She can't be serious. "I-I don't have anything else to wear."

"You're wearing shoes, maybe a bra. Underwear is not your thing, is it."

Sandra rose to her feet again, shifting her weight to her fingertips on the desk surface. "I will say this one more time.

Take the dress off, or I will call the police and report you for theft."

I got up and faced her for the first time today. I pinched the hem of the dress, my fingers shaking, and waited for her to change her mind.

I reminded myself that dreams are not for the living and slid the dress over my head. Keeping my feet planted, I hung it delicately on the back of the chair. Then I removed my high heels from my feet and stooped closer to the ground.

I stood in front of the chair in my bra and underwear, hands folded in front. And I let her see me, my encircling stretchmarks that sprouted from my dark underwear to my belly button. I showed her that I had nothing to offer. Perhaps that was what was the most insulting to her.

She looked right through me. "Get out."

"B-but . . ." *I need something – a scarf, anything.*

The back of my legs hit the chair in reaction to her next look.

I turned and exited her office. I used my purse and heels to cover my stomach. Entering the lobby, there was chatter on the other side of the glass doors stops. Dozens of eyes landed on me.

I made way for the stairs. Claudia held the doors of a packed elevator open.

I unzipped my purse and found my wallet and removed a graduation photo of Jackie. She was twenty-one. It was one of the few graduation photos where she was alone, in front of an old university building. She wanted me in every photo. That day, she hugged me tight in her long dark gown and mortarboard. She wanted me with her. Back then.

I turned the photo over and ripped it once. Turned it over and ripped it again.

CHAPTER THIRTY-SIX

M y landlord was early.
And knocked again.

I may as well get it over with. "Coming," I muttered. I dragged my feet across the rug.

I looked through the peephole. *Isabella. Why are you here?*

"I know you're in there," she said.

Let her say goodbye. You owe her that. I unlocked the door.

Isabella sighed and peered behind me. "You're leaving?" She brushed past me into the living room. Her curls were bouncing on top of a crisp cherry-red t-shirt. She stuffed her hands into her front jeans pockets and approached the floor-to-ceiling window that provided a west-facing view of the city.

"Gave my notice," I said.

"Moving back out west?"

I nodded.

"You're better off away from here. Away from DMI." She opened the blinds and looked out when the dust dispersed.

"Are you better off at DMI?" I asked her.

"You know why I stay. And you also know with every year, my exit comes closer." She turned to me. "Heard about the bar. I'm sorry, I forgot to replenish the morning special drink."

I made her miss her sister's birthday party, and she's apologizing to me? I might miss this girl. "Not your fault."

"Also heard about the Titan interview." She moved to the diamond shape in the centre of the living room rug, tracing it with her toe. "I thought you were insane." She looked up and grinned. "But I would take on the worst clients in a heartbeat to see Sandra's face at that interview."

I almost smiled.

Her playful tone vanished. "You asked me something at the spa."

I shrugged.

"You asked me how DMI's second business got started."

I did, but now I don't care.

"Sandra's mom's cleaning business. That's how she built her client roster. She made Sandra watch, so when the right client came along . . ."

"Daniel."

"Yep. A better life was the hope."

"You came to tell me that?"

"No. I heard you were walking the streets in your underwear." Isabella approached me. "Sweetie, are you okay?"

Well, let's see. This second line of business cost my sister her life. And those that were responsible got away with it. I'm trying to uncover everyone responsible, but all I've come up with is a walk of shame. "I'm fine. Really."

"I had to pry a towel from your death grip at an all-women's spa. What in God's name happened?"

I remained silent.

"Don't tell me it was because Sandra fired you," Isabella said.

"It's a long story."

"I've got time." She sat on the couch, pulled dirty socks from between the cushions and folded them.

She really wants to hear this after all I put her through. I'm confused. I used her to cause a shitstorm in our boss' marriage, went behind her back to work in the business she prohibited me from and got her pulled from a family celebration to sleep with the goblin king.

Should have taken advantage a long time ago.

I took the seat next to her and waited until I felt her

warmth. "Me and Daniel got involved."

She waved her hands and blurted, "It's my fault, I should have warned you better. He preys on DMI girls."

You did warn me. "It wasn't one-sided."

"You like that douchebag? Sorry. He *is* handsome, before you get to know him." She held up her hand. "Continue."

I'm still trying to figure out that one, too – my impulsive attraction to the same person I'm trying to put behind bars.

"When you told me your former co-worker got hurt, it freaked me out. I asked Daniel who did it, so I could stay clear of that client when I entered that line of the business. He wouldn't tell me."

Her fingers danced with the ringlets in her hair.

"You warned me. I didn't listen." My voice trembled. "Daniel threatened to set me up with him if I didn't give him what he wanted."

She got up and circled the coffee table. "What did he want?"

Think of something good. The weirdest shit I'd seen was on the S and M chat sites that me and Jackie visited in high school. "It's really weird. Rather not say."

"Tell me. I won't say anything."

My head sunk to my chest. "It's humiliating." Through my hair, I saw her eyes widen. "Like, foreplay with stuffed teddy bears soaked in urine."

"What!"

"Can't make this shit up. And he wanted them delivered to Sandra afterward, gift wrapped and all."

"Oh, God, I didn't know Daniel was that sick."

"When I tried to break things off, he threatened me, said he'd bring that monster back. And not just for me. For you, Hillary, Christine, Claudia."

She gasped. "He can't be serious."

"At the party after the baseball game, I begged Daniel to tell me who it was, so I could warn you. He got angry, *Daniel-*

angry, that I kept asking."

She nodded in recognition.

"He said he was going to set one of us up with the psycho." I shook my head. "He taunted me with those spa pics. Said he would send them out if I didn't pick one of you."

"You sent them to him?" Liquid pooled around her eyelids. "That doesn't matter."

"The thought of us going to the hospital . . . I lost it. Sandra found out about it all . . . Daniel, the wine. Then the Titan interview came up. I was pissed. I shouldn't have been there."

Isabella picked up my story. "So she punished you for protecting her employees by tossing you on the street half-naked."

I covered my eyes with my hands. "All that's left for me is to pack."

Isabella marched, hands behind her back, paced in circles around the kitchen island, bracelets jingling. "That's because you were looking in the wrong place."

I sprung off the couch. "What do you mean?"

"I knew this would come back to haunt me. I'm going to do what I should have done a long time ago." She halted in the living room. "I'm going to figure out who this son of a bitch is."

I felt the corner of my lips rise.

Don't get excited. She hasn't thought this through. "If this works, the firm will be ruined. Your income, your family . . ."

"I'm not exposing the firm. That's not necessary." She clapped her hands together. "We find out who it is, and we protect each other."

"Even if you know who it is, Daniel could still have his way."

"You're right. That asshole needs to know his secret is not safe. That we can expose him at any moment. I'll talk to my cousin, arrange for a physical reminder, for the coward and

Daniel."

The culprit and Daniel wearing black eyes was a first step. It wasn't enough. They needed to lose everything. This had to go to the police. Once we uncovered who it was, I'd take it from there.

"I don't want your extended family brought into this."

She brought her face inches from mine and clamped my cheeks with both hands. "I need to protect myself and the other girls. My safety is my livelihood. How do I pay my family's bills if I'm in a hospital bed?"

I nodded.

She let go of me. "Why do you want to be part of this?" she asked. "DMI isn't a threat to you anymore."

Fair question. "Like you said, Daniel needs to learn a lesson. You know what he did to me. I want to help make him pay."

She smiled. "Good. I can use a quick thinker." She walked over to the kitchen island and opened my laptop.

I scurried over to it. "What you are doing?"

"Moving AleAngels documents."

"VPN doesn't work anymore."

Isabella fixated on the screen, eyes roaming. "Yes it does."

Of course. Her IT background.

"Won't they see me tampering with the files?"

She rolled her eyes. "What do you take me for, some amateur? Remind me to remove your VPN access later on."

"Why trash the AleAngels files?"

"I'm not deleting them, just moving them to where no one can find them."

"Okay, why move them?"

"Insurance. Claudia will need my help recovering the files you *deleted*. We might need her to turn a blind eye at some point."

CHAPTER THIRTY-SEVEN

"What took you so long?"

"Honey, I'm doing my job, your job, this new endeavour, and then my other job in a few hours," Isabella declared. She stepped around me, bouncing into my apartment, clutching a brown paper bag.

"If we had met at my condo, it wouldn't have taken this long." She slid off navy blue platform heels and lined them next to my shoes in the entrance closet. "I don't know what freaky shit you think I'm hiding."

I rather do all four of your jobs for the rest of my life than set foot in your condo building.

"Sorry."

She slapped my bum. "Don't feel sorry for me, honey. Feel sorry for the girl who went to work with a teddy bear."

"Hilarious. Did you find anything?"

Isabella made her way into the kitchen. "Do you have wine glasses?"

I took a step away from the tall brown paper bag resting on the kitchen counter.

"Chill, bunny, it's non-alcoholic. I'm as excited about this as you."

"This place came furnished." I pulled two wine glasses out of the kitchen cupboard.

"And here." Isabella pulled a cookie out of the brown paper bag. "It's made by some sustainable, local, organic, never sinned company."

To my surprise, I giggled.

Isabella filled the glasses, then raised hers. "Cheers."

I half met her salutation.

Isabella took a long drink of the faux wine, then removed a book-sized whiteboard from her bag and attached it to the wall. She faced the board and wrote on it. I leaned back, trying to get a better view of the whiteboard. She flipped herself around with a triumphant grin like she'd just won a cheerleading contest.

Boyson was written on the whiteboard.

"What does that mean?"

"This is what I found." She beamed.

"That doesn't mean anything to me."

She nodded. "Nothing suspicious came up in Sandra or Daniel's e-mails six months after Jackie was assaulted."

Hearing her name sent blood rushing through my ears.

"I didn't expect to find anything," Isabella continued. "But if you're trying to cover up something, you don't put it in e-mail."

What's her point? I already know this.

"But then I thought Sandra might have needed help to cover this up. In-house help. And whoever she enlisted wouldn't necessarily know what needed to be hidden. So I thought, let's check her deleted e-mails. The ones she didn't author. The ones that only I would know how to recover."

She hit the whiteboard with the marker. "I would have thought nothing of it had it appeared in a regular e-mail. It was an e-mail from Joan to Sandra, confirming she processed the Boyson payment a month after the attack. I know all of our clients. Never heard of Boyson."

"Maybe Sandra and Claudia worked with the client . . ."

She shook her head. "The invoice was bull. They billed for stuff that can be done over the phone. Do you get where this is going?"

"The company where the jerkoff works sent Sandra hush-money. And a dirty accountant helped with the transaction to make it look legit."

She squished my cheeks with her fingertips. "So much more than a pretty face."

I knocked my face to the side. "Can we focus? How much was transferred?"

"Have you always been this much fun?" Isabella put her hair back behind her ears. "Forty thousand."

She watched me as my throat tightened. I couldn't remember anywhere near that amount in Jackie's bank account when she died. I thought the lawyer mentioned a few thousand.

Isabella continued, "Doesn't seem like a lot, considering what happened, but there could have been more. Staggered payments to avoid audit flags. But the asshole doesn't work for Boyson," she said. "That's a fake company set up by the real one to cover its tracks. There's no need to hide legitimate business. That's why Joan sent that e-mail with no details. She knew it was important to Sandra and wanted to confirm she got the job done."

"Why did Sandra delete the e-mail? Wouldn't that draw more attention than leaving it in her inbox?"

"Sandra isn't an idiot, but she's not tech-savvy. There's a misconception at DMI that if you delete an e-mail within 24 hours, it's gone forever. That's not accurate."

A misconception that you haven't bothered to debunk.

"Sandra and the company the guy worked for put in some extra effort to keep this transaction a secret."

"How are you going to find the real company?"

"Great question." She grabbed her now-empty glass and the bottle, made her way to the living room, and flopped on the couch. She moved food coupons and flyers to the side before stretching out her curvy legs covered in shimmering nylons and resting them on the coffee table without a sound.

I followed, but remained standing.

"Hacking passwords is easy," Isabella said. "Uncovering deleted e-mails is complicated, all the more so with Claudia lurking around in the evening. But I did it." She took a long gulp of her drink. "It's very difficult to track bank records. But it can be done through the IP address."

"Can you do it? Trace the payment?"

She clapped her hands and kept them together. "Bout that. It would take me a long time to do it. Multiple sessions on Joan's computer. It would be much faster if I brought in an expert."

"Let's do that. Do you know someone you can trust?"

"So . . . yes, but it won't be cheap. Like fifty thousand."

"What?"

She held the tip of one pinky finger with her other hand. "You have to pay up for shit like this. Taking this on is a big risk. It's not a light crime. I have some expenses coming up for my dad." She filled her glass. "This operation will have to wait until I can get the money."

I've been waiting long enough.

"I'll get the money. All of it."

"No." She built a wall in front of her with straight hands. "You don't have a job. Where are you going to get it from?"

I have no idea. "I'll borrow it from family."

"Katey . . ."

"End of discussion. Now, how do we find the employee once we know the company?"

"Sheesh. One step at a time."

"Tell me. I need to prepare. Sleep with everyone at the company until someone slips?"

"That would work if it was a solo job. By moi." She took a drink. "Once we know the company, we need the HR records. I can't hack the system off-site."

"You think this is noted on the company's HR records?"

"Not the way you're thinking." She topped up her drink. "I tried to convince Sandra to tell the other girls about what happened to Jackie. She insisted this guy was no longer a threat. I pushed her on what that meant . . . like, is he at the bottom of a lake somewhere? Anyway, she didn't say. My guess is he was fired."

She finished the glass, lifted the near-empty bottle, and examined what was left. "Really wish we could invite some booze to this party."

"What made you come to that conclusion now?"

"The credit goes to you. I overheard Sandra talking about the Titan interview. She said she would never let it happen again. Maybe it was her tone or . . . I don't know, but right away, it reminded me of our conversation from nearly two years ago. About the guy who hurt Jackie no longer being a threat. Different words, but it was the way she said it."

"Is that the best we've got? Your hunch based on sound pitches?"

"I know, it's not rock-hard evidence. But it's our only lead. And believe me, I know her."

Okay, if that's all we've got, then that's that. "How do you plan to break into the company's office?"

Isabella pulled my arm, sat me next to her, and put her arm around me. "That's where you come in. Honey, it's best if you don't know in advance."

CHAPTER THIRTY-EIGHT

Fresh air, green grass and a tree overlooking a pond should inspire me to figure this out. And if the stupid sun would screw off, I might find a way to get the money faster.

"Chips for you because I like your feet." I threw flavoured potato chips to three quacking ducks that pecked at crumbs in the soft, trimmed grass.

If I used all my savings, didn't pay my rent, electricity, phone, or Internet bills, and didn't buy groceries, I figured I'd still be several thousand short. And Isabella could insist all she wanted. I wasn't letting her pay for this. Not one cent. And not because she needed the money for her family.

I need to pay for this.

That Rolex *would have come in handy right now. Where am I going to get the money?* "Where?" I asked the ducks. They waddled on their webbed orange feet, eyeing the chip bag. I turned it upside down. "Enjoy. I can't afford these anymore."

David wouldn't give the balance without a business plan and approval from a financial advisor. And Mom wouldn't do it without his permission or a long interrogation process, and I didn't have that kind of time. Nor did I want to reveal that I blew my savings on therapy, charities that helped those who had lost family members, and a dirty Toronto hotel.

I can get a job as a bartender. They make thousands in tips. I don't know how to bartend.

My lycra shorts rode up my bum when I slid back into the shrinking shade provided by the maple tree. I snapped my underwear—wet from the unusual stifling spring heat—back into place. I peeled my black cotton t-shirt from my skin and waved the fabric. Sweat trickled down my spine beneath my shorts. Removing an elastic from my wrist, I tied my hair in a ponytail.

I should have brought water. The pond, beaten into a grey-blue by the sun, was calling. I kicked off my cork-soled sandals, got up and headed for a pond the size of a *Costco* parking lot. The sun screamed into the back of my neck and left my skin streaked with moisture.

The grass transitioned into dirt and sand, then to water.

The water was freezing cold. October water, we would call it back home. I stepped farther into the water and ran my fingers through the still surface.

Deeper.

Strong strides. It was so shallow. The sun had more of me than the water. I felt so exposed. No one else was in there. Parents were watching their kids, who were catching minnows. Hipsters in dark tight jeans smoked up at the water's edge.

Further I went, gentle ripples disturbed the still water. So cold. I was no longer thirsty. Deeper. Hips immersed into the opaque mass, spine pinched, clothes were heavy.

My chest rose and fell slowly, out of sync with my quick breath. I couldn't. My eyes levelled at the water. Dark liquid flooded my eyes. And I went under. The last time I swam, it was with Jackie at a cottage north of the city. The neighbour told Jackie her bathing suit was too slutty. I almost drove that wench's forehead into the rocks supporting the dock. Jackie got rid of her first, the way she did. And we never saw her again.

My hands touched the ground and sifted through the loose earth.

How did you end up like you did, Jackie? I know. And this is the only place I can tell you. Pride. You had to be the best at everything.

Dirt and pebbles found their way under my fingernails.

Clay brown and orange surrounded me. I couldn't see far in front of me.

There are so few places where no one can see you.

One hand gripped the bottom, then the other, as if I was looking for a rope to keep me underneath. There was nothing to grab onto, nothing to help. My chest flattened against the bottom. Water filled my ears, and air bubbles escaped my mouth. Head filled, pressure built. My lungs burned. I didn't want to go back.

I broke the surface and gasped for air.

Treading water, I changed directions, not sure what side of the pond I entered.

"Are you all right?" a distant voice called.

I turned to the sound. A small crowd lined the shore.

I looked around. I was in the middle of the pond. *When did I get out so far?*

One of the spectators wearing a neon yellow t-shirt entered the water. *You can stay there. I don't want your help.* I headed back to shore.

I sat back down in the shade with my things. Water dripped from my hair and arms onto the grass and my cloth purse. Black specks of dirt covered my wrists and ankles.

The crowd dispersed.

Jackie. I can't avenge you as long as I hate you for who you are. There was no chance. I couldn't have given you what you needed, neither could our parents, your friends, some boyfriend, or DMI.

"My mommy said you can have this." A kindergarten-aged boy with a cartoon face held out a striped blue-red-and-white beach towel. "You're really pretty." He giggled.

I took it, wiped my face, chest, and legs, and squeezed my hair dry. "Thanks."

The cod-fished mouth boy watched me. "My mommy says it's too cold to swim."

I looked for the owner of this twinkie. To the right, four women holding e-book readers and stemless wine glasses waved at me. *Probably a dumb book club.*

They raised their glasses at me. "Good for you, honey. We are about to do the same," one called.

I half waved to the group and turned back to the little boy. "Why don't you go into the water and see for yourself?"

"I can't. I don't have my water wings." He pushed his pale baby-curved stomach outward as he swung a red plastic bucket.

Me and Jackie could swim by the time we were five. "You should know how to swim on your own by now."

He looked down. "I'm taking swimming lessons."

I have thinking to do. "Here's your towel back. Go away."

The little boy dropped the towel on the ground. "Do you want to build a sandcastle?"

I exhaled loudly. "Does the castle come with an ATM?"

"Uh."

"Then no."

"Please." He stomped his feet, smacked the bucket against his knee.

"Why don't you make a friend your own age to play with?" *A friend that has some pills.*

He whined. "It's my birthday."

That was loud. Other people in the park turned my way. *Little shit.* "Okay, fine."

I climbed onto my knees and heard a crunch. *No.* I opened my bag, took out my extra-dark sunglasses, now with a cracked frame and one lens missing. "I need these," I mumbled.

"Broken," he said.

"No shit, Sherlock." I tried to pop the lens back into the frame. No dice.

"My name's Noah, not Sherlock." He paused. "Maybe you can wear my mommy's sunglasses."

I looked over at the sorority on the blanket. They were wearing Chanel aviator sunglasses. Beside them lay designer purses and wine bottles.

"Sweetie, go put on your mommy's sunglasses, okay?"

The kid waddled back to the real housewives of the city park. He took sunglasses off a tanned face and put them on. They fell off onto the blanket. He put them back on and held them on his face. *Good boy.*

The group laughed and told his mom how a baby in *Chanel* is just the cutest thing. He ran back to me.

"I got them," he squealed.

"Where are you? I hear you, but I can't see you."

He waved his arms like attracting a search and rescue helicopter. "I'm right here, right here."

I got up, stretched my arms out front like I was walking in the dark. "Where is he? I can't see anyone."

He took off the sunglasses.

"There you are." I clapped my hands. "Those sunglasses are magic. I can't see you when they're on."

"Really?" He jumped in the air.

Mommy must have been drinking with you in the belly. "Really."

I pulled my phone from my bag. "See this. It's broken, too. If you get me one, I'll build you a huge sandcastle."

"How big?"

"So big. The size of the Playboy mansion."

He opened his mouth, niblet corn teeth shone between apple-shaped cheeks.

"And one more." I pulled out my wallet. "See this girl." I pieced together the four ripped pieces of Jackie's photo. "She's pretty, isn't she?"

He raised his bucket. "Yeah."

"Your mommy would love this pretty girl in her wallet. If you get her wallet, I'll build you a giant wall around the castle. No one will be able to get in."

The squirt froze, jaw dropped.

The women opened another bottle of wine, and the chatter volume escalated.

"Go into your mommy's purse and put her phone" — I held my phone in the air — "and wallet" — I held up my wallet — "in the bucket very quietly. Like this." I placed my phone at the bottom of the red bucket so it didn't make any noise. "And wear your sunglasses, so no one sees you. Go now."

The boy trotted off. Back to the blanket, picking up a black structured purse. He undid the zipper and turned it upside down. The contents spilled onto the grass and the corner of the blanket — makeup, wallet, keys, tissues, toys, and phone.

Idiot. I waited for his mother to scold him.

But no one said anything. They didn't even look at him.

I held up my wallet in his direction and shook it. Mom's wallet went into the bucket. *Yes. Good boy.*

The women down their drinks and cackled as if they were at a drinking contest.

He grabbed a toy airplane from the blanket and threw it. *C'mon, focus.*

The phone was in hand.

He stood up. *No, no, sit down.* He dropped a phone into the bucket, creating a loud smack. *Oh, geez.*

I waited for a reaction from the adults. There was none. I waved him over.

I plucked the wallet and iPhone from the bucket. They went straight into my purse.

"Noah!" His mom stood, a toy airplane and a compact in her hand. *Crap.* The Mom crew got on their hands and knees, searching the blanket.

"Take this towel back to your mom. I'll meet you at the water to build the castle."

His mom called again. "Noah, come here."

"See you soon." He waved goodbye with his bucket.

I took off into the sparse woods, breaking into a run and heard my useful friend squeal, "She made me do it."

And that was exactly how my sister lost far more than a phone.

They had to pay and could never get back what they had.

CHAPTER THIRTY-NINE

I could do this. It was only an hour on my own.
I could entertain these schmucks while she broke into the law firm's office with an employee ID card.

Of course it was a law firm.

Isabella's cousin came through and found the name of the real company—the law firm—Sandra had worked so hard to keep a secret. I only had to steal ten iPhones from my condo gym and swimming pool to pay Isabella's cousin the snoop fee. Boysen was a shell company set up to float the hush-money transaction with Sandra. Exempler was the law firm that the culprit who hurt Jackie worked for. To find out the identity of the criminal, we needed access to Exempler's HR records which could only be done on-site without paying another third party.

As long as the card was on him, it was easy pickings for Isabella. If everything went to plan, I'd have all the answers I needed tonight.

Walk faster. Don't be late. The four-inch heels I was wearing were not made for walking.

Isabella axed using a private location for our rendezvous. She said the more secluded the location, the more likely the client was to demand their *tastes* be addressed. She wouldn't tell me what these lawyers liked to sample, because if I knew, according to her, I would be even more awkward and would scare them away before they had the chance to freak us out.

My role was simple—chat, distract, and collect. And only act like myself at the planned times.

Isabella, of course, had to run this event by Sandra, even though Sandra was out of town. She lied about the company we were meeting—naming Exempler would have raised a blood-red flag. But Isabella promised to make it worth their while, and the law partner agreed to not discuss the event with anyone else. If the company name came up, they'd use a false name which was apparently something they'd had practice with. Isabella also made Sandra an offer she couldn't refuse—a generous price tag and a promise of new overpriced business.

But Sandra was no fool. She sent her spy.

Isabella was positive Claudia would play along with my *coincidence attendance* by threatening to expose any of Claudia's many secrets Isabella had become privy to.

The meeting spot was a rooftop patio. New venue for me, but same black suits and black cocktail dresses occupied the space.

"Katey!" Isabella squealed from a high round table. She was with three guys and Claudia.

Isabella kissed both my cheeks. "Katey, what a coincidence. This is my friend, everyone. Would you mind if she joined?"

"Please, join us," the more senior member of the law firm responded.

Then Isabella introduced our target. "And this is Saud, the managing partner."

He looked much older than his company photo. Thick frown lines, shaven head, and dyed dark eyebrows—I had put him in his late forties.

Isabella put names to the others. "And Graham and Robert. They work for Saud."

I smiled at them.

"Nice to see you again," I said to Claudia, her face titled upward as if she was watching an air show.

She raised her glass. "What a beautiful dress you're wearing."

I got straight to work, squeezing myself between Isabella and Saud. His cologne was strong and musty, but it helped mask the scent of his bourbon.

"We're talking about the serial killer who targeted couples," Isabella said.

"Are you involved in the case?" I asked.

Saud turned his head as if he was about to shake it. "There was a conflict of interest."

Hmm. Isabella told me their client recruitment strategy was shadier than DMI's—wait for the arrest, sleep with the cop, and pay the prospective client a visit in jail.

"You'll have to forgive me," I said, touching his forearm, "I don't know the case."

"In eight years, he got fifteen hipster couples on road trips. They found the couples on hikes—the suckers all used cowbells to scare the wildlife. Fools."

"I thought law firms got around conflicts of interest?" Isabella asked. "The lawyer on the other side of the floor takes the case."

"We needed a higher wall." Saud grinned, rolled his glass in his hand and slapped one of the young lawyers on the shoulder. "I expect it built by Monday morning."

"Okay," the young lawyer squeaked.

"Katey, my apologies." Saud flagged the waitress pretty quickly, given the size of the crowd. "She'll have a dry martini."

I made eye contact with the waitress—an acknowledgment of our arrangement. Isabella slipped her a few hundred dollars to keep booze out of my drinks.

"I'll order some apps," Saud said. "The sliders and . . ." He scanned the menu.

"Crab cakes, hummus, goat and artichoke dip," I blurted.

The list was out of my mouth before I realized it.

Saud laughed and nodded to the waitress.

Claudia's eyelids fluttered like butterfly wings.

"Your scar." Isabella traced a rubber-like hairless patch of skin stretching from the inside of Saud's wrist to the other side of his arm. "What happened?"

His arm sat in my hands for another beat, and then he pulled away. "You don't want to hear about that."

"Tell us," Isabella begged. "I'll come over so you don't have to yell over the noise."

She passed behind Saud — his eyes blinked hard. *Did she get his work ID pass from his wallet?*

"You have our full attention," she said.

"I was building my Muskoka cottage deck. A bear the size of a Hummer approached. Was this close." He reached behind Isabella and touched her opposite shoulder. "Tools were everywhere. I didn't want him stepping on a power saw." He was only talking to Isabella. "The saw was safe, and so was the bear. But" — he tapped his scar — "two for three that day."

Uh-huh, the bear was the threat. Not your waxed hands handling power tools.

Two drinks arrived, my fake martini and Saud's bourbon. Before the fumes from his drink poisoned my airways, I turned to thank the waitress and caught Isabella's eyes. Her head nudged to the left, then right.

Crap. She said picking his pocket would be like stealing lunch from a French teen model.

"What did you do? Hope you weren't out there alone?" Isabella asked.

"Drove myself to the hospital."

"Don't mind me." From beside him, Isabella bent at the waist — the whole table watched her chest spill from her dress into full view — and grabbed her phone sitting in front of me.

"I could have got that for you." He leaned into Isabella as she squeezed back to her spot.

She whispered something in his ear.

I took a sip of my drink. Isabella shook her head again as her full red lips tickled his ear.

Ugh, c'mon.

The crab cakes arrived. I grabbed a knife and fork and cut.

The lawyer with the squeaky voice asked me to share.

I considered slipping a cake into my purse.

Long fingernails landed on my lower back. "Let's save some for everyone else," Isabella said.

My knife screeched on the plate. Perfect circles turned into shapeless bits.

"Wouldn't want to be on an island alone with her," one younger lawyer said.

"Or a buffet for two," Claudia chimed in.

"The last time we went out" — I waved my fork at Claudia and Isabella — " Claudia was so good. Made sure everyone was full."

"Oh?" the lawyers said.

Claudia stiffened.

I cut a new crab cake, stabbed it with a fork, and waved it in front of Junior's mouth. "She's so generous. Spoon fed everyone the whole night. Didn't let anyone lift a finger."

Claudia was ready to pounce on me like a raptor in Jurassic Park.

"That's how my two-year-old nephew is fed," one of the boys said.

The artichoke dip arrived. I scooped it up and hugged the round bowl to my chest.

Isabella weaved her arm under Saud's. "We'll leave you two alone." She pointed to me and the food and led Saud away from us.

"Do you guys want some?" I asked, pushing the dip and bread plate toward the lawyers.

"We'll pass," the boys said.

"You don't like this?"

The gap-toothed one cracked a smile. "We're waiting for the sliders."

"Sliders," I shouted. "Where's our waitress? We ordered sliders." Sliders that Isabella asked the waitress to delay delivering. "I'll get them."

I pushed my way through the crowd. There wasn't a lot of time.

I reached the bathroom and held my stomach. Three women in black strapless tube dresses stood by the mirror, applying lipstick.

"Do not eat the crab cakes," I said loudly and bolted into a stall.

I grabbed toilet paper and ripped it into three piles. One by one, I dipped them in the toilet water. *Eww.* I rolled the dripping mush into balls, and tossed them into the toilet. They splashed and sprayed water over the seat.

The women shrieked and exited the bathroom.

I took off my shoes, walked to the bathroom door, and turned the lock.

It was only the three of us now.

Soft moaning seeped from the farthest stall. I moved towards my target in bare feet. I took a deep breath and kept it inside while I crouched to the floor and peered under the stall. Isabella was standing. I think her belly was hitting the wall. Saud was behind her, his pants around his ankles.

Please don't look down. I balanced on three trembling limbs and reached under the stall door toward his crumpled pants.

Don't look down. Don't look down.

Crap. His wallet was in the pocket on the other side of his pants. I laid on my side on the floor and reached into the stall as far as my arm would go — neck strained and tendons in my hand protruded. My fingertips nearly brushed his pants. *Closer, closer, almost there . . .*

Shit, I'm too far away. I needed to go into the adjacent stall — I'd be directly behind him. If he saw me there, I wouldn't be able to escape easily. He could run over Isabella and block me in the stall. She might play dumb and sell me out to face a top criminal law firm. *Stop it. Focus.*

Bang, bang. My arm retracted as if it landed in an alligator's jaw. Someone was at the door. *Find another bathroom, asshole.*

Bang, bang.

The moaning stopped. *Shit. Am I far enough back so he can't see me through the cracks?*

My heart thudded against my chest. We waited. I wrapped my face with my arms.

Isabella giggled, and more breath-filled moans ensued.

She migrated to the ground, knees on the floor.

The sound of wet skin against wet skin quickened. He groaned while her hand found the back pocket of his pants piled on the floor. With two fluid motions, she pulled out the wallet and tossed it underneath the stall door.

Scrambling, I picked up the wallet, opened it, and plucked out credit cards, a driver's licence, a health card, and a gym membership. Isabella said the access card should be attached to something, like a clip. *Where is it?* I checked the cash compartment. Nothing.

I clamped the wallet, spread my fingers to feel for the attachment, rotating and holding it in each position a little longer than an object lit on fire. Flipped it upside down. Hundred and fifty-dollar bills floated out, but there was no bulging clip.

I snatched the bills off the floor, rubbed them together between my fingers, and stopped my urge to smell the healthy amount of cash before returning the bills to the wallet.

His moans escalated. *Hurry.*

I turned the wallet around and unzipped the change compartment. Saud's photo appeared on a white card. I unhooked the clasp that held two cards — the photo card with the Exempler logo and a plain white card. Isabella said the plain card permitted access to the office, while the photo card was proof of identity. Isabella made her own picture ID card — she said it wasn't difficult to replicate since it only proved visual identification.

It took me two attempts to stuff the photo ID card back into his wallet. Then I crawled right up to the stall wall and lowered my head and chest to the floor.

Oh, God. I shot my head towards the floor after catching Isabella's bare bum bobbing between red stiletto heels.

I reached for his pants, but they were too far away. I used the floor for leverage to stretch my arm further.

She pointed her finger at the floor.

He moaned louder. His breath was shorter.

She waved her hand rapidly, cupping it toward her.

Oh, I get it. I reached further and dropped the wallet next to Isabella.

He moaned and heaved, one long guttural satisfied noise.

Isabella stuffed the wallet back into his pants.

We did it. Well, she did it.

CHAPTER FORTY

Isabella had been gone far too long. Something must have happened.

Her only text message since she'd left for Exempler's office was, *Watch him. Stay put.*

Yeah, I'm doing that. I was mostly staring and wondering what his role was managing the aftermath when his firm nearly killed Jackie. I wondered if he'd established a protocol for when it happened again. If he set up a precautionary slush account. Or gave a glowing reference and a generous severance package to move along the culprit bastard to another firm.

Speculation had gone past the rabbit hole was where my focus had strayed because it wasn't needed elsewhere. After Saud got what he wanted from Isabella, there was no need to top off my drink or order appetizers. He joined a table of six guys. He knew them. They were like him. They took turns slapping their hands against the table and shouting about themselves.

I didn't think he knew that I was still there, hunched on a high stool and peering in his direction like a driver checking the rear-view mirror of a car.

Saud didn't know I was there, but the piercing high-pitched squeals from behind me did. From the edge of the patio roof, Claudia raised a glass to me, sandwiched by the baby Exempler lawyers. She was spreading her arms on the metal railing, ribs jutting through her satin dress. When she laughed, the horizontal bones in her chest took turns protruding like pressing piano keys.

"Do you want to join us?" the one on her right called.

Claudia snorted. "She prefers the company of chips and bread crumbs. They can't run away."

I checked my phone again. Nothing from Isabella.

She told me not to send any messages while she was there. I texted her anyway. *Where are you?* She'd been gone more than an hour.

I turned to check on Saud. The noise at his table had died down. *What's going on in bro-land?*

All eyes were on one of the suits and a waitress leaning over him and reaching for glasses on the table.

With both hands, the guy pulled up and scrunched his white dress shirt near the belt.

The waitress laughed. Her long ponytail flipped back and forth like a horse flicking its tail.

"You stained my shirt," the guy accused.

I strained my neck for a better view. I couldn't see anything on the guy's shirt. It was dark, but there was probably nothing. *He must know Daniel. Go to the bathroom and scrub.*

The waitress picked up a rocks glass lying on its side on the table. "Oh, well, you know."

The table was silent.

The waitress hummed a song, rounded the table with a bounce to her step, and a zig-zagged path.

"You know what?" The guy pulled his shirt toward her.

"I dunno," she replied, speaking in another direction and moving her head in an *s* shape.

He pulled his shirt further away from him so that the front was no longer tucked into his pants. "Get some club soda," he barked.

She flipped her ponytail to the side and posed, one hand on her hip.

"You spilled a drink on my custom-made shirt, don't

apologize and do nothing to make up for your incompetence." He stood and pushed the table aside.

"Get the manager. Now." Saud ordered the waitress.

"Coming right up." The waitress said, and pointed her thumb and index finger as if she were firing a gun.

Is this Isabella's doing? Did she pay off the waitress to stall them? The manager will probably offer them free drinks, and that will keep them here longer.

I glanced at my phone. App icons and blue rising bubbles stared back at me.

A short guy with dark, slicked-back hair and wearing a striped suit, approached Saud's table. "I'm Pete Vincello, the manager. You asked to speak with me."

"Yes," Saud said. "Your employee spilled a drink on my friend's shirt and didn't apologize. We asked for club soda. And she pranced around the table."

The stained-shirt guy with a wide wet circle over his stomach stomped back to his seat and remained standing.

"I spoke to Nicole, your server. This is a big group. And there's no women at the table," the manager told them.

Saud slammed his rocks glass against the table. "What the hell does that have to do with anything?"

"It's important our employees feel comfortable," the manager said.

"This is fucking ridiculous. We planned a company party here . . . Exempler law firm, sound familiar? Damn right."

"No."

"It's cancelled," Saud screamed.

A black cheque folder landed on the table. Saud held out a credit card without checking the bill.

Wait. No, no. That wasn't supposed to happen. He was leaving. *Shit.* I checked my phone again. *Fudge. How are we going to get the pass back in his wallet when he's asleep at home? We're not.*

I tore after Saud across the patio.

I couldn't see him at the entrance to the elevators. *Where did he go?* I had hit the elevator button three times to go down. *Hurry up. I had one job, one job.*

When will he figure out his ID card is missing? Tomorrow morning on his way to work. The whole night was sketchy — Isabella *randomly* running into him near his office and inviting him out. And then the bar bathroom. Everything tonight was rushed. He'd add it all up, check his access card records and the security cameras. Then he'd report the break-in. Isabella changed her appearance as much as she could in the cab ride over, but if Saud looked for her on the security camera footage, he would recognize her.

Before the doors fully opened, I flew out and sailed down the building stairs. I looked to my right, then left. Couldn't see him.

Claudia, half covered by one of the boy scouts, blew cigarette smoke my way.

"Which way did your boss go?" I asked the boy.

Claudia put her fingers over his lips. "Don't tell her."

I don't have time for this.

I pulled the small fry by his shirt collar and whispered, "I'm taking your boss to heaven and back tonight."

Our lips met. Whistles and cheers erupted in the background.

I broke away. He swallowed and pointed south. His voice cracked. "Adelaide."

"Thank you." I took off my heels and bolted down the street.

Where is he? He couldn't have gone far. So many people were in my way. It was hard to see, hard to move.

There. Big back, white rolled-up sleeves. That was him. "Saud," I yelled.

He stopped and turned my way. I caught up.

He looked at my feet. "You should get a cab."

"I'd prefer to walk. With you."

"I don't live far," he said without breaking stride.

"Sorry about the end of the night."

"Didn't know you were there."

I picked up the pace to keep up. "Is that normal behaviour from the bar?"

"I'll never return."

"I'll never go back, either." I sounded stupid.

He veered to the street side of trees planted in the sidewalk.

I checked my phone. Nothing.

Between the trees, I wrapped my arm around his waist. "The ground is a little rough."

"Put your shoes on."

"I can't stand another minute in these heels."

His back muscles tensed. My arm slid down his waist, and stopped at his belt.

Think, think.

"I know an amazing show on Netflix about criminal lawyers."

"What's it called?"

"Can't remember. I'll show you. It will only take a few seconds."

"Not interested."

I can't let him get away. Jackie and Isabella would know what to do.

"This is me," Saud said. We stopped in front of a white high-rise condo building. Saud twisted free from my grip.

Forget them. My eyes searched the ground. *Nothing comes easy to me. This hasn't been easy. And it's not going to change.* "It was great meeting you," I told his back.

I ran to the mailbox, took a deep breath, and stomped my foot into broken glass from a beer bottle scattered on the sidewalk.

I screamed as the glass sliced the ball of my foot.

I hit the ground, landing on my hip. A sharp, pulsing pain took over my foot. Blood trickled from the arch of my foot onto the concrete.

I raised my bloodied foot higher. Rocking back and forth, I cried out. Saud returned to my side, looked at me, my leg, and the glass on the ground. "I'll call an Uber. You should go to the hospital."

"No." I winced. "I just need a bandage."

"You need stitches." He pointed to the ground, decorated with red drops.

A crowd formed around me. "Are you all right?" a voice asked.

"It's fine." I tipped my head to Saud. "My friend is helping."

Holding my arm up, he crouched down.

Saud's hands moved towards my foot. I shrieked. He pulled a triangular, bloodstained piece of glass from my foot and threw it onto the sidewalk. My foot throbbed like it was strapped over a flame.

"My concierge will clean this up." Saud lifted me up by my armpits and rested my arm across his shoulder.

CHAPTER FORTY-ONE

Seated on the edge of a bathtub, I lifted my legs one by one over the side and turned on the tap. I placed my foot, which was dripping blood, directly under the running water.

The stand-alone soaker tub was spotless before I got there. Not a watermark anywhere.

Ow. My foot snapped back from the running water.

"Apply pressure to stop the bleeding," Saud said.

"I will. First it needs to be rinsed."

We watched the blood run over the tub's white surface and swirl around the drain before disappearing.

Saud checked his watch.

"Do you have a topical antibiotic?" I asked.

Saud opened the vanity doors beneath the sink and half-assed rummaged through the contents. He made a displeased sound and left the bathroom. I grabbed my purse from the floor, checking my phone. *Nothing from Isabella.*

I grabbed the bar of soap from the dish caddy and patted the broken skin crisscrossed with red lines.

Ow. I washed off the red-stained soap bar and returned it to the caddy.

"Don't have any. Your foot is rinsed," Saud said when he returned, one arm hanging on the top of the door frame.

I swung one leg back to the floor, straddling the side of the tub. "Do you have alcohol?"

I can't believe I said that.

He tapped his foot, still in a shoe, on the floor, then disappeared back into the hallway. *Back to my phone. Unlock the screen. C'mon.*

He returned with a crown-shaped bottle and tissue and handed me both.

"Could you pour some on? I might fall over."

He unscrewed the top over the tub. I leaned away.

I took the whiskey-soaked tissue and rested the outside of my ankle on the edge, with my foot dangling over the tub.

I held my breath. Whiskey coated my palm and dripped from my knuckles into the tub. "Ouch. I can't, can you?" I held the wet mush ball beside his hand.

Water roared out of the faucet and down the drain.

He grabbed the mush ball and pressed it into the ball of my foot like he was creating a sponge painting. I retracted as blood smudged over his fingernails. My fingertips drew four straight lines on the back of his hand. "Gently," I said.

He tossed the tissue into a garbage can. I screwed the cap on the whiskey bottle while he ran his fingers under the water.

"That's cold," he said.

"I don't mind the cold," I told him. *What I mind is the whiskey sewage odour emanating from your garbage can.*

The corner of his mouth rose, and his expression froze. *Weird.*

He got on his knees, poked his head into the vanity under the sink, and came out with several large, brown fabric bandages. "To stop the bleeding." He handed the bandages to me.

Why didn't you take those out before? Whatever.

My phone went off. I reached into my purse on the floor. It was Isabella. She messaged, *Done.*

Yes. The relief momentarily eclipsed the pain in my foot.

We were almost there. She just needed to return the card to Saud. And I just needed to keep him occupied for a bit longer.

Now, Isabella, don't freak out. I texted back Saud's address and let her know the door was unlocked.

"Sorry, letting my roommate know I'm okay," I told Saud.

He was watching me. Arms folded, leaning back against the vanity.

WTF Get out now Isabella messaged.

A spot of blood soaked through the brown fabric of the bandage and grew.

I shrugged at Saud. "It's better than nothing." *It'll probably take her twenty minutes to get here from Saud's office.*

"Do you have a clean tea towel you don't mind parting with and some duct tape?"

He burrowed his head back in the vanity cupboard. "Aha." He pulled out a white plastic package with rolled gauze.

Maybe he took a shot of whiskey while I wasn't looking, but he no longer seemed to equate me with a cockroach that wouldn't leave his luxury condo.

That will stop the bleeding. "I don't know if that will work. I have to think about it."

"My friend used one. Worked like a charm." Saud took my ankle in both hands, re-covered my foot with the bandages and looped the white fabric in a crisscross pattern. He fastened the two ends with a knot.

"Ow. Too tight."

He fiddled to untie the knot, reversed the loops, and rewrapped with less pressure. "Good to go."

"Thank you so much."

"No problem." He offered me a hand. I took it and pulled myself up on my good foot. Our hands were still together.

"Can I use your balcony?"

He raised an eyebrow.

"I need to shake out my dress. Bits of glass got caught."

He turned his back. "Follow me."

The living room was massive—six people could live in that room alone. Make that ten, there was only a single couch. The wall window stretched the length of the condo, showing one, two, three . . . six high-rise condo buildings lit as unevenly as the sky.

The glass balcony doors slid open.

Unlock the front door. "My purse." I retreated back to the front door quickly not giving him a chance to question why I needed my purse to shake out my dress. I think he started to say something.

The front door lock clicked, but the sound was indistinguishable from the street noise.

I hobbled back and joined him on the balcony. He was facing the street, gripping the railing. *You can do this.*

"Sorry, did you say something? I didn't want the air conditioning to escape."

That weird lopsided grin returned to his face.

"What a beautiful view," I said when the silence and his smile were getting too weird for me.

The other condo towers blocked what could be a decent view. I looked up at the sky and saw a few stars peeking through the haze. "What's the most interesting thing you've ever seen from here?"

His focus remained straight ahead, like he was driving. "The best things always happen at this time of night."

Twenty minutes, then never this city or these people again.

He described some drunk-fest sightings he'd witnessed from his balcony.

It was too dark to see my scars. I pulled my dress over my head and shook it out over the railing, using the fabric to absorb the sweat from my palms.

Saud continued rambling but was now talking about himself. *Does he not see I'm wearing nothing? Or is he that unimpressed?*

He stopped talking, but his focus remained straight ahead. *It's not enough.*

"It's too warm out here." I retreated inside. He didn't follow, but I sensed I caught his attention.

I threw my dress and purse on the couch. With courage I didn't have, I unhooked my bra with one hand behind my back.

Footsteps approached from behind. I felt his presence grow in the dark open room.

He was close but not making any sound. It was unnerving.

I spun around. Before I could make the full turn, he took my hips in his hands and turned me back the other way. His hands found their way to my thong, but only momentarily before it dropped to the floor. The rough touch of the lace fabric lingered on the top of my feet as the sound of a belt unbuckling and the undoing of a zipper followed.

His touch felt hurried and foreign. It sent my heart racing.

A metal object connected with my inner thigh. I jumped at the cold sensation against my hot skin.

My head gravitated toward the front door. *No, stay.*

My knees collided.

He pressed one hand on my shoulder. The metal object was a belt buckle—the cold, smooth surface climbed to my stomach then up to my breastbone. "Put it on," he said.

Do it, or go home.

I fastened the belt around my hips.

Less than twenty minutes before Isabella gets here.

His voice volume rose. "Higher." He was no longer touching me.

I slid the belt to the small of my waist, tightening it.

"Higher."

I raised the belt until it was strung across my chest, covering my nipples. He wrapped his arm around me fast, the leather strap belt tightening.

He pulled the belt flap hanging in front of my chest until I was facing him. Hard bare chest, his stomach broken up into six pads. He lifted me by my waist onto the back of the couch. Wrapping the belt flap around his hand, he pulled me close with strong arms until he was in position between my thighs.

Both his hands slipped beneath me. I took him between my legs, crossing my ankles on his other side. He was ready and danced for entry.

No, not so soon. And not here.

I broke away and jumped off the back of the couch. "Let's go to your room."

He paused, eyes empty, then he then unbuckled the belt around my chest. It dropped to the floor, the metal ringing against the hardwood.

Oops. "Or, whatever you want."

In the dark, he made me feel like I was in a room with fluorescent lights.

He approached, took my hand in his, and held it firmly. Taking his lead, we arrived back in the bathroom.

He climbed into the high-walled bathtub, squatted, and turned on a tap. A high-pressure stream of water roared out. He lifted his head, looked straight ahead, eyes steady.

I was a bit relieved he wasn't looking my way, since it was a lot brighter in there, and I had nothing but my arms crossed against my chest to cover up. *What's going on now?*

He stepped out, defined thigh and calve muscles contracting, peeled both my hands from my chest, and led me over to the tub.

Water rapidly filled the porcelain bowl.

"No more than fifteen minutes," he said.

I looked down and out. *You want us to take a bath together? Okay . . . could be a lot weirder.* My breathing was calm, and my arms weren't scrambling to cover my marks. I wasn't the one who needed to be embarrassed. *And this will definitely kill a good chunk of time.*

"We can do that."

Ink black eyes received my assumption.

He moved behind me, stroking my arms with the back of his fingers. I straightened between him and the water as he told me what he wanted. "Just you." He drew out the *S* like the hiss of a snake.

Something's not right. The water in the tub rose.

251

"I'll turn it off when it's full," he said.

Something was wrong. My eyes lifted to the soap, to the faucet, then the tap. It was the tap. The cold water was running. Only the cold.

Oh shit. I've swam in October. The water was freezing. You needed a wet suit.

I looked at him. Pupils feasted his eyeballs. I told him, "No suds."

He offered his hand. I took it. I sat on the thin ledge of the tub, my feet perched above the rising water.

I lowered my good foot into the water—that's cold, too cold—and I yanked it out.

His hand was flat, applying pressure on my lower back. "It's easier if you get right in." The front, then the back of his fingers, caressed my spine.

My foot sank back into the water. The cold ticked up in notches, like an ice pick at work.

Get in. Or watch your face reflect off the water.

Holding both sides of the tub, I saw her face in the stirring liquid. The freckle on her left earlobe, hair side-part and strands too short to tuck behind her ears. I propped my injured foot on the caddy and slid down into the water.

I thrashed. *Holy shit. Fire. It feels like fire. I can't breathe. I can't do this. I can't do it.* I threw my arms over the side. Water splashed on the floor.

"Get me out of here." My chest screamed, torso writhed. I scrambled to my feet. Goosebumps coated my skin. My nipples were so hard they could have cut the mirror. I clutched the tub wall for balance and pulled one leg out of the water.

He sat on the toilet, forearms on his thighs and sucked in his cheeks. "You girls. Keep getting weaker."

Both hands clamouring the bathtub edge, my shivers quieted. My elbows bent and water shook from my hair to the floor.

With a snap of the wrist, he tossed a bright white bath

towel onto the floor in front of me.

I picked it up, squeezing it in my fist. And with an over-hand motion, I threw it back at him.

The water reached the brim. I shut the tap off, sat on the edge of the tub and used my feet and the slope of the tub wall to slide down and sink underneath the icy water.

It was worse than I imagined. The cold felt like a thousand stabbing knives, one inch at a time, searing parts of my body I forgot existed—eye creases, the back of my ears, web of my fingers.

In normal-temperature pool water, I could hold my breath for four minutes. *I'll try to last for one.*

A disjointed dark face waved above the surface. He was only a blur, but I stared back as long as I could.

The pulsing pain in my ribs grew more intense. It was different from the external hammering pain. It pulsed to a slow hard drum beat. Then the drumsticks turned to mallets. The motion halted, and the pressure that built in my chest felt like it was under the weight of a boot heel.

He grabbed me by my arm, pulling me up. I wasn't ready. *Gasp.* My throat burned, and I let my breath be harsh.

The way he looked at me took my focus away from the cold. Like he knew me and was waiting for me to say something familiar to him.

A minute or so later, I couldn't take any more of his presence. I shook him off and submerged myself again—arms, chest, hands, hips, thighs, knees, and feet under the water. I kept my head above.

I couldn't stop shaking. *That's a good sign.*

My breathing stayed short, shallow.

On his knees, he glided his fingers through the surface of the water along the length of the tub, first one way, then the other. He whispered something in another voice, higher pitched. I couldn't make it out. My teeth chattered.

"You're doing great." He was back to his normal voice.

I swallowed water. Cold rushed down my throat and chest. I coughed. *You're fine, stay down. Stay calm.*

He mumbled again. "Life jacket."

He talked to himself again, but I couldn't make out anything over the sound of my own air that was begging to escape my body.

He pointed one finger, reaching into the tub. There was that voice again. "Don't you see it?"

He ripped his arm out of the water. His voice was different now, not as high. "Where is it?"

I pressed my head against the tub wall.

He pointed to the far end of the tub, by my toes, which were now blue at the tips.

"Right there." His hand dove back in and out of the water. He shuffled to the other end of the tub on his knees with a renewed energy. He hovered over the water as if he saw something, but nothing was there.

His face was submerged in the water. He yelled something from under the water, then screamed. Both arms plunged into the water. He didn't touch me.

His arms emerged first. His head snapped back. Water dripped down his forehead, off his sharp nose, and onto his lips. He didn't wipe it away. He gasped, bare chest pumping.

We stayed in silence, listening to him breathe. Listening to the cold seize my body until I couldn't feel it anymore.

My neck turned. His hand was on my knee. My knee wasn't shaking. My shoulders were still, my feet were still, and my hands rested on the bottom of the tub.

"Do this." His thumb and index finger formed a circle.

I lifted my arm out of the water and tried to imitate him, but my fingers wouldn't bend.

He linked one arm beneath my legs, and the other around my shoulders.

I was in the air with a hazy view of a white ceiling.

I heard music—a piano and bass.

Now the white had turned to a surrounding dark. My back made contact with something soft. A duvet. I tried to sit up. Couldn't. I tried to bend my knees and arms. Couldn't. I was as stiff as a corpse.

He was lying on top of me now, facedown, smothering my cheek. He was a weight, but not heavy. His chest moved and trembled when he inhaled deeply. Besides his breathing, he was motionless.

I stared up. My eyes blinked, my fingers twitched, and my toes curled.

He rose, his weight still on my lower body, and pressed a palm against the center of my chest. "Not yet, you're too cold." He got up. Cold, sharp air broke my skin. I gasped, but no sound came out.

I needed him. Needed his body heat. "Come back," I squeaked.

He rifled through a drawer behind me.

I clawed at the duvet. It lifted.

He pulled the duvet corner back in place and smoothed the dark surface with his hands. Then he straddled me, lingering on his knees.

"You need t-to warm me up."

He held up a condom in its wrapper between two fingers, and raised his dark eyebrows.

That will get my temperature back up.

I nodded.

He broke the wrapper and rolled on the condom.

An hourglass figure appeared in the bedroom doorway. *Isabella.*

I remembered. She was there to return his security card, but his pants were in the living room. She gave me a thumbs-up. Then she mouthed something and looked at me, concerned.

She did it.

He was back on top of me, holding up his weight with his arms and hesitated, slumped his head. Light from the street caught his bare scalp, created a cone shape, concaving on his shoulder. His body heat loomed. My pelvis moved toward him.

I flicked my wrist at Isabella. *Get out of here before he sees you.*

He touched my hair. Scrunched it into his fist. Cold water trickled onto my neck.

"Close your eyes."

I did.

The music stopped.

"Stay still."

His torso pressed against mine. Heat. He helped me wrap my legs around him. His arms slithered around me and lifted my upper back off the bed. He held me in a tight cradle. Our damp skin collided, my cheek on his shoulder, and we rocked back and forth.

He prodded between my legs but couldn't enter. I shifted my leg to the side.

"Don't move," he commanded. He buried his face in my neck and breathed deeply.

We continued to rock together, back and forth. The scent of his cologne returned. My breathing got deeper, and my fingers flexed.

He let go abruptly. I fell and hit the duvet.

His knees competed for space between my legs. His tongue slid from my collarbone to my cheek.

I get it. I won't move at all this time.

He took my hands, folded them on my chest, then he entered me.

I felt him inside me, but no other sensation. He didn't make any noise—not even the air coming in out of his airways made a sound. The sheets and bed matched his silence.

When it was over, he left the bedroom. He returned in a

dark robe, dropped cash on the bed without looking at me, and left the room.

CHAPTER FORTY-TWO

"Get your frigid ass under a hot shower," Isabella said as she connected a USB key to my laptop.

"I'm fine." I pulled the hood of my sweater over my head.

"I warned you," she said. She took my hand, pressing her nail into mine. The flesh underneath my nail turned white. "Drink some water."

"I'm fine."

She retracted away from the laptop, filled a glass with water, and placed it in front of me.

"Can't believe you did that sober."

I would have slipped into hypothermia if I was drunk.

"Do I ask what happened before the necro session?" She pointed to my bandaged foot.

"Doesn't matter." I couldn't stand still, even with a bum foot. I rocked on my good foot and focused on the laptop.

"Maybe this will warm you up." Isabella grabbed her purse from the countertop and pulled out cash from a white envelope. "Here. You earned half."

"No." I pushed aside the cash. "He paid me."

She split the pile of bills and shoved half of it back my way. "Think of all the travel mugs made of recycled metal that you could buy. Cause you'll need new ones when the others fall apart."

"What's taking so long?"

"Chill, honey. I'm sorting the spreadsheet. It'll take a few minutes." She poked my ribs with a shiny fingernail. "You should have taken something from his fridge."

I tapped my good barefoot on the floor.

Her hands slapped her lap. "I'm not doing anything else until you take the money and order a damn pizza. Look at you. I could take a straw and drink from your neck." She scooped the dip above my clavicle with her thumb.

"Fine." I snatched the cash from the counter.

Isabella turned back to the laptop and straightened up. Her fingers flew on the keyboard.

I took out my phone, opened a food delivery app, and ordered a pizza.

I hovered nearby. She sorted columns with names, addresses, salaries, employee ID numbers and employment dates. The information changed so fast that my eyes couldn't follow.

"You're killing me," I said. "Tell me what all this means."

"Why don't you clean . . ." She ran her hands on the counter and inspected her fingertips which had collected nothing. "Nevermind."

"Isabella."

"Okay," she said. "These are all the schmucks that worked for Exempler and were terminated within three months of the assault. Employees in the New York, Boston, and U.K. offices."

There must have been sixty names on the list. "I thought the money transfer came from the Toronto office."

"It did. Don't shit your pants, okay." She clicked *Toronto* from the sort menu. "These are the terminated Toronto-based employees." The data on the spreadsheet disappeared to blank cells.

"That's why I don't want to show you yet. I need to think." She dropped her hands on the laptop, silver bracelets crackling.

"What about expanding the time frame?"

She nodded. "Maybe six months." She clicked the mouse.

Two names appeared with the revised criteria—Rebecca Lee and Heather Ferro.

My heart sank. I took a step back and pulled my hair from the roots.

"We'll go back to the employees from other offices," Isabella said. "I can talk to my cousin. Maybe she can trace flight records."

"You think he's from another office?"

"Could be. Toronto headquarters could have handled everything."

I gripped the edge of the kitchen island, lowered my head, and breathed deeply.

How are we going to repeat this ordeal in the UK?

"We're not there yet."

"If we Google the names, could you recognize him from the night it happened?"

"I told you. I was with a different group." She paused. "You have no idea how many times I think back to that night and wonder why I didn't turn my fucking head around."

"What are we still doing?" I asked. "We're done."

"We're stuck, not done. I understand if *you* believe getting fired is the only way to leave a company. There are other ways." She tapped her index finger over her lips. "What if he left the job another way?" Her fingers hovered over the keyboard before landing on the mouse.

"I thought you said he was fired."

"I did, and I think I'm right. I should have thought of this earlier. The company wouldn't record it that way."

She was right.

"Here." Her new search that captured employment end dates without a reason yielded three names. He was one of these three.

"I know you didn't see him that night, but I want to see them now," I said. "Google their names."

She didn't say anything, logged into her LinkedIn account,

and typed the first name in the search field, *George Therow*.

A picture of a man with white hair, a deeply wrinkled forehead and thick, round glasses appeared. He must have been in his seventies.

Really? She could have taken this guy out.

"Too old," Isabella declared. "Sandra doesn't do geriatric business. They're a liability. Ya know, could go any time."

"After tonight, I don't believe Sandra does any kind of risk assessment, just a strict dollar-for-dollar cost analysis." I folded my arms across my chest. "If they're willing to pay, she wouldn't say no."

She threw up her hands. "I'm telling you what I've seen for more than five years."

Isabella opened a second browser window. "This guy sounds familiar, though." She searched for the second name in Google Images. Several photos popped up, including a few that showed him in a wheelchair.

Next.

Isabella copied the third name into the search bar. She stopped before hitting *Enter*. Her eyes narrowed. "Son of a bitch!"

"What?"

She straightened her arms, smacking the countertop. "Holy shit."

"What is it?" I searched the screen. *I don't understand.* "Tell me." I turned my head away from the screen to face her. "What!" I squeezed her shoulder with gnawed nails.

"I know this guy. Felix Warren." She pointed to the screen. "You don't recognize the name?"

"No."

She opened *LinkedIn*, entered the name into the search field, but not Felix Warren. She typed Jon Warren.

CHAPTER FORTY-THREE

M y eyes zoomed in on Jon's photo. A styled beard hid his chin and neck and distracted away from his narrow, light eyes — eyes that pained when we spoke about Jackie.

"I know him," I whispered.

"You helped with the asshole's wedding."

"Daniel called him Jon."

She flipped back to the spreadsheet and revealed the *Middle Name* column. *Jonathan* appeared.

My words came out muted. "We went to his house. For the photo. He said he was her boyfriend. That she'd dumped him for another guy."

"That would be a ballsy move by Jackie to break Sandra's rules. No dating clients. Ever."

Isabella looked at the screen. "The guy is sick, but not stupid enough to tell you his real relationship with her."

That was it. Of course there was more to it. That's why Daniel got up in the morning that day. "The photo. Ex-lovers flashed to the PR world right before his wedding. That was never the problem, was it?"

"Not from Daniel's throne," Isabella said. "Jon probably saw it as a reminder of what he did. Thought his secret got out. He was probably losing it. That's why Daniel ran to circle jerk with him. Ya know, blamed it on a tech glitch, re-assured their dirty little secret was still safe."

Jon sat across from me. I drank his pain.

"At his house, they wanted to talk privately," I said. I gripped the surface of the counter. *This can't be the first time it happened. What are the chances of only my sister going through this?* "How long has he bought DMI girls for?"

"Could be since the business was launched or before since he knows Daniel."

This isn't adding up. "When we picked the photos for the website, Claudia didn't mention he was a client. She said he was an artist. Daniel's friend."

It was Jacob who told me Jon was a client. I thought he'd gotten his wires crossed.

Isabella tapped the screen. "His LinkedIn profile doesn't mention he worked at Exempler. Look." She scrolled down the job history section. She was right. His employment at Exempler had been omitted.

"Claudia knows what happened," I said.

Isabella shrugged. "Hard to say. Sandra wouldn't trust anyone with that information. I only know because I saw the aftermath."

"Sandra told me to stay away from Jon. Help with the wedding only."

"Yeah. She's cold, but she doesn't want us hurt. That's lost revenue." She pressed her fingertips together. "You say Daniel ignored Sandra's command that you stay away from Jon?"

I nodded.

"That's weird. You said Daniel threatened to send Jon after us. Including you."

Shit. Remember the story you told her. Fool. "I forgot. I was going to help with his business. The work was far in the future. Then I got fired."

She looked like she was about to say something but stopped. "Right." We stood in silence.

Daniel knew what Jon did. He offered me to Jon to make amends. I held my stomach, but it wouldn't comply. I ran to the sink and threw up the water I drank.

"Sweetie." Isabella rubbed my back.

I rinsed my mouth. "When does this guy get what he

deserves?"

"Slow down, honey. First things first. Get some rest. You've been through a lot, for you, in one night."

I knew it. She wanted to find out who it was so she could find out who the bad apple was. And then carry on, knowing her paycheck won't be at risk because she could avert a hospital stay.

"How are Jon and Daniel going to pay?"

"I know all signs point to Jon. But I'm not sure it's enough."

"What more do you need? He buys young women, lied about his relationship with Jackie, and left his job after he beat the shit out of her. And the payout. And Sandra told me to stay away from him. How is that not enough?"

"Chill. We have enough to warn the other girls. That's the most important thing."

It is not.

"I know he's married now," Isabella continued, "but trust me. These guys take a break, but they always come back."

She doesn't want him to pay. She never did.

"Hey, look at me." Isabella turned me around to a face that didn't look like it had been up all night. "I think we found the right one, but there's a chance it's a coincidence. If we beat the shit out of the wrong guy and Daniel, it creates a shitstorm for us, not for him."

I smacked my hands against the granite counter. *We are not having doubts. You are.* "What would convince you? If he fessed up after threatening to sharpen a knife on his balls?"

"And what if he doesn't?" Her face was hard. "We have his personal information." She pointed to the screen—birth date, address, SIN number. "I can access his credit card statements. If he was at the bar that night, that will be enough."

She didn't hear the doubt in her voice. Jon wouldn't get what he deserved. Not if it was up to her.

Isabella paused. "There's some-something I need to tell you." She scraped one fingernail with another. "It doesn't make any of this better, but I want you to know that forty thousand was transferred to Jackie."

But Jackie didn't have that in her account when she died. I overheard the estate lawyer say it was like a few thousand. She didn't have any investments or retirement savings. That would have meant she spent nearly the total amount in less than two weeks. I needed to look into her estate records. They were at home. I'd figure that out later.

"Go to bed," Isabella said. "You look like you went through what you went through tonight."

"Hillary was with Jon. Did anything happen to her?"

"Nah. Hillary would blab to the world." Isabella peered at me. "You look disappointed."

Not even close. Jackie went through what no one should go through. And the last person should be my sister. Anyone else, me, any of the girls at DMI. Not my sister.

"Worried. You said he'll be back."

She cupped her hand on top of mine. "We'll be prepared."

You're wrong. Wrong again.

CHAPTER FORTY-FOUR: JACKIE

Early October 2016
I was almost done. Custom-made gift bags with the latest iPhones, spa gift cards, and skin care products that cost more than Sandra's personal fitness trainer. Clients were going to love it. And I would be the one giving it to them.

I wore a Vince Camuto burgundy dress and Gianvito Rossi over-the-knee boots and black glossy tights to match the baskets. Clients had to remember me.

"Well done." Sandra entered the boardroom and lifted one of the stuffed wooden treasure chests to eye level.

It took her a long time to make her way to the boardroom. I sprayed my scent in the hallway over an hour ago—Chanel No. 5.

She lifted it higher, twisting the box to the side. "Perfect."

It wasn't perfect. The chocolate she ordered from Spain was missing.

"Tell Rupert to pack the car with the baskets by eight AM."

"You're on the seven AM flight tomorrow morning. Business class was only available at that time."

She swiped her fingertips over the top of the gift and examined them.

I smiled, knowing she wasn't going to find a speck.

"I'll deliver the gifts when I return," she said.

"I'll reschedule right away. Clients are expecting us tomorrow."

She froze her position in displeasure. But it didn't matter because I knew how to deal with Sandra by that point. Trying

266

to get her and Daniel to compete for me was idiotic. Trying to leave DMI through a boyfriend, even dumber.

The answer was right in front of me. I learned it in New York. But I didn't use it correctly because I didn't understand what it yielded at the time.

I gathered my hair in my hand and pooled it over my shoulder.

Her hips twitched under the taupe three-quarter sleeve length dress.

That was how I wore my hair. When she watched me with clients.

She would leave my side and close the boardroom door. She never looked me in the eye during those times.

I sat down with my back to her. She took my hair into her cool smooth hands, combing it with her fingernails. I leaned into her touch that altered between dominate and submissive and must have taken nearly a lifetime to master. She separated my hair into three pieces.

The first time I invited her to watch, I asked her to French braid my hair before the session. It took the spot held by Katey when we braided each other's hair as children. It was worth it. Watching her need for me grow with every pull and cross, I knew I was going to get everything I wanted. It was the only thing that distracted her from her business.

"The client was pleased last night," she said.

I felt her heat through the back of the mesh chair.

She leaned in, and we met through the fabric separating us.

I lowered my voice. "Were you pleased?"

She pulled my head backward. Her fingers writhed through the layering motions.

Every time I let her watch me with a client, my credit with her built. It was the only way she could be satisfied. And Daniel knew it. He couldn't give her what I could. And he hated her for it. He might have hated me more.

It was Sandra's mother's fault. Made her little girl watch Mommy perform those extras when it was time to clean the bedroom.

She moved faster, leaving the braid with loose strands.

"You were far away. Could you see well?" I asked her.

Her nails glided on my neck and curved to my shoulder blades.

She walked out a few times before I was done with the client. Before I figured out that I couldn't look at her.

The night before that changed. She was in the corner of the room, hidden by the dark. She needed to feel just as important as the client. The client laid down while I faced her with my hair wrapped around in front. I found the right angle. The streetlight crept in through the curtains. Two parallel lines marked my chest like paintbrush strokes. She stood up. Our eyes met in the dark. And she didn't leave.

In the boardroom, it was time to make her remember that moment. I took her hand beneath my dress, to the bra clasp between my breasts. I held her hand there, forbidding access to what she ached for most.

Her breath was quiet, off-beat. I traced her fingers carefully along the border of my silk bra until she couldn't bear it and plunged herself farther down until her hand was full of supple, vibrant flesh. She sunk her nails into me, and each one left their mark.

The pulse from her wrist raged against my chest. Her rose scent spilled over me like rain.

She bent at the waist, moved her grasp over to the other side, and encircled my breast with hands that knew hard labour. She squeezed hard, harder—devouring the generous mound. I threw my head back, the braid slinked over the chair, and our eyes met.

She collapsed on the back of the chair and broke from me. Then she stood, twisted the chair so that I faced the wall, and rushed out of the boardroom.

I swivelled and caught a glimpse of her long red waves flying off her back.

That was what I wanted her to remember. It made her want me for her. And when that happened, her eye was off the prize.

CHAPTER FORTY-FIVE

"Katey, I'm glad you called," Evelyn told me. "Haven't heard from you in a while."

"I tried you three times."

"Sorry I missed you this morning. What did you want to talk about?"

My hand went to my wrist and touched Jackie's gold bracelet—the one I found in her room in the home we once shared.

"My contract is over in Toronto." I stopped. "I want to leave, but I couldn't bring myself to come home. This is time sensitive. My apartment lease is up."

I wasn't lying. I needed to leave. There was nothing left for me to do. Isabella confirmed Jon used his credit card that night and lined up her cousin to beat the crap out of him. She didn't want me there. When she told me, I pictured brass knuckles beating Jon into Jell-O, but I felt nothing.

"Let's take a moment to reflect on your time in Toronto. You went to Toronto for work. And to find closure with losing Jackie." She paused, giving me a chance to jump in. I had nothing to say. "What are the positive experiences from your stay? First thing that comes to mind."

I found out how my sister died. You were all sold that a freak accident took her out. But you were all wrong, like I always knew. "I'm not sure."

"When did you last laugh?"

When Claudia flirted with clients by singing a lullaby. "With a friend I made here."

"That's wonderful. How do you spend your time

together?"

That's a loaded question. "My colleague, Elizabeth. We do girly things. Go to the spa, restaurants. You know, normal stuff."

"Reflect on your time together. The moments that brought you close, forming a connection."

"What does this have to do with me not wanting to go home?"

"Your last close relationship with a peer was your sister. It's natural you feel apprehensive about separating from Elizabeth. Recognizing the tools that built the friendship will help you build similar relationships moving forward."

Isabella is nothing like Jackie. Doesn't matter. Let Evelyn do her psychobabble bullshit. "Elizabeth didn't give up when I didn't want to be her friend."

"Tell me more about the times when you didn't seek her company."

She knew the answer. "When I couldn't do all the normal things. Like go out and drink alcohol."

"Besides alcohol, is there anything else that prevented you from participating in activities with Elizabeth?"

I took a deep breath. This was more than what I'd planned to reveal. "Elizabeth lives in the same building Jackie did. I can't go near there."

"Your dreams of Jackie and the condo. Have they continued?"

"Yes."

"Tell me about them."

I'll make an exception because maybe if I give her something, she can use it to get me home. "They're more vivid, more graphic." My phone was slipping out of my hand. This wasn't helping. "I don't want to talk about it."

"When you return, we'll continue to address the triggers. If there are any other stresses you can think of, write them down." Her words were blending into each other—that meant she was anxious. She knew what I was feeling was more than anxiety over separation from a friend. "Spend time with Elizabeth. Don't be alone. Book the ticket with someone else present."

I spun the gold bracelet around my wrist. "What if it doesn't work?"

"Call me. I'm always here. We'll discuss other options if our plan doesn't work out."

"There's no other way to address these triggers? I have to talk about my dreams?"

This is bullshit. Why am I even listening to her? If I listened to her in the first place, I would never have learned what happened to Jackie. "You weren't right about my sister. So don't tell me that talking about my dreams is the only way to get home."

"Katey, I want you to see someone in person. I have an associate in Toronto, Samantha Gold. She works downtown. Let me get the address. It's a beautiful modern building, faces a park on the north side."

She gave me the address. I typed it into my phone to estimate proximity from my condo.

But Samantha Gold wasn't the first business that appeared. The first business that appeared was what brought me there. And it was going to get me home.

CHAPTER FORTY-SIX

The sign said I'd found what I was looking for—Dr. Colin Catsbury, Certified Hypnotist, with the worst online reviews.

"I have an appointment. Victoria Stanton," I said to the girl with painted eyebrows sitting behind the algae-filled fish tank front desk.

"Right on time." She smiled. "As indicated in your online assessment, we ask first-time customers to settle before the session. How are you paying?"

I pulled out two hundred-dollar bills. From Saud.

"If you refer someone, you'll get fifteen off your next appointment." She handed me a receipt and led me to a narrow and deep office. More murky tanks filled with blue, orange, and yellow fish marked the corners of the room. "Make yourself comfortable. Dr. Catsbury will be right with you."

"The fish tanks need cleaning. Or a visit from animal services," I told her. She left quickly.

I made my way to dust-covered plastic blinds and adjusted them to block the sun screaming into the thirty-fourth-floor space.

A petit man with a blue sweater vest and a short gray-and-white beard entered. "Hello, Victoria. I'm Dr. Catsbury."

"Hi, Colin." I continued fiddling with the blinds and coughed as the dust spread.

He opened one arm towards the furniture. "Please make yourself comfortable."

I took a seat.

"Very nice to meet you. How did you hear about my practice?"

"Let's get started," I told him.

He pushed his thick-framed rectangular glasses further up his nose. "Your initial assessment indicates you're looking for help overcoming anxiety induced by a traumatic event. Tell me more."

My throat constricted. "I found my sister dead in her condo almost two years ago. I can't go back into the building."

He folded his hands and rested them on his belly. "I'm so sorry for your loss. How old was she?"

"Twenty-seven."

"Just horrible. Have you seen a grief counsellor?"

"Yes."

"Did your counsellor suggest hypnotherapy to supplement treatment?"

"I moved away from my therapist. I've had other successful experiences with hypnotherapy."

"May I ask why you previously used hypnotherapy?"

"Let's focus on why I'm here." I checked the clock on my phone. "We don't have much time."

"Of course." He crossed his legs, a high-reaching blue striped sock and black hair took over the raised leg. "Do you need to re-enter the condo building?"

I'd like to tell him that I felt handcuffed to this city, but I was holding the key. Evelyn concluded that my anxiety about Jackie's building was making my nightmares worse and that I needed to get them under control before they kept me from enjoying a girl's night out. I couldn't talk about it with Evelyn, and I didn't need to talk about it. I needed this clown to do his job.

"I'm an event planner. Events are held in the condo's commercial space. My job depends on being able to access the building."

"Have you tried to enter the building since your sister passed away?"

What do you think? "Of course not."

"How do you feel when entering the building is proposed?"

"Sick to my stomach."

He wrote a few notes on a pad of paper. "I'll explain the process. The goal of our first session is to gain a deeper understanding of your anxiety. I'd also like to speak to your therapist. Subsequent sessions will include forty-five-minute hypnotherapy sessions, using a number of techniques to change the negative association you have of the building."

"There is an event at the condo building tomorrow. I need treatment today."

"Unfortunately, hypnotherapy doesn't work that way. It will take at least a couple of sessions to determine which techniques you best respond to."

"I plan to speak about your services at the event tomorrow. It's on quitting smoking."

He stroked his beard. "A large conference?"

"Over six hundred people."

"I can't guarantee anything after one session."

I moved to the wide worn-out leather seat covered in strands of short black hair. I pulled a lever at the side of the chair. The chair reclined as my feet were raised to the level of my hips. "Let's get started."

He dragged a stool close to my chair. "I'm going to bring you back to the night your sister died in the condo. Can you describe the building to me? The entrance, lobby, condo unit."

I described it.

"If you become too distressed, the session will cease."

"I'm ready."

"Could you take off the bracelet? It's distracting you."

I looked down to see that I was twisting the gold circle around my wrist. I took it off and rested it on my thigh, with the engraved nine-digit number facing me.

He pointed to a corner of the ceiling. "Do you see the red square?" A square about the size of both my hands was painted on the opposite wall. "Focus on it."

I concentrated on the red square.

"Good. Let my words guide you." He drew them out like he was giving instructions to a child.

I took deep breaths, keeping my eyes on the red shape.

"Let the chair relax you. Melt into it."

He spoke slowly. "Relax your toes, ankles, feet, knees."

His uneven-pitched voice pushed my concentration on the red square harder.

"Focusing and relax your hips, chest, and shoulders. Good."

"Your neck, mouth, and eyes."

My legs felt cool, hard to move.

"Slowly, sink deeper."

My eyes felt heavy, wanting to close.

The red square popped out of the ceiling.

"Deeper. Slower."

The sound of pumping water through the fish tank dissolved.

I closed my eyes.

"There are glass, double-doors ten steps ahead of you. Walk toward them, counting each step. When you reach the doors, push them open. Count each step with me. Ten, nine, eight, seven, six, five, four, three . . ."

The door was held open by a guy carrying a hockey bag.

"You did very well."

I lifted my head from the chair, then slowly swung my body out.

"Based on your reception, another session is essential."

I got up, slowed by the lingering faux weight in the legs, and made my way to exit the room.

"We'll be in touch to schedule your next appointment," he called out. "Take some brochures for the conference tomorrow."

He rushed out to meet me as the elevator doors closed. " Wait until dark," he said as the doors slid closed.

CHAPTER FORTY-SEVEN

I'd walked for hours under the sun on the concrete sidewalk. When I lapped Jackie's condo building, a switch turned on. I wasn't sick or hyperventilating. I could only think of what was directly in front of me—a sidewalk crack, a pedestrian, an e-scooter whizzing by.

The pink and orange sunset hues in the sky were almost gone. It was time. I scanned the intercom names outside of the building until I found a name on the twelfth floor. With each resident, I cross-checked the name on Facebook until I found someone who looked around my age.

I waited for my feet to lead the way. They'd know first.

My feet came through and pushed me forward to catch the entrance door as someone exited. I didn't look like an intruder. I knew the building, the lobby, where the elevators were.

I knocked on Jackie's door.

"Yes?" A woman in a spaghetti-strap maroon cocktail dress answered the door. She seemed unreal, like she was some figure from a dream.

"Sorry to bother you. My friend Celane lives on this floor," I said. "She's running late. Do you mind if I use your bathroom?"

The girl scanned me while fingering her white pearl necklace.

"Celane is a sweetie, but not punctual. This isn't the first time she left someone waiting. As long as you're not drunk, you can come in."

"Thank you so much."

The woman opened the door wider and ushered me into Jackie's living room with new jade-green curtains. I stopped.

"The bathroom is this way."

The tea kettle boiled water. My heart drummed a steady beat. I clenched my teeth to the rhythm, two beats, one step, two beats, another step.

Something moved in the corner of my eye. It was an orange-and-white cat, scratching the arm of a beige couch. I listened to the breaking threads as claws dragged, snagging the fabric. The feline stared at me, stopped scratching but kept its paws on the couch, arms stretched. Then it ran into the kitchen on the other side of the island facing the oven and sink, out of sight.

Out of sight. In this small space.

I caught up to the new occupier of Jackie's space. She flicked on the bathroom light switch.

"Don't mind the clutter. I'm getting ready to go out." She left.

With eyes shut, I closed the door behind my back. When I opened them, everything was blurry. Vague, unsteady outlines of the fixtures appeared. I focused first on the vanity. I started from the bottom, like an upside-down waterfall shutting off, and four legs came into focus. Lines climbed, formed the cupboard, and circled for knobs. The white sink followed. Then the silver faucet, cylinder makeup case and a hair straightening iron.

The toilet, standing shower, and tiled floor appeared at the same time, like watching a photograph form in a dark room.

But the bathtub wouldn't come into focus. The rim of the tub was shimmering, like heat radiating off a sidewalk.

I took a step forward.

Jackie was under the water, almost at the surface. Her eyes were closed, her hair spread out and floating in hundreds of tendrils.

I leaned forward and grasped the edge of the tub with one hand. I wanted to get on my knees, but they locked.

I reached my arm out as her dark hair dissolved into the water. Her skin disappeared as water drops hit the still surface.

Please don't go.

I watched her vanish until the bathtub was empty.

I kissed my fingertips and touched the edge of the tub.

There was a knock on the door. "Are you done?"

How long have I been in here? The coloured city lights blared through the window.

I opened the door and met the woman at the threshold.

"You best get going." She peered over my shoulder.

"I'm done here." I switched off the light and turned around. I wanted to remember how this room looked in the dark.

Wait a minute. I stayed at the threshold. In the window, I saw the woman's reflection in the glass. The reflection was an opaque and dark shape, but her outline was clear. She turned, and I focused on her hairstyle—loose waves were gathered at the crown of her head.

I whipped around to face her, then looked back at the window and her reflection.

"Is something wrong?" she asked.

It can't be.

"Who else wanted to use your bathroom?" I asked.

She told me, giving me more of a description than I needed.

But deep down, I already knew long before today.

CHAPTER FORTY-EIGHT

"Ben, I have a favour to ask."

"Not a word in months," he accused, but his tone was from the same place where he laughed. "Tell me you're sick of the gas-guzzling SUVs and noise and are coming home."

"We'll have to catch up at another time."

His voice shifted to his business tone. "What's going on?"

"I need you to go into my parents' house and get something."

"Not what I expected." He paused. "Why can't your parents give it to you?"

"They're away for the week. I need it now."

It was true. My parents *were* away on vacation. But I would never ask them for it.

"I'm not breaking into your parents' house."

"You're not. I know where the spare key is. I'll text you the alarm code."

"This is illegal."

"You promised me that if I needed *anything* . . ."

Ben was silent.

"I'll tell them it's for work, and you're going to pick it up. They won't mind. They love you for everything you've done for me. Their friends get stuff from the house all the time when they're away."

He sighed. "You're asking me to steal from your parents."

"You don't have to take it out of the house. Just take a photo, and send it to me."

Please, Ben, please. I know I'm right, but I need your help.

"I'll think about it," he finally said. "If I were to agree, and it's not looking good, what would I look for?"

CHAPTER FORTY-NINE

She was aboard, according to the yacht's manifest. I'd already ventured there today. I crossed the third gangplank to board *Amore Ares*, a yacht suited to entertain five hundred passengers.

The sun would hover over the water a little longer. Then the boat would leave the harbour and sail out on the night waters.

As I circled the main deck of the boat, I ran my fingers along the expanded railing that the dancers I hired for tonight would use like gymnasts on a balance beam once the party got going.

It took time to circle the main deck in the heels I was wearing. She'd hear me. She'd come.

I stopped to admire the four-pedestal waterfall at the bow. The water shot up straight from a firehose hole and fell into the birdbath-shaped pool. It would be lit up at night.

She wasn't inside the dining room or the indoor center of the main deck. The tables were set with the décor I ordered. The black, white, and rouge colours matched the invitations I'd sent out. The table linens had changed. They were coal-black instead of off-white.

Any moment now, she'd hear me. My — Jackie's metal and wood heels — made a distinct sound. One that could not be forgotten, no matter how much time had passed.

I stopped and faced the water. Endless water, interrupted by an island with an airport. It was always windy by water, even on a hot day like today. The breeze was cutting through my long flowing dress, encouraging me onward.

When I felt her presence, my eyes stayed fixed on the horizon. She was coming from the upper deck, where the band would play. The party would start when the yacht was far out on the water. It was the perfect venue for tonight's main event.

The initial scent of roses cut off faster than usual. "I wasn't expecting to see you here," she said from behind me.

I turned around and stepped forward until we were an arm's length apart.

"I thought you were Isabella." She looked down at my feet.

Isabella isn't coming tonight. And she isn't the original owner of these shoes — you know that.

"Hello, Sandra."

She hiked the fallen strap of her off-the-shoulder, floor-length shimmery gold-coloured dress. It fell right back down to rest on her arm.

"You look beautiful." She eyed the package I held. "What is this?"

I moved closer to her. She stood her ground. I held up the cream-coloured box wrapped with a scarlet ribbon. "It was a gift for my sister, Jackie. I want you to have it."

The concave curve under her cheekbones deepened. She turned toward the water and rested her relaxed hands on the railing. The wind lifted her hair off her shoulders. She already knew I was Jackie's sister. Of course she did.

She took the box, placing it on the railing. She untied the ribbon with a single pull and lifted the flap. She draped the floor-length black dress closely against her. "It would have looked stunning on her."

"How long have you known?" I asked.

Her tone softened as if she was forgiving me. "Seems odd. I let you stay after the first time you tried to ruin my company. I let you pursue my husband. I felt bad for you. For what happened to Jackie. Then the interview happened."

She never felt bad for me. But she was right about one thing—I was always after her, or her company—same thing anyways. That was why I did those things, including her husband. It was such a relief that I could make sense of why I wanted him—it was never about him. I wanted her all along, to ruin her. I just didn't know why until I revisited Jackie's condo.

But she missed one more thing. At the time, I'd missed it, too. I thought it had nothing to do with me and her. I knew now. She'd find out soon. And she'd also learn what it meant not to forget.

"Why are you here?" she asked me.

I waited until the breeze carried her scent into my lungs. "I wasn't expecting you, either, the night my sister died."

She didn't move as the hair on her arms rose in the humid air.

"When I arrived, you moved around me. Who would have thought there were so many places to hide in a one-bedroom condo? You found them. Behind the curtains, the couch, the island."

She stayed focused on the water.

"You could have fled, but it wasn't enough," I continued. "You came to the bathroom because you knew I wouldn't take my eyes off my sister. You watched from the door as I pulled her from the water. It wasn't enough for you to watch her drown. You needed to know that it was too late. That your problem would never return."

We stood in silence, listening to the waves crash against the boat. I let her stay focused on the water.

"I left the party with everyone else that night. Ask them yourself."

"You came back. You knew I was coming and that the front door would be open. You came back to her home to let her know how you really felt about what she told you. You saw her fall beneath the water. Then you hid when you heard me."

I captured her focus.

"And why would I do that to my *favourite employee,* as her colleagues described her to the police? Ask anyone. I treated her like my own daughter."

"Jackie told you that night she was setting up her own business. A public relations firm."

Even as I said it now, Sandra looked the way I felt when I woke up from my dreams of Jackie.

I owed Ben the world for retrieving Jackie's estate files from my parents' basement. The papers confirmed she established a business in her name.

Her voice was steady, strong. "You have no proof."

"I have the business number of the company, Ontario Inc. eight-zero-four-two-six-zero-six-three-six. She already used the hush-money from Exempler to pay for start-up costs. Concealing a brutal crime complicates the noncompete clause in DMI employee contracts, doesn't it?"

Only inches of space separated us.

"What would the police think about the escort business that landed my sister in the hospital?" I whispered in her ear. "Be sure to mention your maternal tendencies."

She turned her back to me. "I did not kill her."

I walked around her and stopped at her side. Her eyes were glassy.

"Why have you not gone to the police?"

I took another moment to savour our time together. It had always been more than DMI. It started as a girl pleasing her customers after they watched her scrub the toilet. Daniel, Claudia, Isabella, even Christine and Hillary. We were all in her life to remind her what she no longer had to do.

I wouldn't experience the moment when all her reminders could no longer serve their purpose.

"There is an alternative to the police," I said. "A deal. The kind you have experience in negotiating."

She swallowed. "There's over two million in a vault, behind a façade in the change room," she said. "Cash and jewelry. I will give you the code."

I pulled out my phone and then gazed up, giving her permission to speak.

"Seven-five-two-zero-five-six."

I recorded the digits into my phone. "There's one more thing."

She waited.

"I want you to wear the dress tonight."

She strained the lace fabric at the shoulders between both hands. She nodded once. "Go. Guests will arrive shortly."

I memorized her hunter-green eyes drowning in wasted energy. And her scent — the nauseating stench of fear.

That's how I'd remember her. The way she started.

"Goodbye, Sandra."

Chapter Fifty: Sandra

Like sponges, the guests soaked up Sergei's words.

His performance could have been the campaign—gliding on a stage in a black Brioni suit, shaking vodka on the rocks in a glass with an ivory bottom in one hand, carrying a microphone in the other, and speaking with an accent so thick no one could make out half his words. They loved him. He made them feel like they were worthy of being there.

This event would put DMI on a new map. Companies would seek us out. No more bidding for contracts. The other PR firms wouldn't know what hit them. Their staff would come to me—competent staff that could finally replace the barnyard waste that was representing my company.

Sergei, your performance better be enough to make them forget about this revolting vodka.

"After one taste, you can guess what Ogon represents." He shook the metal ice cubes in the rocks glass and waited for the crowd to stop laughing.

They had the nerve to gag out loud. They needed a reminder what he was paying to have them here tonight. To eat this food and be amongst this company.

Sergei resumed once he had their attention again. "The easiest translation is *fire*. But it's not that simple. Where I'm from, Ogon is used to describe what you might call here, a way of life. A life that doesn't seek serenity. And never does it choose the easy way."

He walked along the border of the elevated stage. "The best way to show you what I mean is to tell you a story from when

I was a little boy. To get to school, I walked through the woods. Sometimes it was dark. I could take the route with a clear path, lit by the snow and with other people. Or, I could take the path where the tree branches scratch your face, and the roots trip you to the ground. And when you run, you see two small round circles flash near the ground." He pointed two fingers at his eyes, then stretched them out to the crowd. "Which path to take? It was never a question for me. That's how I've lived. Because taking the hard way is the only way to learn who you are."

The dining room became silent.

"When you drink my vodka, you think, this is crazy. My throat is on fire."

The crowd burst into laughter, four seconds long. That was enough.

"But then, you go back for more. And why is that?"

Not a sound from the audience.

"You're risking it all. It's what the core of our nature craves."

He shook the rocks in the glass, creating the only sound in the dining room.

"These days, weakness is encouraged. I hear it all the time — relax, slow down. Doing nothing tells you that is all you are. Ogon is a reminder not to waste what you're given. It's only when we reach our breaking point and then go further that we know what we can do."

He raised his glass in a toast. "Ogon"

This was it. They would either fall for this repulsive substance like they had for him or would move to the upper deck to hide their shameful presence.

The crowd raised shot glasses in unison. "Ogon!" everyone cried. Down it went.

Faces scrunched. *I told you not to do shots unless you have a mixed drink to cancel the straight vodka taste.*

Cheers erupted on standing feet. Glasses clinked.

289

He did it. Son of a bitch pulled it off.

Sergei turned to me, arms lowered and spread. "I want to thank Sandra, Daniel, and their team at DMI for giving me and the most beautiful company here tonight." He grabbed two vodka bottles by the neck, one in each hand. The audience laughed. "Let's see how you all do after a few more."

More laughter followed. Only he could pull it off using insults as a sales pitch.

The frosted bottle with thread-thin twining flames, my selection, was the best feature of the product.

"Sandra, stand up."

I slid my chair back and rose to four hundred and eighty-seven guests, including seven of my staff seated at forty tables. Ten guests cancelled last-minute. Three were still unknown. The audience roared with applause.

Daniel put his bread roll down—crumbs spilled over his bread plate. He rose, half-sheltering me from the crowd. He wore the wrong suit.

"As you enjoy dinner, I'm making rounds," Sergei said. "Each table will take a shot with me to celebrate this fine drink."

More cheers.

Daniel's ivory cufflinks clinked my plate as he reached over me and grabbed an oyster.

I scanned everyone who mattered at the table to ensure they did not witness Daniel's sloppy behaviour.

Daniel leaned back and snapped his fingers at Claudia, sitting on my other side. "Do a walkabout."

"I just did one."

I looked her way.

"But no problem," Claudia squeaked in her shameful high-pitched tone.

"Is there something I should know?"

Claudia's voice rose another octave. "No, all good."

A lie. "You can go home now."

"But you need me to . . ." Claudia motioned to brush hair behind her ears, even though her hair was pulled up. "The interns saw Katey earlier today."

This is nothing to worry about. "I saw her, as well."

"What was she doing here?" Daniel slurped the oyster shell. "Begging for her job back?"

No, that is not what happened. And that whore got it wrong, too. I am the only one who knows. And it will remain that way.

The night Jackie died, I returned to her condo after the ungrateful bitch told me about the PR company she established. A clone of DMI, of *my* company. Specializing in crisis management, social media campaigns, branding, event planning, and media training. Unbelievable—she couldn't come up with one original service.

She wanted to let me know what she was taking from me. She started to plan on the night everything changed. That night, I knew something was going to go wrong. *I wasn't there.* Daniel promised his silver-spooned prep boy Jon our best girl for the night—Jackie. She was the one he had his filthy eyes on since day one. I never allowed it. He was prohibited from going near any of my girls. Not even allowed access to the loose twins. But Daniel never learned *no*, even when it didn't apply to him. He waited until I was out of town.

I returned. My prodigy embodied what *no* meant to Daniel. Black, blue, and crusted. I sank to my knees and begged her to go to the police. But Jackie refused. Instead, she asked me to sit on the bed and hold her underneath the bleach-white hospital blanket that was stained crimson red. She told me she wanted to protect me and the business I'd bled for. She said involving the police would have meant an investigation, and that would ruin everything and harm me more than Jon. She told me to make Jon's law firm pay up. And to never talk about it again. There was tape on her hand to hold the IV tube in place. Then she squeezed her hand on top of mine.

I did what she wanted and more. I earned two million in hush-money from Exempler over two years, far more than what Jackie asked for. I could not believe I got that much out of them, a top criminal law firm. It was not the first time I learned image construction was a far more useful skill than memorizing legislation.

I had been negotiating with Exempler all night and returned to the office ready for an eighteen-hour workday. And there was Jackie, spending the money before she knew it was settled.

I should have known. She always wanted what I had — my clothes, my car, the food I ate, the company I surrounded myself with. And I favoured her. I gave her far more than top pay. I shared behaviour and etiquette tricks Daniel's old-money grandmother taught me. I invited her instead of Daniel to VIP events. She flourished. The girl with nothing but stunning looks brought in more clients than all the other girls combined. And she brought the clients that Daniel originally recruited and lost, back to me.

She found my shame — I failed to protect my girls. She was waiting for that day to come and reveled in it. I hesitated to *ask* her one day why she was printing client contact lists. She said she was organizing DMI's top clients in a way that would make me proud. I told her she was the only one who made me proud.

But it wasn't enough. She had my love, my influence, and my protection. And she wanted out, while living a kept life off my back.

She played it well. If her PR firm had taken off, she would have hung the assault over my head every time we competed for a client. I'd have no choice but to back down and only submit proposals for contracts that she did not want.

I left Jackie's condo that night. Walked around the block. I did not have the words yet.

It was so cold out. I refused to put my coat on.

Isabella saw me from the window of a restaurant. She could not leave me alone and followed me back up to Jackie's condo. I would never forgive her.

I knew Jackie's sister was coming, that her flight had been delayed. The door was unlocked. Jackie thought I was her sister and heard me enter the bathroom. I told her starting her own PR firm was in violation of her contractual obligations and that I would see her in court.

She threatened to go to the police with the assault. I told her to go ahead, go the police. *See how quickly your business grows when it comes out you exploited your sexual assault to advance your career.*

She was livid, screaming and thrashing at the water. She told me the DMI girls would rally against me and go public that I forced them to please my husband and our clients. I told her to go ahead.

And I was ready to leave. But then, she made the next move. And I was not ready for what happened next. She leaned back into the wall of the porcelain-white bathtub, squeezing her hair over her shoulder. "I hoped it wouldn't come to this," she said. "You're right. I'm not going to the police about the assault. That might scare my clients. But I will still give them a call with a question. Is it illegal to accept money from drug smugglers and send them fake invoices?"

That time, I still did not have the words. Nor did I give myself time to think. I went for her. Before I got there, she stood up. She stood too quickly and slipped. She hit her head on the edge of the tub and disappeared under the water.

She was gone.

I could not see anything. I was bombarded by things that did not matter at that moment — eating a small bowl of plain spaghetti as a ten-year-old girl, wearing the same baby blue lace-trimmed dress every day to school, borrowing Daniel's aunt's wedding ring on our big day because he had lost mine.

I did not know what happened. When I could see again, my hand was on Jackie's head, holding her under the water. Isabella was there. She screamed and pulled me away.

Isabella was about to call nine-one-one, but I told her to think of her family. And she did. Then she left me and Jackie alone one last time.

I sat on the floor, listening to the bath bubbles pop.

Then I heard someone at the front door. It had to be her sister. I hid. I could not be seen there. Katey should have found Jackie right away, not searched the bloody closet. If that stupid bitch had gone to the only room with a light on, Jackie would still be alive.

I looked up from my plate and watched the lilies suspended in a vase of water on top of the table. They stared back. Three white lilies stood with a gentle curve through the long green stems in a tall oval vase. The petals spilled toward me as if they were listening.

"She is moving home. Did not want to leave on poor terms," I told Daniel.

"Did she forget how to use e-mail?"

"She likes the water."

"Good riddance."

Just like her sister. She came to steal from me.

My mistake was keeping her on after I secured this contract. She got the better of me when she pitched to AleAngels. I thought, *she is using me, I should do the same.* Then no other invitations to pitch came. Time passed. I waited and was humiliated on a live broadcast.

Daniel, stop eating like a cow.

The summer salad was meant to remind guests of the season that we were in—colourful, light, and cheerful. My favourite. The salad was not an invitation to ruin the best season of the year.

My eyes veered back to the lilies. I saw why Katey selected this display — the flowers looked like a body preserved in liquid. *She did this to me.*

"And Isabella?" I asked.

Claudia almost raised her phone above the table. "She hasn't returned my calls or texts."

Isabella did not pass on high-priced client opportunities. "Did she have a family event?"

"I can't access her schedule for some reason," Claudia whined.

I got up with my mixed drink, lifted the side of my dress and weaved around ten tables to join Sergei at the other end of the dining room.

"Ogon!" he shouted. My guests echoed his toast before downing shots.

They cheered, congratulated themselves, and formed a circle.

"Where is your shot?" he asked me.

I raised my tall, red-tinted glass. "I would like to celebrate with you until the end of the night."

Sergei moved closer to me. "Everything is so beautiful. It's almost perfect."

"Almost perfect. Whatever is wrong?"

"Look at the middle of the table."

Christ. The oversized vase was filled with water. Olive glass pebbles sat on the bottom. No flower. And no one on my team had noticed. *How did I not notice?*

At the adjacent table, the lily was in the vase. And the lilies were in the vases at the other nearby tables, as well.

It was only one table. Still, unacceptable. My girls would explain this by dawn tomorrow.

"My apologies. How embarrassing. We have never missed one."

"One? Turn around."

The table on the outer edge of the dining room was missing a lily. The one behind it also held an empty vase.

"Excuse me." I lifted my dress and tracked the tables lining the west window. Two tables without lilies. *How did this happen?*

I followed the trail.

Three tables were missing centrepiece flowers.

I rushed forward, hoisted my dress higher. Four.

Another one. Five.

I stopped at the bulky imposition in front of me. *What is he doing here?*

"Sandra."

He placed his wretched lips on my face.

"Hello, Jon."

CHAPTER FIFTY-ONE: JACKIE

Mid-October, 2016

Crouched on the balls of my feet like Gollum, I didn't move an inch. My earring stabbed the back of my head as I pressed against the wall of Daniel's private room at the bar.

A sneeze crept. I licked the roof of my mouth, and it was gone.

I plugged my other ear to better hear what they were talking about. The music hadn't started playing in the bar, but the noise from the happy hour drunks was getting louder.

"We look forward to doing more for you," Daniel told someone from the sketchy trucking company. "As you expand."

I would have done whatever anyone and everyone at the bar wanted of me if it meant deleting the memory of the last time I met with Daniel and the company on the other side of the wall. Daniel still made them look like gentlemen.

It would never happen again, I thought, as long as I could get the right dirt. Then I could make a clean break and have enough leverage to keep the distance I wanted. At least, the closest thing to clean at DMI.

The first thing I was gonna do was book our flight to Fiji. Business class. Katey always wanted to go there—warm water, palm trees, sun, heat. The opposite of all her likes. I never understood it, but she always dreamed of things she was afraid of.

My thigh muscles contracted, and I pressed my fingertips to the floor for balance. It wasn't a good room for private talk.

There was plenty of space above and below the wide sliding barn-style doors for sound to escape.

The shaking rippled to my knees. *Don't fall*, I warned myself, I was so close.

"We are happy with your services. The way things are," someone in the room said.

"It won't stay this way when we're audited. It needs to be public, something that's seen. At least mark your trucks," Daniel said.

"We don't want attention. We'll be searched. If that happens, then there will be no business."

I knew it! I didn't know what was in the trucks, but it wasn't mangoes that would get them searched at the border.

"What does Sandra think?"

They stopped talking. Didn't matter, my work was done. My bones cracked as I jumped to my feet and dusted off my hands. And that was my first mistake. I victory-lapped outside the door—bent at the waist to one side, then the other, rolled my head in half circles. I repositioned the slit in my dress to the front and was ready to move on now that I had everything I needed to do so.

I took one step forward, and was pulled back so fast my feet didn't land on the floor until I was in the private room I'd been spying on. The door slid shut behind me.

I screamed and dug my nails into whatever flesh wasn't mine.

The back of my head hit the wall with a smack. Daniel. I almost called for Sandra, but I remembered that she wouldn't hear me. She wasn't in the city.

His hand slammed the wall next to my ear. "How long were you out there?"

His cologne-infused bourbon blocked my airways.

"Go to hell," I yelled and tried to duck underneath his arm.

"What did you hear?" His other hand slammed the wall. I

was trapped between his arms.

"I'm not interested in anything you have to say." I ducked under one of his arms.

He pulled me back. We were so close that his face blurred into a heat-emitting bronzed mass.

Our chests rose and fell out of sync. I tried to make myself puke all over his too-tight Tom Ford suit.

He didn't care that I was eavesdropping — it wasn't the first time. But things had changed between us. Sandra told him I was off-limits to his clients. And even better, she told him why. When she told him, I knew because he could never face anyone who defeated him.

"What will Sandra think?" he asked. "Why don't I call her now and ask?"

I felt my lips stretch across my teeth. "Tell her. She'll take the next flight home. To be with me and her client." Still less than an inch away from him, I focused on the space in front of his ears and visualized the nervous blood rushing to his temples. "Sandra will call you when we're done."

His arms still caged me in as his eyes drilled into mine. I opened my eyes wider.

His breath roared. He bent his elbows, and I flung my hands in front of my face. He pushed off the wall and sighed. His shoulders fell, then he clapped his hands once.

He took his phone from his back pocket.

"Girls like you get what they want," he said to me, his tone flush with amusement.

"Remember that more often." I turned to make my exit. The door wouldn't slide open, and I jiggled it with one hand, then added my other. I pulled the vertical bar and fiddled to find the lock. It was dark. Nothing moved.

"The party is just getting started." He grabbed my wrist and forced me to turn around.

"Don't touch me."

The door on the other side of the room slid open, and a broad figure entered. He came closer. It was one of Daniel's douchebag friends—they all had the same desperate ivy league haircut and just-shaved look. He was one of Daniel's friends who used Sandra like a rag doll as a teenager. This asshole was always at our parties. Creepy as fuck. His hands always found their way to the you-didn't-pay-for-that-zone. And then the jail zone, when no one was watching. But Sandra found out, and then he went quiet, but not away.

What the fuck was Santa on steroids doing here? I tried to make way to the exit again, but Daniel held me by one arm.

"You wanted a client tonight, right?" Daniel asked me. "Remember my friend Jon? He's all yours." He turned to Jon. "You've liked her for a while." Then he turned back to me. "You're right, as always. Sandra wouldn't approve. But Sandra isn't here."

Daniel tossed me out of his grip.

Jon eyed me up and down, opening his mouth, small teeth razored over his bottom lip. *I'd rather take a wire sponge as a client than spend a night with him.*

It was time to get out. I sprinted toward the door. "Get off of me," I shouted as Daniel grabbed me and dragged me back to the center of the room. He let go and pushed me into Jon's chest.

"Get away from me," I screamed. He closed one arm around my waist, and that was more than enough to keep me where he wanted.

"I kept my promise to my wife that I wouldn't lay a finger on you," Daniel said on his way out. "You two have fun. Don't go too easy on this one. I'm talking to both of you."

"Don't touch me," I yelled at the beast suffocating me.

"Easy. I don't bite," he mocked.

I pushed, slapped his barrel-chest and tree-trunk arms, and clawed at his skin. He held me tighter.

I raised my hand, but he grabbed it and twisted it behind

my back. He laughed and closed his other arm around me. He stood as still as stone as I flailed like a rabbit caught in a trap. The more I struggled, the harder he crushed me into him.

Stop, I told myself. Remember what Isabella taught you — violent clients want you to fight back. Don't react, and neither will they.

Everything in me wanted to spit in-between his eyes that sat too close together, but I listened to Isabella and stopped moving.

He placed his hands on my hips, gripped hard, then moved them upwards like he was trying to burn me with my clothes. He lifted me in the air by my armpits. "Would the camera help you smile? You didn't seem to mind posing with me in the summer."

I stifled my cries, but not because I was in pain. Not yet.

The amusement he carried in his eyes was gone. He lowered me to eye level, stretched out his tongue and licked my cheek from my jawline to my eye.

He set me down on a bar stool, stood in front of me, smashing into my knees, and lifted my chin. I looked at the ceiling.

"Cat got your tongue?"

I tried to read the labels on the bottles behind the bar. *He's going to get bored*, I told myself.

His hand closed over my jaw. I kept my eyes on the alcohol bottles. He directed my face away from his, released me with a discarded toss and clicked his tongue. "Can't believe they get the most for you."

He walked behind the bar, and my chest heaved.

"Want a drink? I'll make you whatever you want."

I tilted my head downward to meet him. "Make two. One for you and another to shove up your ass."

I heard glasses clink. "I'll make you a Cosmopolitan." The sound of liquid running into a glass came after.

I thought of Sandra and what she would do when she found out about this. The Sandra today, and not the teenage cleaning staff Daniel and Jon still saw.

Two pointy black leather shoes slipped underneath mine, and I wished the floor would crack and he would disappear into the ground, like a piece of shit does.

A full martini glass with two olives was set down on a table next to us.

"I've offered you many drinks," he said. "You accepted, then moved on to the pretty boys."

He lifted my chin with one finger and narrowed his eyes. "Do you enjoy humiliating me?"

My neck stiffened.

"Share one drink with me. Then I'll consider your debt repaid. I'll help you."

What happened next was difficult to remember clearly. I was on the ground, surrounded by the smashed martini glass. The room rang with a high, static pitch. I clutched my ear, it was warm. I hovered my hand in front of my face and twisted it until the red liquid reached my wrist.

Then I blinked and couldn't see.

I scrambled to feel the ground surrounding me. My hands throbbed, and my legs were wet with cold and warm sensations. I told myself I was okay.

He came into my view. His features were blurred, but I could see him grow and then tower over me. His feet threaded my legs.

"What do you want?" I shuffled, my hip ground into the glass shards.

He crouched, placed one knee on the floor, like a man did when he was proposing, and picked up a piece of broken glass shaped like a triangle. "My initials" — he lifted my dress, circled my inner thigh with his fingers, and traced F-J-W — "carved here."

My free hand trembled violently — the other hand pressed my dripping wet ear.

I took the glass triangle from his hand, and hovered it over

302

my thigh, right where he wanted the inscription. I shifted my dress up high, exposing much more than I needed to. He watched, and I watched him. He licked his lips. I swung my wrist back, leaped forward, and plunged the glass into his chin.

Blood flew down his neck, the fall not slowed by his chin.

I got up as vomit hosed through my mouth. I limped toward the unlocked door. I was almost there.

My knees hit the floor first. I screamed as I was dragged backward. My nails clawed at the floor, but there was nothing to grip. The glass bits pierced the skin beneath my dress — my thighs, stomach, and chest.

He flipped me around. I kicked. He hooked my legs in the crook of his elbow. He lifted his foot, the sole of his shoe suspended in the air.

Then the door opened. A loud noise came through. I knew I would be left alone on the ground. Everything flashed into a sheet of white, then faded to black.

Chapter Fifty-Two: Sandra

"Thank you for having us tonight," Jon said.

I did not invite you to the most important event I have ever thrown.

"Claire and I are having a great time."

"Enjoy yourselves."

Claire did not move. Spoiled bitch. I approached her and her lavender cowl-neck dress that clashed with her dark hair. We kissed, and I turned my back to Jon.

I leaned to him. "You are glowing. The thick beard is working."

His face, half-hidden by hay-coloured facial hair, turned the colour of the napkins.

I returned to my table. "Why is Jon Warren here?" I asked Claudia.

"He's on the guest list. I thought you or Daniel invited him."

"I didn't invite him," Daniel said as the fillet mignon settled between his teeth.

I went over the list again last night. There was no way I would have missed that disease.

"Find out when he was added," I told Claudia.

A hand reached my lower back. "Take a seat. Relax," he told me.

I remained standing. This was Daniel's fault. Because of him, every time Jon came up, we had to treat it like an Amber Alert.

My husband waited until I left town to teach me a lesson.

It was not the first time. *I* was not the first time.

So I protected Katey from Jon, even though I knew why she had come to my company.

I had to use all my discipline to stop myself from telling Katey what I did with the rest of Jackie's payout money. Afterall, Exempler still owed a debt. And DMI deserved a fresh start when Jackie died — new furniture for the office and my home, new clothes, shoes, and jewelry for the dressing room. I even replaced the office floors she walked on. I chose stone floors to remind myself that we saw the same thing when I looked down, and she looked up from her new home.

My focus retreated to the tables with the missing lilies. *The empty vases should be tossed overboard with that repulsive dress Katey wanted me to wear.* The dress was at the bottom of the lake by now — where they both belonged.

"Go to the bathroom. You don't look good," Daniel said. "I'm going up top."

"Stay for dessert."

"The band won't wait." He got up, tossing his napkin on the chair, and breadcrumbs spilled on the seat. I picked up the crumbs, one by one, and folded them into the napkin.

I rose, and Claudia followed but sank back down when our eyes met. "Watch the dining room," I said. "Report to me if anything is off."

The fresh air was all I needed. My guests would not let me pass without gushing my name and complimenting my work.

My guests cleared the dining room, creating a bottleneck on the stairs to the upper deck.

There was a line coming out of the women's bathroom. A long line. There must have been ten people waiting on the deck. *This is not good.*

I passed the line and entered the bathroom. "Pardon me, ladies. I am touching up my makeup."

I applied lipstick matching the colour of my hair and used the bathroom mirror to survey the space. Horrible retching came from the stalls behind me.

Sergei and his shots.

The second round was louder. I turned to the women with too much glitter on their eyelids standing next to me. "I will have water brought. Would you like some?"

They smiled at me. "Yeah. You're the best, Sandra."

"Anything you need."

I exited as Claudia hastened toward me.

"Go get water for these guests," I said.

"Okay." She bounced from one foot to the other. "The captain wants to speak with you. He says it's urgent. People are sick."

"Did you ask the captain if he has attended a party before?"

"Uhh."

"He should know better than to set off an alarm at this type of occasion. You deal with him. I have guests to attend to."

She hurried off in a zigzagged path.

I proceeded up the stairs to the upper deck. What lay ahead was better than I imagined. The dancers on the railings were radiant in red, yellow, and white bejewelled, one-piece bathing suits. They twirled, did splits, tossed batons, and flipped over one another like varsity cheerleaders.

A crowd congregated around the bar. Guests pushed past one another for another drink and crowded the stage, jumping to the band's music.

A model dressed in a black sequined dress offered me a mixed drink.

I moved closer to her. "Ensure those waiting at the bar are being served. Let the other staff know."

"Of course."

"Thank you."

I spotted Shane Eglinton, the CEO who would pay any price to secure his success. And he was coming over.

"Sandra, what a lovely evening."

"Shane." We exchanged kisses. "Thank you for coming."

This man had said no more than two words to me before to-night, even though we have attended the same engagements for years.

"I'm impressed," he said, raising his drink.

I scanned his attire while he scanned the deck. This was what a smart man looked like. He showed up wearing a Dsquared2 suit. A Toronto brand would prop up the Toronto-based vodka we were selling.

"The band is second to the gut-twisting juice, of course."

I laughed, inching closer to him. *It is coming.*

"We're launching a new clothing line. A higher-end line. We're in talks with Holt Renfrew, Nordstrom, the Bay. I'd like you to come in and chat with us."

"I'd love to," I said.

He turned before I could continue.

"Sandra, I need to speak with you." The captain with my useless manager approached me from behind. *She knows who I am talking to.*

"Excuse me for one moment," I said. Shane was already gone.

I marched to the railing. The captain and Claudia shuffled my way. "Ma'am," the barely five-foot-five sailor began, "many guests are ill. The bathrooms are full. They're throwing up overboard into the water."

"These few instances are unfortunate. Is there any damage to the yacht?"

"No damage, ma'am. But these are not a few people. Look." He pointed to the main deck below. A dozen bodies were lined up with their heads slumped over the rail. "This is food poisoning. We must head for shore."

"Cut the night short because your crew overserved a hand-ful of guests." I almost broke into a sweat at the thought of ending the night early because of that incompetent moron.

"She's right. It's fine," Claudia screeched.

"Ma'am, I have a responsibility. These people require

medical attention."

"What are you getting paid for the night?"

"Ma'am, I could lose my licence."

"I will pay whatever you make in a year. The cruise stays on schedule. Understood?"

The captain looked away, then back at me, and nodded.

"Keep an eye on him," I told Claudia.

She turned to follow him and smacked into a stone pillar with flowers resting on top. *Idiot.* The thin cylinder vase secured to the pillar took more out of the clumsy fool than vice versa.

I inspected the vase for dirt from Claudia's face. It held only a single red and a single yellow lily. *There should be more.* "Why are there only two flowers?"

"I-I don't know." She squinted, rubbing her nose. "I checked them earlier. Everything looked fine."

Something was not right. "The centrepieces in the dining room are missing lilies."

Claudia scanned the deck. "Look, that one and that one," she said. "They have lilies."

"Check all ninety-six arrangements on the main floor and upper deck. Tell me how many flowers there are in each vase."

"There aren't ninety-six. Maybe half that. I counted earlier."

"How many are there? There should be ninety-six. Who changed the order?"

"I-I don't know. Isabella is ignoring my calls."

A guest stumbled into Claudia, bent over at the waist and threw up on her. Claudia shrieked as the liquid and chunk mix slid down her sapphire-red coloured silk dress. She lifted her hand—it hung from the joint. Pink chunks dripped onto the deck.

She could not have done this. Impossible. She left the yacht right after I saw her. "What time was Katey here?"

"Uh." Claudia looked down at her soiled dress that sagged between her thighs. "You saw her."

She is hiding something. "Did you see her?"

Tears mounted in her eyes. "Yeah."

I grabbed her by the shoulders. "What time? Answer the question."

"This a-afternoon."

I did not see her until the evening. "What was she doing?"

There was a splash, followed by shrieks, on the other side of the boat. The dancers were on the railing, but they stopped performing.

Claudia's eyes widened, showing a patchwork of stretched blood vessels. Her hand covered her mouth. *No, you do not get to be sick until you tell me what the fuck happened.* I grabbed her by the ear. "What did she do?"

She screamed. "Sh-she was in the kitchen. With the flowers."

The deck vibrated from panicked footsteps.

Lilies are poisonous. The salad had red, yellow, and white petals in it.

The music stopped. The dancers jumped off the railing.

I let go and looked at the empty dance floor, now dotted with red, brown, and black puddles. Bodies flooded the stairs. Some stopped to take photos with their phones. *No, stop. This can't get out.*

Nausea hit. *It's not nausea.*

The upper deck was cleared, and my guests had dropped to their hands and knees, sinking in fluid highlighted by the red and yellow lights from the stage where the band performed.

More screams.

Daniel. I need to find him. I ran over to the bar, weaving around curled bodies and pools of vomit. My stomach lurched. I stopped, leaned over, and clutched the agonizing pain.

I heard cries and screams. *This can't be happening. It's a bad dream. I'll wake up. I always do.*

A cold hand touched my back. "She blackmailed me," Claudia cried. "I'm sorry. I didn't know what she was doing."

I landed my wrist on my mouth, right in time to catch the blood. "My dinner plate. It had my name on it."

She nodded and used her wrist to wipe the new colouring off mine.

I removed one arm from my stomach—it felt like a fishhook was being dragged through my intestine.

I shuffled forward. My right knee wouldn't bend. My focus stayed on the ground. The bottom of my dress was soaked and torn. I saw ivory cuff links and then his body in a fetal position on the ground.

I dragged one leg behind me until I collapsed and continued to crawl towards him on three. I rolled him onto his back. His lips were covered in foam. I felt his neck. His pulse was weak.

I got to my feet. In the bright light, I saw the deck covered in bodies.

I'd been there before.

I felt a stabbing pain in my chest. I fell. I closed my eyes and heard another splash and one last scream.

CHAPTER FIFTY-THREE: ISABELLA

Images and videos of the vodka launch went viral on TikTok and Instagram. The shot of the dancer with a fiery baton falling into the crowd and engulfing a man wearing a tuxedo into flames had the most hits.

What have you done, Katey?

I turned up the volume on the TV to hear the news coverage. Whatever Katey slipped me that induced a twenty-four-hour coma was a dream compared to what she brought to the yacht party.

"Three are confirmed dead—Daniel Maile and Sandra Maile, the owners of the Public Relations firm who were hired to run event, and another party attendee, Felix Warren," a female anchor intoned. "Police are treating the deaths as homicide."

What have you done? I covered my face with my hands but peeked between her fingers to watch what was supposed to be the event that cast a safety net around me for years to come.

"Over a hundred people who attended the event are in hospital from food poisoning. Police suspect foul play," the newscaster continued.

"Dr. Emmett Andersen, a poison specialist, has joined us. Dr. Andersen, we've heard unconfirmed reports that calla lilies were found in the salad served on the ship. Have you ever seen lilies cause death before?"

"Erin, I've only seen evidence of small animals dying from ingesting calla lilies or lilies of the valley," the expert said. "Lilies, despite their common use at special events, especially weddings, are poisonous plants. The medical condition of the guests likely became exacerbated because they were out on the lake. Accessing medical aid on the water is challenging."

"Based on your experience, if the lilies are not the cause of death, what else could be?"

"It's too early to say. The coroner's examination will determine that. There are a number of poisons that are easy to access and easily disguised in drinks and food."

This is my fault. I begged Sandra to fire Katey from the get-go, before she ruined everything—for me, my family, all of us. Sandra wouldn't because she wanted me to investigate, get close to her and find out what Katey knew to assess the threat. I told her no good could come from the girl whose sister died while working for her. And I still tried to get rid of her—I didn't send any proposals her way or bring her out with clients. No recruitment, no future at DMI. But it wasn't enough, and I failed to do what needed to be done. Sandra, as usual, was blindsided by the opportunity when Katey won *this* contract. She kept Katey around.

When Sandra finally came to terms with the fact that Katey wasn't there to bolster DMI sales, it was too late. When I visited Katey at her apartment, it was clear as day that she wasn't going anywhere. She came for answers, so I gave her one. And she deserved to know half the story. The knowledge benefitted me, too—I wanted to know who could put me out of commission and into debt. I gave her someone to blame. I thought she would accept the discovery with pride, find closure and leave. Then things could go back to the way they were.

Knock, knock.

I rose, made my way to the door, and peered out the peephole. No one was there. I opened it. A gym-sized duffel bag sat on the floor outside my door.

I grabbed it, shut the door, and placed the bag on the kitchen counter. I unzipped it and pried the flaps open. My jaw dropped. The bag was full of stacks of cash.

What on earth?

I checked the side compartments and found a sealed white envelope. I ripped it open.

Dear Isabella,

Thank you for everything.

Katey

I squeezed the letter against my chest with both hands. When I was ready to let go, I reached for my phone and called my little sister to tell her I was sleeping over tonight. I'd always have my sister.

CHAPTER FIFTY-FOUR

A dinosaur. A bunny. This wasn't so bad, observing the cloud shaped from a hammock beneath a coconut tree in Fiji. The long leaves were shaped like swords. And when I blew smoke from my joint, the leaf became a hose putting out a fire. *Cute.*

I didn't regret not sticking around to see my final touches on the vodka party. I could create a story of what happened every day with the help of the clouds, trees, and whatever I was smoking.

That cloud looked like Daniel. Where the cloud broke, that was the body part where he felt excruciating pain. The one over there, where the pointy leaf hit the cloud, that was the organ that failed Sandra first. The sun hit the part that burned from the inside out.

When I travelled to my new residence, I didn't bring much with me—a beach dress, bikini, sunglasses, and a baseball cap. And Sandra's book from her mother. It was meant to be shared and passed down.

My burner phone rang. I fished it from my bag lying beneath the hammock. *Telemarketers have infiltrated burner phones. What's next?*

The screen displayed the Russian name from Sergei's crew, *Vladimir Lebedev.*

ABOUT THE AUTHOR

Andrea has lived in several areas in Ontario and currently resides in Toronto. In the warmer months, Andrea spends her time writing and snacking with her friends and dog. During the cold months, she does the same thing. The story is inspired by Andrea's experiences working in just about every sector, including advertising.

www.ingramcontent.com/pod-product-compliance
Lightning Source LLC
Chambersburg PA
CBHW062113170626
46813CB00002B/423